The Fixer Upper

Lauren Forsythe

PIATKUS

PIATKUS

First published in Great Britain in 2022 by Piatkus
First published in the US in 2022 by Putnam,
an imprint of Penguin Random House, New York

1 3 5 7 9 10 8 6 4 2

A CIP catalogue record for this book is available from the British Library.

ISBN 978-0-349-43207-6

Typeset in Caslon by M Rules
Printed and bound in Great Britain by
Clays Ltd, Elcograf S.p.A.

Papers used by Piatkus are from well-managed forests and other responsible sources.

Piatkus
An imprint of
Little, Brown Book Group
Carmelite House
50 Victoria Embankment
London EC4Y 0DZ

An Hachette UK Company
www.hachette.co.uk

www.littlebrown.co.uk

For the women who learned, sooner or later,
that selfish is not a dirty word.

It took me a while too.

Chapter One

'I'm afraid we aren't able to accommodate a table for one this evening, madam.'

The concierge at The Darlington was handsome in a bland sort of way. He had the sincere, apologetic look perfected, almost. But he couldn't hide the irritated wrinkle above his eyebrow, or how his gaze kept shifting to the couple behind me. The kind of customers he wanted, dolled up to the nines, and more importantly, not alone.

Here we go.

I bared my teeth in a fierce smile, trying to ignore the embarrassment staining my cheeks. Giving me away. *Not now, Aly.*

'Well ... I mean ... you took my reservation, so ... could you please see what you can do?' Hearing myself nervously babbling made me wish I was someone else. An Amazonian warrior, perhaps, desperately in need of a steak and a quiet night. Or someone like my friend Tola, who would never take no for an answer. *Yes, what would Tola say?* I straightened my spine. *'Especially* as it doesn't say anywhere on your website about not accepting solo diners.'

'Madam, it's simply not ...' He sighed and turned his attention back to the reservations list in front of him. *Say what you like, pal, I'm not going to slither away.*

Looking past him to the high vaulted ceiling, opulent chandeliers, and soft rose crushed-velvet seats of the restaurant, I finally allow myself a slow, soft exhale. I deserved to be here. I deserved an evening of decadence, of perfect wine pairings and statement food prepared by one of London's leading chefs. And just because I was dining alone didn't mean I was going to miss out.

It's simply not profitable. That's what the concierge wanted to say. And he was going to try, ever so delicately, to shame me into giving up. If it had been any other night, I might have let him. But tonight was *my* night. Tonight was Third Thursday.

The third Thursday of every month, I bought a delightful meal, drank something delicious, and read my book at a restaurant in London. And I did it 100 per cent alone, whether I was dating someone or not, safe in the knowledge that for a glorious few hours no one was going to ask me for anything. Third Thursdays were circled in bright orange in my calendar. I had never missed a single one, and I wasn't going to let a snooty waiter ruin my record now.

'Look, man,' I felt the man in the couple behind me lean forward, finding myself overwhelmed by a sudden cloud of cologne, 'Find her a table, OK? Otherwise I'm pretty sure it's discrimination.'

The concierge pressed his lips together, and I could tell he was weighing up the likelihood of a social media storm: *Diners in London restaurant come to aid of lone female who just wanted to try the chef's award-winning tortellini.*

I briefly considered bursting into tears. The concierge seemed to sense that was my next move.

'One moment,' he snipped, and disappeared.

I turned to the aftershave fiend behind me to thank him, and blinked in surprise.

'Jason!'

'Aly!' His face lit up, and he put out an arm so he could sweep in and kiss me on both cheeks. The woman at his side smiled, tilting her head slightly in a way that suggested she expected an introduction *immediately*.

'This is my wife, Diana.'

I nodded at her, uncertain. She looked so chic and I tried not to scan her as she was scanning me, taking in her luscious dark hair and painfully-stylish-yet-understated outfit. We seemed to come to the same conclusion at the exact same time: Jason had a type and he had definitely upgraded.

I pulled a hand through my dark curls, suddenly self-conscious.

'Married! Wow! Congratulations!' I was a human exclamation machine. I paused, looked at him again and blinked. 'Honestly, I barely recognise you.'

This man had slicked-back blond hair, a fitted shirt and smart black trousers. I squinted a little and wondered if he'd had his teeth whitened. The Jason I knew five years ago had lived in cargo shorts and oversized T-shirts with holes, and tied his scraggly strawberry-blond hair back with a piece of string. He'd lived in his parents' basement, teaching guitar to local kids without much more in mind for his life than that. There were no hard feelings when I ended it, it had just ... run its course. They usually did, one way or another.

I'd liked him though. He was my exact opposite: hippy, easy-going. His cargo shorts had hundreds of pockets that always held cardboard protein bars in case of emergency. He used to misquote philosophers and pretend he was making it up on the spot.

I couldn't remember if that was what finally pushed me to end the relationship. That or the pinkie fingernail he always kept long for strumming – that super-long nail always freaked me out.

'Oh, I'm sure; I had a bit of a ... well, an epiphany, I suppose?' He turned to his wife. 'Aly and I dated when I used to be a lazy bum living at my parents'. In fact, I owe it to her that I finally grew up and got my act together!'

Diana raised an eyebrow and looked at me quizzically. I half shrugged in response.

'How's that?'

'All that talk of potential, and that I could really *do* something with my life if I found what I was passionate about!' He still talked with his hands, and I noticed his gold wedding ring glinting in the light. His nails were all cut short.

I laughed, feeling myself blush. 'Sorry, that's my particular brand of enthusiasm. Love waxing lyrical about potential. It gets old.'

'No,' he reached out to touch my arm, kindness in his

eyes. 'I kept thinking about what you said, and I decided I wanted to get my own place, you know? And then I got that email from that free course you'd signed me up for and thought *why not?* I got a job, met Diana, and now we're here celebrating buying our first home!'

'Wow!' I breathed, blinking again. 'All that in five years? That's amazing.'

I suddenly realised where the conversation was about to shift, and there was no way to avoid it. I rallied my energy for the inevitable: Who's doing better now? Who's winning at life?

There it was, that ever-so-slightly pitying head tilt, and then ...

'So what about *you*, what have you been up to?'

Apart from arguing with a concierge about being able to dine solo in a restaurant on a Thursday night?

'Oh, you know,' I waved away his question casually, 'still living in London, working in marketing. Getting turned away from fancy restaurants.'

They laughed politely, and I watched in horror as a queue started to form behind us. The concierge was busy raging at his manager, sending me death glares.

'So are you still at the marketing agency? You wanted to be ... brand manager or something, right?' Jason prompted, and I tried not to wince.

I was taken aback by the fact that he remembered. I shouldn't have been, Jason had been sweet, after all. He'd taught me to surf one weekend in Cornwall, and we'd sat on our boards in the ocean while he told me I was an old soul. He played guitar beautifully and wore these little woven bracelets he made when he got fidgety. But the basement and the fact that I'd seen him once blow his nose into a sock because he couldn't be bothered to find a tissue were the fingernails in the coffin. And now he was a married home-owner with coiffed hair.

I reached for the prepared statement I always turned to in this kind of situation. The statement that made me sound busy, potentially important, but not stuck-up. The statement that said: I'm having such a great time living my life I'm not even considering competing with you and your family and your marriage and your home. I am H-A-P-P-Y.

'Head of branding, yeah!' I yelped. 'I'm on my way! Still at Amora, ever so busy, we're really growing from a boutique agency to a place with lots of big-name clients. I'm working with some great tech firms right now! I'm ... still living in London, loving it, breathing it all in, *you know*? Every day is an adventure! The interviews for head of branding are in a couple of weeks, actually ...'

Oh God. I had been talking about that promotion to Jason five years ago. And as much as my boss Felix promised me I was close, I was still in exactly the same place.

'We'll keep our fingers crossed for you,' Diana said kindly, clearly recognising I was absolutely no threat.

'And what about beyond business? Are you seeing anyone special?' That eyebrow wriggle was starting to annoy me. His wife tapped his shoulder with her clutch.

'Don't ask people that!' she hissed, and for a moment we shared solidarity.

I shook my head and smiled to say it was fine, assuming a sing-song voice, 'Everyone is special in their own way, Jason.'

'So, no one more special than anyone else?'

Even Diana looked irritated that time.

Why did the happily coupled always insist on parading their status in front of everyone else, like we were the last ones left in a Musical Chairs semi-final? *Better hurry up or there'll be no one left* ...

I winked winsomely. 'I guess I'm just having way too much fun.'

I could almost see them think it: *Fun like dining alone in a fancy restaurant that won't let you in?*

I winced, looking around for the next topic of conversation, but luckily Jason had that misty look in his eye and took care of it for me.

'I really do want to thank you, Aly. Honestly, if you hadn't pushed me, I'd never have changed my life for the better.' He gestured at Diana and she laughed.

'Unrecognisable,' I said tightly, then smiled. 'I'm really happy for you, Jason.'

He tilted his chin at the returning concierge and lowered his voice, 'And if he won't let you dine, you're welcome to join us. You shouldn't be denied a dinner just because you got stood up! Feminism!'

I tilted my head at him and looked at his wife, who gave me a bemused shrug.

'That's very kind, but I wasn't stood up, I only booked to—'

'Miss Aresti, please follow me,' the concierge gathered up the menus and nodded his head towards the dining room.

I turned back to Jason and Diana, speaking a little too loudly. 'What a *relief*. If I hadn't been able to review this place tonight, my editor would have *skewered* me!' I almost felt the concierge twitch and saw that smile on Diana's face again. Good for her, she deserved a Jason 2.0. 'Congratulations on the house!'

I followed the concierge, head held high, and then paused, looking back. 'Hey, Jason, do you still play guitar?'

He shook his head, good-natured as ever. 'Nah, I don't really have time for that stuff any more.'

I nodded and turned back, unsure why I'd needed to ask.

The concierge raised an eyebrow, as if I should be eternally grateful for his attention, and I followed, taking a seat and ordering without a pause. I always looked at the menu online before dining out.

I could tell he wanted to tell me he wasn't a waiter, and wasn't going to take my order, but he simply assumed a long-suffering smile and listened. It felt like a win.

When my order was accepted, my glass of wine arrived, and I got out my book. Finally, I could breathe.

Third Thursday was meant to be a treat, not an ordeal. It was the one time I didn't have to pretend to be anyone else, didn't have to do anything for anyone. Didn't have to go on a date with someone, fizzing with hope, only to find they were thirty-five and hadn't dealt with their childhood traumas, didn't know how to ask a question *and* listen to the answer, and still weren't wearing matching socks. It was easier to date myself.

Besides, I was still licking my wounds after Michael. I'd met him at the farmers' market on a Saturday morning, buying fancy olives. He'd looked across at me and simply said, 'Hello, you,' in this surprised delight, as if he'd been waiting for me and hadn't believed I'd ever appear. Michael had a really lovely smile, and he made the best cappuccino I'd ever tasted outside Italy. Which, in hindsight, wasn't really a good reason to fancy someone.

I'd helped him find a new flat after his horrible house-share came to an end. And then I spent a week helping him move and painted his walls and helped him set up his council tax payment. We spent a lot of time walking around IKEA and building his furniture. After that, he said it was moving a little too fast, and I was 'exhibiting girlfriend-like behaviour'. But he thanked me for getting a great deal on the movers.

And so here I was again, returning to myself. Making an effort. The solo dates could feel awkward sometimes, but I kept doing them, hoping that one day it would get easier, until I looked like that woman I'd once seen in New York, dining alone at the bar. She'd looked so relaxed, so confident, sipping her wine and reading her book, occasionally taking delicate bites of asparagus. I'd decided I wanted to be like that. No matter how many times the waiters looked at me with pity.

Normally, after the first five minutes of feeling on display, I settled into it, but tonight my eyes kept straying to Jason across the room, so well groomed, so successful. Five years had passed, and he'd turned into a completely different person. While I, Alyssa Aresti, identifier of potential and nagger into self-actualisation, was still in exactly the same job, the same damp London studio flat, and still single at thirty-three. I still had none of the markers of thirty-something success to my name.

I wasn't sure why seeing Jason succeed irritated me so much. Perhaps because I'd spent so long trying to encourage him, trying to help him figure out what he wanted. How many hours had I scoured the internet and done job quizzes with him? How many times had we had conversations about personal hygiene, and not yelling upstairs to his parents that we were having *alone time* whenever we'd been about to have sex?

The race through your twenties and thirties wasn't meant to be a competition. Success looks different for everyone, and we're not all looking for the same things. Logically, I knew that. But as I watched Jason and his wife drink from their bottle of champagne, toasting their new home, I knew I was lying to myself.

Whatever game we were playing, he'd won. And I had a feeling I'd helped him do it.

Chapter Two

'And so now he's a project manager!' I told Tola and Eric by the coffee machines in the communal kitchen at work the next morning. I lied that I'd met a friend in a bar, and as I was leaving, Jason had appeared. I didn't want them to know about my solo dining exploits. They were the closest I had to real friends, even though our extra-curricular activities only went as far as after-work drinks and the occasional drunk kebab. Even so, I didn't want them to know my sad self-care ritual was gorging on handmade pasta and drinking an overpriced Rioja on my own once a month.

'Was this the one who was shit at the ukulele?' Eric asked.

I shook my head. 'Guitar. And he wasn't shit.'

'Must have been one of the other man-children you've dated,' Eric stuck out his tongue at me, and I raised an eyebrow, passing him his coffee.

'I have never dated a ukulele player. Greg used to build ocarinas, but that's not the same thing.'

Tola burst out laughing. 'I don't remember this one. Oh wait, was it the guy who didn't speak at all?'

I shook my head. 'Before your time. About five years ago.'

'And he thanked you for making him into a capitalist Ken doll?'

Eric jumped in, pointing at me, 'She had her work cut out with Jason. He once spent fifteen minutes telling me the plot of a film that *I'd told him about*. And he thought surfing was a personality trait rather than a hobby.' Eric always had quite a lot to say once he got himself going. My terrible taste in boyfriends was one of his favourite topics. 'Oh, *and* he always referred to the sea as a woman. *I watched her bountiful waves caress the shore* . . . douchebag. He had to be the worst one, right, Aly?'

I rolled my eyes and pretended it wasn't bothering me. And that I hadn't immediately gone home last night and looked up Jason on LinkedIn.

'But hey, they only last a few months, so if you didn't like 'em, there's no time wasted,' Tola brought me back to the conversation at hand, her fuchsia lipstick refocusing my attention, 'I respect that.'

'Really? You respect Aly's absolute failure to commit?' Eric rolled his eyes, and I pouted.

'It's not like I do it on purpose!' I yelped, 'I put myself out there, I try to be kind and loving and . . . it just falls apart. It's not always me doing the dumping.'

Eric raised an eyebrow. 'No one is choosing those men on purpose. Unless your type is hopeless baby. You're not dating for keeps, sweetheart. Those are time-wasters.'

'You're mean today! Did you go on another Grindr date looking for romance and end up with meaningless sex again?' I sang, hoping to redirect the conversation.

Out of habit, Eric looked around the office to see if anyone had overheard, then glared at me. 'There is nothing wrong with wanting a real connection with someone.'

'No, but you can't go looking for a comfortable knitted cardigan in Ann Summers and then complain about it being a bit chilly around the nipples.' Tola looked at me. 'Am I right?'

I snorted. 'You are always right.'

Eric and I had known each other for quite a few years. When he'd started at the company, not long after me, I was intimidated by him. Here was someone my age with a fancy suit and a home and a beautiful fiancée. He had swishy hair and spicy cologne and always knew how to talk to people. He was always laughing. Everyone in the ads department loved him, hanging around his desk in the hopes of a good story and a bit of banter.

It wasn't until he'd been there about six months that I left the office late, found my bus had been cancelled and bumped into him in the pub. He'd been a few drinks down and was worse for wear. He clearly wanted someone to talk to. That's when I found out his beautiful perfect life was all a lie. Because Eric was gay, and he needed to tell his fiancée and move out of his flat and figure out how to start his life over. I happened to be the first person he told, and it's hard not to be friends after something like that.

Tola only joined us a year ago, and we weren't really sure why this bold, gorgeous twenty-something wanted to hang out with us. She was this absolute force of nature – she'd left school and got a job designing costumes for the West End musical *Cats*. When she got bored of sewing furry jumpsuits all day, she ended up reinventing herself as a social media expert. I got the sense she thought me and Eric needed her, that we needed someone with that Gen Z energy to stop us being two bitter Millennials, constantly bitching about everything. And she was absolutely right. She also brought the triple-strength dose of tough love when we needed it, which can't be underestimated.

'So, why is this annoying you?' she asked as we walked over to my desk.

'It's not, I wish Jason all the best.'

'Aly, you are very good at lying to yourself, but I don't go in for all that. Indulge me.' She leaned against my desk and gestured with a bright blue fingernail.

'Because he's doing better than I am!' I whined, putting my head on the desk in frustration. 'Five measly years, and he reinvented himself, got a new career, met the love of his life, got married, saved a deposit, and bought a house. What have I done in that time?'

'Earned the respect of your peers and clients? Terrified an entire office with your efficiency?' Tola offered.

'Drunk about eight bathtubs full of wine?' Eric added.

'Not helpful!' I threw a pencil at him.

I sat back in my chair and looked at them. 'Should I have held out longer with Jason? Did I quit too early? I thought he had no drive, but clearly he has it now. Maybe I'm throwing away perfectly good relationships just because people have flaws? Maybe I'm being too picky?'

Eric made a face. 'There's flaws and then there's … whatever's up with the guys you date. You're not being too picky – you're not being picky enough! Like that guy Nathan!'

'Nathan was really lovely!' I objected. 'He had big dreams, he wanted to be an actor!'

'Yeah, and you ended up paying for his acting classes and booking his gigs for five months!' Eric threw his head back. 'And you didn't take a commission!'

Tola nodded. 'Eric's right, babe. You know what your problem is? You're not dating men, you're dating projects.'

I could see Eric doing a mental tally of the men I'd dated and watched as the smile on his face grew.

'Stop it! You look way too smug.'

'No, she's right, Aly! You take on these little broken birds, put all your eggs in their basket, and then the omelette ends up rubbish.'

'Stop mixing metaphors!' I rolled my eyes. 'What does that even mean?'

'It means you date men who aren't fully formed grownups yet, put all your energy into making their lives better, and then you get exhausted and tap out before you get any of the rewards of your labour.'

'Oooh,' Tola wiggled her eyebrows, 'rewards of your labour. Sexy stuff. He's got a point, though – Jason said it himself, he's better off for dating you. New and improved.'

'He's not *improved*, he's . . . different, that's all,' I argued.

'He's more successful than when you dated him. And hopefully less of a pretentious knob, but hey, you're not a miracle worker,' Eric snorted. 'Face it, Aly, this is what you do. You date guys who aren't worthy of you, and then you do everything for them. It's a pattern.'

15

I threw up my hands. 'What did I do for Jeremy?'

Tola laughed, holding up a hand. 'Easy, you dog-sat his demon poodle for a week and toilet-trained it. He didn't even say thank you!'

'*And* you got him on the line-up at Belle's to try and launch his music career, and he missed it because he got drunk with his mates.'

I winced. 'OK, we can stop this now.'

Eric's eyes widened. 'No, he's the perfect example! I heard him on the radio last week! Untalented bastard could barely get himself out of bed and now he's got an album out!'

Eric grinned at me, and I shook my head, unsure of what was coming next but certain it wouldn't be good.

'As a man of data, I sense we've got a pattern here, and I want to investigate. I bet you fifty quid that if you give us a list of your boyfriends, we'll find all of them have gone on to be successes.'

Tola was frowning, and I hoped she was about to defend me. But then she smiled, that full-beam, megawatt smile of hers, and it was clear she was about to make this worse. 'We need a proper measurement system. *Success* is relative. We need a numerical assignment to each value. And it can't be like *all* the boyfriends Aly's ever had. Only the short-term, hopeless ones?' Tola turned to me, like she was asking my permission.

'Thanks,' I snorted. 'What's the point of this?'

'Confirming a theory I have.' Eric tapped the side of his nose and walked off to his desk.

I looked at Tola. 'What's in it for me, exactly?'

She shrugged. 'Self-awareness? Giving your mates some-thing to laugh at? Send me a list of names, OK?'

My mobile started ringing, and I held up my hands, waving them away, 'OK, OK, whatever. We want to play *make fun of Aly*, that's fine. I've got to get this.'

I took a deep breath and answered the phone. 'Hi Mama, I'm just about to go into a meeting, everything OK?'

'Of course, you're busy, too busy for my nonsense.' My mother's voice was soft and self-effacing, daring me to agree with her. I knew her game, though. *You're never too busy for family, Alyssa, don't forget that.*

'Mama!' I huffed, reaching for a pen, 'I'm here, what's up?'

'It's your father.'

I let the silence hang there.

'What did he do?' *This time.*

She paused. 'Maybe I was being oversensitive.'

'Mama—'

'No, you go, clever girl. Lots of people counting on you. You'll come for dinner this week, yes?'

'Sure. Let's go for Sunday lunch, my treat,' I said, and heard her squeak of delight. I could imagine her clapping her hands in celebration of a good idea. Of course, we'd spend more than half the time talking about my father and what he'd done most recently, but we'd have a good time the remaining 20 per cent that was just for us.

'Sounds good. I love you, darling,' she said, making a kissing noise down the phone, and then she was gone.

For a while I'd thought loving and supporting her would be enough to help her get over him after he left, but it didn't work. As my grandma used to say, some people have to keep making the same mistakes over and over until it bites them in the arse hard enough.

My father had always been a bad husband, and I'd spent most of my childhood covering for him. I remembered being armed with his credit card, dropped off at the shopping centre when I was twelve with instructions to find something nice for Mummy's birthday and to write a card from Daddy. I still wonder if things would have been different if I'd simply refused.

Luckily, I didn't have enough time to think about it. I had appointments and meetings, then meetings about the meetings, until the day was almost done. I did my usual eleven o'clock rounds, making sure to ask Matilda in finances about her holiday and compliment David in HR's haircut (short back and sides, every two weeks, did I know it was only fourteen pounds?). I did a tea round for the far corner of the office, listened to Justine's love-life drama and told her she deserved the best. The tiny things that didn't matter on their own but that added up, made people feel appreciated. And suddenly the day was almost gone, and the weekend was almost upon me.

Almost.

Oh, crap.

Of course. There he was, on the dot, the same as every Friday afternoon when I was about to make my escape. I pretended not to see him approaching.

'Aly Pally!' Hunter boomed next to my desk, forcing me to look up fully and take my headphones off.

I smiled, trying to hold in a sigh. 'Hunter! How are you today? Looking forward to the weekend? You'll be out on the golf course, I'll bet.'

Even with people I hated, like Hunter, I couldn't help but remember those details. It was like a compulsion, and right now, I hated myself for it.

Hunter looked at me with pleasure, running a hand through his caramel hair. 'I absolutely will be. You're always so ... attentive, Aly. You know how to make a man feel special.'

I clenched my teeth, though whether I was swallowing a sarcastic retort, or actual vomit, I couldn't be 100 per cent certain.

There were a lot of things I hated about Hunter. How he talked about playing the stock market for fun, how he still referred to his father as 'Daddy' and for some insane reason the fact that he liked to wear a cravat really pushed my buttons. Orange, spotty, pink striped. There was one for every outfit. Considering how many awful things there were about Hunter, it was shocking that was the one that got to me.

He'd joined the company two years after me, but was now a manager, like I was. Except he was incapable of following through, working to deadlines or telling the client 'no'. He always walked impropriety like a tightrope and, as yet, the bastard hadn't slipped and plunged to his death at the hands of HR. There was always a safety net. More's the pity.

So, no, he wasn't a great manager. Or a great team player. He was, however, rich, posh and charming. And so full of hot air and bullshit he could have been a Zeppelin powered by fertiliser.

He was my mortal enemy, and he had absolutely no idea. Which was just how I liked my enemies.

'How can I help today, Hunter?' *Clearly you want something.*

'Oh well, Felix said you might be able to help with that report for BigScreen? I'm having a little trouble making it perfect. And obviously, we want it to be perfect for them. So I knew you were the person to perfect it, because you always present so perfectly.' *Good God, give the man a thesaurus.*

Hunter offered a wide smile like a gift, and I wondered how many women had fallen for this routine before. A charming man who leans into your space and convinces you that you're so special and clever that you deserve the honour of doing his work.

And yet, I knew I'd help. Not because I wanted Hunter's approval, but because Felix had recommended he come to me. And, quite frankly, I didn't want it to be done badly. Hunter knew that was my weakness. It wasn't just that I was a people-pleaser. I was also a control freak. Much better.

'I see ... and how much have you done already?'

'Oh, I've outlined it, so all it needs is a little shading, a little colour. The i's dotted and all that. Felix and I just need Aly to wave her magic wand!' He nudged me, and I stamped down on my rage and widened my smile.

'I'm always happy to help, Hunter, you know that. I can absolutely take a look. When do you need it by?'

'Well, we've got a meeting with their team on Monday morning, so ...' he threw his hands up in a hopeful *what are you gonna do* sort of way. I looked at the clock. Four thirty on Friday.

'Do you ... I mean ...' I sighed, 'it's almost the end of the day, Hunter.'

'Oh, it won't take long, babe! Not with your magic

powers! I know you'll do wonderfully.' He patted my shoulder. 'Now I've got to run, some of the team are going for after-work drinkies, and it's my round. Thank you!' He nearly ran away, and I put my head in my hands.

Why didn't you say no? Why didn't you tell him it was too late to hand this off now? Why didn't you tell him this is the third time this has happened this month and you're not his lackey? I growled a little to myself, tightened my ponytail and got to work. If I was lucky, I wouldn't be here until the evening.

'You could always fuck it up so badly the incompetent arse finally gets what's coming to him?' Tola said, appearing at my side with two cans of beer. On Friday afternoons, the bar cart came round, to try and show we were a relaxed company with great culture. But the shine tended to wear off after so many Fridays working late.

'I did consider it. But it'd come back on me. Hunter is one of those golden boys – nothing ever sticks. It would be my fault for not supporting him appropriately,' I sighed, clicking my neck and opening the Word document. 'And Felix sent him to me. For all we know, this could be a test for me to prove my worth. He's always saying I've got to step up and take responsibility. I think they're going to announce the head of branding role this month.'

Tola raised an eyebrow, unimpressed, and then put the can of beer on the table. 'Didn't they say that last month? Besides, if you take on much more responsibility you're going to be running the company. Go on, thirty minutes, I'll time you. Then you can have your beer and I'll proofread.'

'You don't have to do that! I'm sure you've got big Friday plans.'

She stood up. 'I don't do things I don't want to do. So don't worry about it. Besides, no one goes clubbing until at least eleven p.m. ... Grandma.' Tola winked at me and started to head back over to the group congregating by the bar. 'If you *really* want to thank me, start compiling that boyfriends list. I wanna see how many losers you've waved your magic wand over.'

I was lucky to have her. And Eric. Even if the two of them were insistent on pulling apart my dating life and discovering all my insecurities. What if all of those men were doing better than I was? What if five years had passed and my life was exactly the same, the only progress being my slightly increased savings account and my running personal bests? I'd told Jason to think about the life he wanted and make the decisions to move towards it. So why couldn't I take my own advice?

I didn't want to make that list. Because I had a sneaking suspicion they were right.

I ripped a sheet of paper out of my notebook and started scribbling their names, reverse order, working back in time ... Michael, David, Timothy, Noah, Jason ... until I reached age seventeen, and then I paused.

Dylan. The boy with the bluest eyes and the loudest laugh in the world. The first one I'd grown up alongside and been helpless for, even as he'd smiled at his girlfriends and I'd hung around on the sideline, the hapless best friend. I started to write his name, but stopped and scratched it through. It didn't count. It was history. Nothing more.

OK, so that was twelve entanglements in seventeen years of dating. All that time, that energy, and I had twelve losers to show for it. Not even a cancelled engagement or a horrific betrayal to spark an origin story. I had merely ... spent time, like it didn't matter. And now I was here.

I turned back to my computer screen, relieved that at least one thing eternally made sense: Posh boys would make me do their work for no credit, and I would sit at home drinking wine and stewing over it until Monday morning came.

Just as I always did.

Chapter Three

'And the results are in, ladies and gentlemen,' Eric said in a TV announcer's voice while we sat at lunch on Monday. We were perched on a bench in the park behind the office, most of our colleagues camped out around us, lounging on their jackets on the grass, or sat at the little round tables outside the cafe. It reminded me of school, sometimes, us all rushing outside to catch that spring sunshine the minute it hit, faces turned towards the sun as we ignored our phones and drank our overpriced coffee. Thirty minutes of bliss.

I picked at my sad chicken salad sandwich, so carefully prepared the night before, and huffed. 'Do you really have to take so much joy from this?'

'And do you have to be so miserable? It's not a reflection on you,' he replied, stuffing a piece of sushi into his mouth whole.

'Um, that's *exactly* what it is.'

'Well, it's not a bad one,' he replied, chewing rapidly, and Tola jumped in to play referee.

'Don't you want to know our method? There's a whole

data analysis element to this, it's wicked. So firstly, we had to assess what the metrics for success were. But they had to be matched to what *you* believed was success. So we went for all the traditional stuff – marriage, kids, fancy job, home-ownership, money, all that jazz.'

I didn't quite like how that comment made me feel.

'So then, thanks to my expert social media sleuthing skills—' Tola continued.

'And the fact that these guys were all egomaniacs—' Eric added.

'We managed to assess their lives by those factors. We tried to bear in mind what they were like when you met them, to see if there was an improvement percentage. And there was. Drum roll, please ...'

I rolled my eyes, and Eric tapped the table.

'The average improvement percentage was eighty-seven per cent!' Tola announced, grinning at me. 'We call it "the Aly Factor".'

I blinked. 'So eighty-seven per cent of the guys are more successful now than they were when I knew them?'

Eric shook his head. 'Oh honey, no.'

I breathed a sigh of relief. 'Right. Thought that sounded a bit insane.'

'All of them are,' he explained. 'To be precise, every man on that list improved by eighty-seven per cent.'

They were looking at me with expectation, and I couldn't quite process it.

'You mean to tell me that every single man on that list is in a serious relationship, owns property, or is high up in a business now ... all of them?'

They nodded.

'Don't tell me Adrian finally had that book published that he kept sending me random unfinished chapters from?' *Impossible. No one wanted flying werewolf fiction, even if it was set in an alternative Steampunk Victorian England universe.*

'No,' Tola held her hands up, '*but* he was accepted for an agency scholarship after entering a writing competition that – correct me if I'm wrong here – *you* helped him to enter. Now he runs online classes for newbie writers while holding down a second job as an IT manager.'

My eyebrows were raised so high I thought I might give myself a migraine.

'Aly, we can track their improvement back to you. Your energy, your support, your . . . particular brand of affection,' Eric explained more gently, as if I wasn't getting it. And I suppose I wasn't.

'Eric, people are responsible for their own growth, their own decisions. Maybe I helped a little, but these guys clearly . . . grew up somewhere along the way. Met different people, had experiences that changed them.'

'Or you have some kind of mysterious shagging power that makes men better,' Tola said solemnly, and then burst out laughing. 'Your magic vagina! Seriously though, you can't think this is complete coincidence?'

I stared at her.

'Between coincidence or me having magic genitals, I'd say coincidence makes more sense.' I rolled my eyes. 'Besides, it's like, twelve guys. Hardly a huge sample size.'

'David gave a TED talk three months ago,' Eric said,

palms flat on the table. '*David*. The guy who never spoke. He credits his confidence to an ex-girlfriend who made him go to a seminar.'

'He didn't even go,' I huffed. 'He refused, said it was embarrassing. So I went and made notes and brought them back for him, and he watched some of the videos online.'

'See, you made things happen.' Eric handed me the list. 'Look.'

I scanned the list, seeing accolade after accolade. These men were grown-up, impressive, important people. The opposite of what they'd been when I knew them.

'This is what happens when you date people in your twenties. They tell you they hate marriage and cold weather, and then eight years later you see they had their wedding under the Northern Lights.'

I looked back at the list again and raised an eyebrow. 'Why is Matthew on here? We never dated.'

Tola and Eric shared a look, and then looked back at me.

'What?! We didn't!'

'You spent months helping him with his career when he joined the company, kissed him once after the Christmas party, and now he's the same level as you despite only being here two years.'

'He was new to the industry! I was helping him out!'

'The man is the human equivalent of beige, and he's still managed to move up the ranks. Because of the information you gave him,' Tola argued.

'Well, if we're counting every person I've ever tried to help with their career, we're going to need a longer list!' I growled. 'He doesn't count.'

'Fine.' Tola rolled her eyes at me. 'Stats here can recalculate, right?'

Eric looked grouchy but got out a pen. 'Sure, but I beg of you, go to therapy. And stop helping Matthew, he's secretly a little weasel.'

'I thought he was beige?'

'You don't hear the stuff he says around the guys. Beige is a front for evil. Always.' Eric tapped his pen. 'OK, so the Aly Factor changes to eighty-five per cent. Our point still stands.'

I rolled my eyes and watched as Tola and Eric shared that look again. Like I was being unreasonable.

'What? What about my reaction here is so disappointing?'

'We want you to admit that maybe you had an impact, that's all,' Tola said softly. 'Isn't it a gift to be able to see how much you've influenced someone's life?'

Not if suddenly they're all ahead in the race, I thought, *and I've been left behind.*

'I'm just ... irritated, and I don't know why. I'm not jealous of these men. I'd vomit if I had to give a TED talk. And I definitely don't want to work in investment banking or have my wedding announced in *Tatler*. It's ... I dunno ...' I sighed.

Tola tilted her head. 'Maybe you're wondering where you'd be if you'd spent all that time and energy on yourself instead?'

Maybe I'm wondering why the hell I kept dating projects instead of people. And what that says about me.

All I'd ever wanted was what my grandparents had. That enduring kind of love, where they looked across the room at each other with a secret smile, like they had their

28

own language. I didn't need to be somebody's everything, I just ... no matter what I did, how much I gave, it never seemed to be enough.

I sighed and packed up my lunchbox. 'Well, this has been *incredibly fun*, and well done on your researching rigour, but I've got to get back to a full inbox and a smug Hunter.'

They looked up in concern as I left, and I didn't really know how to feel. So what if all these men I'd dated had turned from hopeless, self-indulgent man-children to grown-ups? So what if I'd put in all the hours listening to their childhood traumas and comforting them, and putting up with their bullshit when they absolutely should have gone to therapy? *So what* if now their current girlfriends and wives were reaping the rewards of my hard work? I'd made the choice to support them, to play at being the perfect girlfriend for the short time I was with them. If that helped, I should be proud of myself. And it *was* nice that Jason credited me with believing in him, and that David remembered the workshop. Maybe I'd been like the fairy god-girlfriend these guys had needed at that time in their life.

But where did that leave me?

Tola and Eric had always laughed when I said I found relationships exhausting. That I was too tired to date. But now it made sense. I'd be better off getting a puppy; at least I'd get affection in return for dealing with shit. But, just once, it would be nice to have someone around to say, 'Don't worry, I've got this.'

As I headed back to my desk, I could hear Becky, one of the women in accounts, talking to some of the others. She sat a few desks over from me, so that we almost always ended up accidentally making faces at each other when we were frustrated or thinking too hard. Catching an accidental eye-roll from Becky, followed by an embarrassed smile, always made me feel better.

She also always seemed to be the wise sage the younger girls came to with their boyfriend drama, which was why their little friendship group seemed to huddle around her desk. But today, apparently, it was her own relationship that was the problem.

'He said he doesn't believe in marriage and he doesn't know why I'm so obsessed with it!' she sighed, and the other women made sympathetic noises. I thought of Jason's likely excuse for his change of heart about marriage – a change of woman. But Becky didn't need to hear that.

'He's probably just putting you off the scent!' said Katherine, who'd watched entirely too many Richard Curtis movies. 'So when he does ask, you'll be surprised!'

Becky shook her head. 'He said we've got a lovely family together, what does it matter? And I don't really know how to explain it, because it *does* sound dumb, saying I want a big fancy party with a white dress. We've got our kids, and we've built a home together . . . he's right, I should be satisfied.'

Something about the aggressive gratitude felt familiar. The feeling that it wasn't OK to want more than what she had, and it wasn't OK to want something other people thought was unimportant. I clenched my teeth as I dropped into my chair and reached for my headphones, but with a start, I found Tola and Eric standing behind me, eavesdropping just like I was.

'Hey, Aly,' Eric smiled at me, 'you know what happens after you come up with a new theory?'

Tola grinned, crossing her arms and tilting her head towards Becky. 'You test it.'

We went to the Prince Regent, a pub around the corner from the office. It was cute enough, with framed portraits of random royal family members and that ever-so-charming spilled beer smell. I had a weird affection for the place, where Tola and I had worked our way through the (limited, and pretty disgusting) cocktail list, and where Eric and I had started our friendship over two bottles of Pinot Grigio and a lot of crying. Sure it had sticky floors and only served salt and vinegar crisps, but it held our history.

Eric and I sat on stools at a high table, watching Tola as she spoke to Becky at the bar. We couldn't quite hear them, but I knew Tola was telling a glorious tale of how I had changed previous boyfriends' minds about marriage, and how I could do the same for Becky's commitment-phobic partner.

'I do not want to do this. I don't even know this man,' I said.

'Well, you'll get to know him. You did a psychology degree, right?' Eric nudged me with his elbow and smirked into his pint.

I snorted, 'No, I did a summer course in counselling and an advanced course in marketing techniques. It's messaging and manipulation, not therapy.'

'Is that what you did with them all?'

'No, I was dating them and was nice and tried to help!

Besides, this is some random guy, so we're gonna have to come up with a play, otherwise he's going to think I'm chatting him up!'

I gritted my teeth as Becky swivelled on her barstool and gave me two thumbs up, a hopeful, grateful look on her face. *Oh God.*

Tola jumped off the stool and swaggered over to our table, pausing to check her hair in the mirror on the way. She held two glasses of Coke and put them down with a flourish. 'We are all systems go, ladies and gents.'

I pointed at the drinks. 'Did you forget one of us?'

Tola wiggled her eyebrows. 'These were a gift from an admirer.'

Eric blinked. 'We didn't even see anyone approach you!'

Tola narrowed her eyes and grinned. 'I test well with the bartending demographic. It's rum and Coke, take it.' She pushed it over to me.

'What's it like to be universally adored wherever you go?' Eric asked, holding up his phone as a fake microphone.

'Well, I really want to say it gets old, but it doesn't.' She raised an eyebrow at me. 'Look at the face on you. Nervous? Drink your drink.'

I took a tentative sip and looked back at her, pleading. 'Did I say I don't want to do this?'

'Yes, and we told you being a coward isn't in line with your personal brand as ass-kicker. You should be thanking us, babe. We're giving you the opportunity to shine,' Tola teased. 'So what's the play?'

'You know the first rule of marketing?' I sucked on the straw, resigned.

'Make more money than you spend?' Eric offered.

I rolled my eyes. 'Give people what they need. Tell them exactly what they want to hear.'

'How do we know what he wants to hear?'

I leaned in, so they could hear me over the rapidly increasing din of the pub, the regulars getting rowdier, the newly off-the-clock loosening their ties. Tola and Eric leaned in too, as if they were intrigued.

'We don't.' I grinned at Eric expectantly. 'Which is why we send in someone to scope him out.'

'Why do I feel like by the end of the night you're going to be Tony Soprano?' Tola asked, hand on hip. Eric snorted.

'Nice reference, bit vintage for you.'

'Look, Eric is going to go in first and get a few answers to some important questions. From that, we'll know how to sway him.'

'And you really think some chance encounter with a random person in a pub is going to change this guy's entire mindset?'

I shook my head, 'No, of course not. It doesn't have to change anything. It only needs to crack it a little. Let the light in, plant a seed. The chance for something else to flower, that's all.'

I looked at Becky, swirling her wine around her glass at the bar, chin resting on her hand, head tilted like she was waiting for something. She looked . . . sad. We might be able to help her. I was doing this.

'And it's got to be me?' Eric asked, frowning, 'You're sure?'

'Um, who never stops telling us about how excellent he

was in *Hello Dolly* at university?' I replied, and Tola joined in, grinning.

'Yeah, wasn't your Teen Angel in *Grease* given a standing ovation? And you won some sort of award for *West Side Story*?'

Eric raised his chin and pursed his lips, as if recognising an adversary. 'Oh *hello*, look who's suddenly invested now.'

I shrugged. 'If I have no other choice, I'd like to do it well. Besides, you're excellent at the "banter with the lads" bullshit. It comes naturally to you.'

Eric looked at me in surprise, waiting for me to apologise, but I laughed. 'Come on, be honest.'

Eric mimed offence. 'Fine, I'll turn up my *straight man likes sport* impression, just for you, sweetcheeks.'

We watched as Becky's boyfriend came in, and I gasped, nudging them all to be silent. But, of course, it was so needlessly dramatic that Tola and I got the giggles.

As much as this was absolutely ridiculous, it was fun. It was an excuse to be out on a Monday evening with my work friends, instead of going home to an empty flat and calling my mother to hear what stupid thing my father had done now. Instead of brainstorming ways to show I deserved that head of branding job. Instead of lying in bed wondering why time was passing so quickly and yet nothing seemed to change.

Becky's boyfriend was wide and muscled like a builder, but he had a sweetness to him you could see in the way he looked at her, the gentle way he stroked her arm. Which meant we likely had someone who was only teasing his girlfriend, knowing how much she wanted to get married, or who didn't believe in it as a concept at all. Either way, the man across from us looked like he'd do anything for her, and I could see a gentle nudge in the right direction wasn't going to be particularly difficult.

'So you know what questions you need to ask,' I asked Eric again, and he nodded. 'OK, go forth. Use the force well.'

We watched as Eric slicked his blond hair back, walked over, and greeted Becky with that million-watt smile he was so good at producing when he needed it. He made a deliberate movement, pulling at the blue tie around his neck before he introduced himself to her boyfriend. We watched Eric in 'sell' mode, shoulders back, broad frame on display as he shook hands, clapping Becky's boyfriend on the back, and then immediately gesturing to the bar. 'My treat!' we heard him insist, throwing his hands up as if he wouldn't hear of anything else, and grabbing the bartender's attention.

'God, he's so smooth,' Tola said by my side, watching it like daytime television. 'We need to find him someone soon, or he's gonna stop trying to date and forget about love altogether.'

'Agreed. The shagging about is getting old, no matter what he says. Do you know anyone for him?' I saw her shake her head out of the corner of my eye.

'All my mates are too young and probably a bit too . . . out there for someone like Eric,' Tola considered. 'He needs, like, some relaxed guy who wears cardigans but makes it look hot. And cooks, because Eric is terrible at that, and I want someone to throw a goddamn dinner party worth going to.'

I chuckled. 'Excellent points. Very selfless.'

After about twenty minutes, Eric came back to our table.

He deflated from his macho persona and fed through what he'd learnt. I kept an eye on Becky and her boyfriend at the bar. They didn't look too traumatised.

'It's the money, I think,' he said, taking a slug of my drink. 'And I think he's a little shy. He just doesn't see the point of some big day for no reason when they've got kids to send to after-school clubs and stuff.'

I clasped my hands together, nodding, watching the couple's body language. OK, I knew how to handle this. 'Don't worry, guys, I've got this. One hundred per cent.'

When I returned to Tola and Eric afterwards, it was like I was a goddess. A celebrated actress who bent people to her will, rather than someone who had a skill for listening and providing solutions. Or manipulating, if you wanted to get technical.

'What did you *do*? His face went white! Are you trying to scare him into proposing?' Eric tried to hold in a laugh as they left, waving at us, Becky's face clearly saying, *Well, thanks for trying*, eyebrow wrinkled, right shoulder raised in half a shrug. This time, her boyfriend did look traumatised, and I tried not to giggle at how shell-shocked he appeared, grasping his pint for dear life.

'I spun a story about leaving my boyfriend of fifteen years because he wouldn't propose. Because he kept saying it didn't matter, that I was desperate, but really all I wanted was to have him show he loved me, to have him *pick* me. That it was easy enough for him to stay when I cooked his meals and did his washing, but he'd never *picked* me. That I didn't even want a big wedding, just something small to show him off to the world, to tell them all this was my man, and I was so proud of him.' I looked off into the distance, hands clasped at my chest. 'So I was going, and now he could cook his own dinner because some guy I'd met at the gym who looked like Jason Momoa wanted to marry me instead.'

Their jaws dropped.

'You came up with all that?' Tola asked.

'More importantly, you fancy Jason Momoa?' Eric tilted his head like a dog who'd found an unexpected titbit. 'Interesting.'

'*Becky does*. And the point is that everything's a narrative.' I shrugged. 'It provided justification for her feelings and created a *hint* of fear. If nothing else, it'll spark a conversation on the journey home, and maybe she can make herself heard.'

Tola blinked at me, almost dazzled. I liked that expression. 'Babe, there is something *here*. You can feel it, right? Like, how many women are in Becky's position? How many women have been putting all this … emotional energy and money and time into being whatever their boyfriends needed? We could help them.'

'By forcing boyfriends to propose?' I wrinkled my nose. 'Not exactly doing the lord's work, is it?'

Tola looked skyward, clenching her fists. 'No, not the proposals. The emotional labour! The hours of extra housework and admin and childcare and being in control of everything all the time. And not getting anything back in return! We have a generation of exhausted women on our hands.'

'You want us to start a company hiring managers for people's lives?' I asked, shrugging. 'I mean, the rich already have personal assistants … maybe it could be an app?'

'You're not listening. Think about the amount of time and effort Becky puts into their family life, right? Think about how many years she's been talking about marriage. Then think about you, breezing in and finding the exact right thing to say and way to play it so the notion could penetrate. All that time, all the emotional energy, saved. We could literally give women the gift of time.'

'By ... fixing their men for them?' I frowned.

'Emotional outsourcing!' Eric yelped, and I could already see our number cruncher trying to find an angle.

'We could really help women!' Tola said, like she was waiting for us to feel this earth-shattering realisation, and we just weren't complying.

'Look, this is fun, and I've loved getting the chance to scheme with you guys,' I started, '*really*. But I want to be head of branding. That's what I've always wanted. It's why I went to uni, it's why I did my masters, it's why I've worked here and put up with the Hunters of the world for all these years. And it's so close now I can taste it. I spend enough time fixing everyone's problems, I don't need to do it as a side hustle.'

'But ...' Tola looked at me in disappointment, 'think about the wives and girlfriends of your exes, how happy they must be that you sculpted these man-children into romantic heroes? We watch all these movies where dudes with abs know how to plan these hugely elaborate romantic surprises, and in reality women across the country are reminding their boyfriends to change their boxers on a daily basis. They deserve better, and we could give it to them. This could *be something*, Aly.'

'So what you're saying is, we'll help womankind by repro-gramming their boyfriends, one underachiever at a time?' I let the sarcasm seep through my words, and Tola grinned.

'That's exactly what I'm saying.' She put her arms around

both of us. 'Us three, having adventures. Affecting change. What could be better than that?'

'You're such a hustler. Let's . . . let's see what happens. But in the meantime, the next round is on me, in honour of Eric, much-loved actor extraordinaire and severely wasted talent in the advertising department.'

Eric gave a little bow and I got a round of espresso Martinis in celebration. It was the most fun I'd had on a Monday evening in a long time. It couldn't last though, not when they realised this wasn't a business plan or a workable scheme, no matter how much Tola wanted it to be. It wasn't going to be a YouTube series or a podcast or whatever it was people used to turn their faults into fame these days.

Which is exactly what I told Tola when Becky found us in the break room the next morning and thanked me for trying, said they had a good chat, but he hadn't changed his mind. I actually exhaled in relief, and then had to cover up by patting Becky on the shoulder and telling her it was nice to get the chance to chat to her though. She smiled at that.

Life could go on as normal, no crazy ideas or plans. I wanted the head of branding role. When I had it, I'd have respect. No more Hunter coming to me to do his work, or the ads guys giving in their reports late, or having to chase every single colleague to give me their work in the right format. I'd finally prove the theory I had based my entire working career on: If you work hard and stay determined, you'll get what you deserve.

Which, of course, all went to hell when Becky turned up on Friday with a sapphire-and-diamond engagement ring glinting in the light.

Chapter Four

Becky dragged us three out with her accounts team for celebration cocktails, lauding us as the people responsible for finally getting her boyfriend onside. I tried to wave it away, but Tola lapped it up, enjoying her moment in the spotlight, a feminist relationships expert, fanning the flames of exhaustion, rage and frustration until they became a huge bonfire.

'He doesn't remember our kids' birthdays!'

'I have to buy his mother's Christmas present every year!'

'I went away for a conference and my daughter went to school wearing yellow polka-dot tights and a Peppa Pig pyjama top!'

'I don't think he was really happy for me when I got that promotion, you know? Like, deep down.'

'I went back to uni to do my masters and now he says I act like I'm smarter than everyone.'

'He came home drunk and pissed in the laundry basket.'

Well, at least that last one was funny.

Listening to these stories spill out of my co-workers as they downed mojitos and white wine spritzers, I wondered if maybe, just maybe, I was lucky to be on my own? To have my own time and agency and no one to answer to? Maybe love wasn't worth the exhaustion. I thought of my grand-mother, preparing the dinner every night for fifty years, and how she never once complained. Maybe she would have, if I'd asked her.

'Are you his fucking mother?' Tola asked one of Becky's friends, pausing dramatically to sip from her straw. 'No? Then stop coddling! Stop feeding. Stop doing anything but demanding what you deserve. Because you are all *beautiful, wonderful women*, and you deserve to be worshipped! Those men should be on their fucking knees, grateful you put up with their badly shaved, unwashed, don't-know-where-the-dishwasher-tablets-are selves.'

There was hooting and whooping.

'This is rapidly turning from an engagement celebration into a potential ritual sacrifice,' I mumbled to Eric, who snorted and leaned in close to me.

'I'm trying not to make too many sudden movements in case they suddenly remember I'm here,' he mock-whispered.

'She's good with a crowd though,' I had to admit, watching Tola holding court. 'She's got the razzle-dazzle.'

'She's got more than that. I feel like she's determined to make this into something, and she's going to take us along for the ride no matter what. There's ambition, and then there's Tola.'

I watched the women talking and laughing with each other, looked at their faces as they joked about their shitty maternity packages and navigating in-laws and bumping into exes. Jealous boyfriends and early-morning runs and dyeing their hair.

These women were tired. And they didn't even realise it. The exhaustion of expectation and disappointment was part and parcel of being female. Like Tola said, they'd been hoping they'd meet someone who was already a fully mature grown-up who could cook his own dinner and knew what his mother's favourite flowers were.

'Excuse me,' one of Becky's friends broke off from the group and hovered at our table. 'You helped Tola, didn't you?'

Eric grinned and tilted his head to me. 'She's the mastermind. Expert in human ridiculousness.'

I elbowed him, smiled apologetically. 'I helped, yeah.'

She dragged a chair over and fell into it.

'I'm Emily. My husband doesn't know how to look after our baby. He offered to be the stay-at-home parent so I could go back to work, but he didn't read any of the books and he calls every fifteen minutes, or he gets my mother to come over and then she criticises me for leaving my baby at home because I want to be a "career woman". I make more money, I had to go back! And then I get home, and the house is a mess and he hands the baby over and plays PlayStation all evening! I know I should be grateful but ...'

I closed my eyes and tried to channel my inner agony aunt. 'Gratitude is an excellent emotion. But it's not a shield that holds off bullshit indefinitely.' *Where the hell did that come from?* I sounded like the daily horoscope on Tola's Mystic Mondays app. 'You just need to teach him.'

'I need to teach him to recognise that our daughter needs

looking after and it can't all be on me? Why can't he know it on his own? Why is it *my* responsibility to teach him?'

I made a face and threw up my hands. 'I have no idea, but unfortunately, if you want the spoils, you're gonna have to do the work – hopefully only briefly, but the benefits will be long term.'

'And you can do that?' Emily asked, suddenly hopeful.

'Well, we were thinking about starting a business outsourcing female emotional labour,' Eric told her. 'Apparently it might be the final puzzle piece in the dismantling of the patriarchy.'

She kept her eyes on me, waiting for me to say the word and solve all her problems. I was shocked to find I felt powerful. I loved looking at a problem and finding a solution. And I couldn't resist a challenge.

'OK, tell me how I can help.'

We had to find a baby, which sounds more alarming than it was. Luckily, Eric's friend Marcus was happy to help.

Marcus was a huge beast of a man, his T-shirt clinging to every visible muscle beneath his two-sizes-too-small T-shirt. The only thing that softened the complete 'gym bro' effect was his baby daughter, strapped to his front in a purple polka-dot sling, grinning up at him like he was the centre of her universe.

'OK, there are a few key points here,' I said as we huddled together in Finsbury Park on a blustery Saturday morning, where we knew Emily's husband took their daughter to play. 'Marcus, we need to show off that you're the ideal dad, and that your baby here is *thriving*.'

Marcus wiggled his eyebrows and grinned, adjusting his daughter in his arms. 'Always happy to be told I'm perfect.'

'As long as you're happy with a little healthy competition,' I teased. 'We need the husband, Liam, to see how well you're doing, how easy you make it look. We need him to want to be like you.'

Tola looked at Marcus suspiciously. 'Why are you helping us again?'

He laughed, and his daughter burbled in delight. 'Because Eric asked. And also because this guy is letting our side down. But mainly because the sooner men become more active parents, the sooner we get a decent paternity package.'

Tola smiled and nodded once, convinced.

'One that doesn't depend on having a female parent in the picture?' she asked, and Marcus pointed at her.

'Got it in one.'

'OK,' Tola rubbed her hands together, 'let's go start some shenanigans.'

Marcus made his way over to the swings, where Liam was half-heartedly pushing his daughter, eyes glued to his phone. We watched as Marcus ambled up, and saw Liam's eyes widen in surprise at the sheer size of him. I could almost see the thought-bubble above his head: *This guy is taking his kid to the park? Shouldn't he be in a gym somewhere? Or knocking someone's teeth out?*

'Is this seat taken?' Marcus smiled winningly, gesturing at the swing next to Liam's daughter.

Tola snorted in my ear, 'Is he *hitting on him?*'

Eric made a face, and sounded prickly when he

responded. 'Marcus is very happily married, he's just friendly.'

Liam stared at Marcus, saying nothing for a moment, and then half shrugged. 'Sure. Go ahead.'

'Cheers.' Marcus turned his attention to his daughter, chucking her up in the air and then sliding her into the swing, making faces and explaining what he was doing in a sing-song voice.

Liam's daughter started watching this new, exciting man in her field of vision intently, smiling and clapping at him more than I bet she ever had for the father standing slightly out of her field of vision with his hand glued to his phone. We watched as Liam seemed to realise this too, and blinked.

'He put his phone away!' Tola grabbed my arm in excitement.

'Shh!' hissed Eric.

'Let's get closer,' I said quietly, 'and stop acting like weirdos! Three childless grown-ups hanging near the kid's play area is not a great look!'

We snuck around to the bit of grass behind the swings, so we could listen to them chatting.

'You got a happy one!' Marcus said, smiling at Liam. He nodded his head at his own daughter: 'This one's already a moody teenager. I feel like I'm going to turn around from making her lunch and find her all dressed up to go clubbing. The time goes so quickly, doesn't it?'

Liam looked at him like he wasn't sure Marcus was actually talking to him. Like he hadn't had an adult conversation in a while, and had to remember how to do it.

'I dunno, sometimes it seems to go incredibly slowly,'

Liam sighed, then looked embarrassed, like he'd said the wrong thing. But Marcus smiled and nodded.

'Yeah, the ever-exciting routine of listening to them cry, waiting for them to shit all over the walls, crossing your fingers that they'll sleep, and then panicking when they do.' Marcus shrugged. 'Or is it just me that's an absolute mess? I kinda figured the stay-at-home-dad life would involve more cuddles and Xbox, you know?'

Liam's eyes lit up, even as Tola raised an eyebrow at me. 'Really?' she hissed.

'He's playing a part!' Eric defended his friend, then paused. '. . . At least, I think so.'

But that was all it took for Liam's defences to drop. Here was someone who wouldn't judge him, wouldn't tell him it was all meant to be a magical experience. He had someone to moan with, and you could see the relief on his face.

'You're a stay-at-home dad too!' Liam exclaimed, 'I haven't met many others. It's . . . yeah, it's a bit more . . . boring than I thought it would be.'

Marcus nodded, keeping his eyes on his daughter. 'Have you thrown up changing them yet? First time I changed her . . . I was sick, she was sick, we were both crying . . . it gets better.'

He looked at his daughter with such love, and Liam smiled.

'Besides,' Marcus added, 'how much of your job before was boring? This way you get to be the person to watch her grow. I get to hear her first words and see her walk. My other half finds that a bit hard, I think. But that's the way the finances go sometimes, right?'

Bringing in the fact that your partner makes more money, that it's a financial choice with no ego. Nice one, Marcus. I was starting to think I hadn't needed to make those flash cards for him; he was a natural.

'Yeah, Emily, my wife, I think she's sad she doesn't get that time. That's why I give her Lila as soon as she gets in, so she gets her one-on-one. I know how much she misses her during the workday.'

I widened my eyes at Tola, mouthing, *'Simple miscommunication!'*

'Yeah, I know what you mean, it must be hard for her. That's why when my partner gets in, I take it as a chance to sort out the washing and tidy up a bit, so they can have that time and not worry. We've got a good military-style system, haven't we, baby girl?' Marcus laughed at his daughter, who clapped her hands.

I caught sight of Liam's face, like it had never occurred to him.

'It's tempting to just dump the kid on them when they walk through the door and take time for yourself, right? But we try and be equals, so my partner takes the baby, I'll get dinner started. They'll do the bath, and then I'll go to the gym ... we both get our time.'

Liam looked at Marcus, and nodded, as if he had decided to reveal something to this mystical guide on his dad journey. He took a deep breath.

'I call Emily a lot at work. I just don't know if I'm doing a good job. Everyone's waiting for me to screw it up. To leave her on a park bench, or get her fingers stuck with superglue or find her chewing on the cat's tail.'

47

Liam rested a hand on his daughter's head, and I suddenly felt for him. He might be completely clueless as to what his wife needed, but he clearly wanted to be a good dad, a good partner. All he needed was a nudge. Maybe a role model. Definitely a community. I wondered if Marcus would catch that ...

'Are you part of a parent and baby group?'

Marcus, you're hired! I grinned at Tola and Eric, elated.

'Yeah, but they were mostly bossy mums and they kept telling me I was doing everything wrong, so ...'

'There are loads of dad groups!' Marcus said, pulling out his phone. 'Here, there's a local one I'm part of on Facebook – shall I invite you?'

I watched Liam's face at that moment, so much hope and relief that I felt myself get a little choked up. That look said *I'm not alone.*

'Oh, bless him,' Tola said softly, and I smiled at her, before nudging them both to shuffle further away from the play area. When we were a good distance from them, we started to speak at a normal volume again.

'That was ... unexpected,' Eric said. 'I thought the plan was to get them into a competition around whose kid was more impressive. I was looking forward to some sort of baby race!'

'We only get one side of the story,' Tola said, somehow more enthused than before. 'Turned up thinking he was some waste of a dad, selfish and whatnot, but the man just needed some community and support!'

'He thought he was helping by chucking the baby at Emily as soon as she came in the door,' I said softly, shaking my head. 'Of course he did.'

'That's cute. I like it. We came here ready to see him fail and found him ready to grow. Love to see it!' Tola waved her hands in the air. 'Come *on*! You two see it now, right? You see that we could help people! There is *something here.*'

'Yeah, OK, but what is *it*, exactly?' Eric countered, raising an eyebrow. 'Play-acting undercover to save people's relationships, when really they should go to therapy?'

I looked at him. 'Strong words from someone who still doesn't talk to a whole bunch of his family members after coming out.'

He threw up his hands. 'They don't talk to me. Which is why you go to therapy to fix *yourself*, not to fix other people. You can't change people who don't want to change.'

'He didn't *know* he wanted to change. Or that his relationship needed saving.' Tola gestured towards Liam looking at Marcus like he'd appeared solely to present him with a genie, three wishes and a deep-dish pepperoni pizza. 'And now he does. Bippity boppety boo, bitches. We're on to something.'

Chapter Five

It moved pretty quickly after that, and Tola took charge. She believed in what we were doing with her whole heart. That we could do good, have fun fixing relationships, free women from their selflessness, and get them to turn that energy inwards. I half expected her to add 'world peace' to the list.

Eric wanted the chance to live out his acting fantasies and distract from his less-than-successful love life, so he was along for the ride too.

And I ... I was being useful. Helping people. A trait I'd been ashamed of was suddenly the key to everything Tola wanted us to do. They couldn't do it without me. And I was enjoying that a little too much.

Tola had a very clear game plan: we'd test our 'fixing up' out on lots of different types of relationship problems and see if there was anything we couldn't handle. At the beginning, we wondered whether we'd find anyone else, but we needn't have worried. Becky and Emily mentioned it to their friends, who had sisters, who had more friends, and by the time three months had passed we had a playbook, a questionnaire, and a booking system.

The men – yes, it was usually men – fell into distinct categories: 1) The unmotivated, 2) the unwilling to commit. They were miserable at their job, but they wouldn't dedicate the time to discovering what it was they wanted. They wanted to start a business or write a book or record a song, but they would rather talk about it than do it. Sometimes the women wanted engagements, but more than anything it just seemed a lot of incredibly strong, motivated women were tired of dragging their partner forward and waiting for him to grow up. These were women who went to therapy and worked with career mentors and ran big companies while setting up side hustles. Women who invested in themselves. And still, they needed to look after their partner. They worried about his happiness, whether he was content, whether he was bonded with his kids, whether he was satisfied in his choices. They left endless Post-it notes and set alarms and wrote on calendars. They ran their shared lives with the efficiency and diligence of an army general. And still, they worried about being a nag – the worst thing a woman could be, after a spinster, of course.

There were a few honeytraps – women wondering if their husbands were cheating – but we decided early on those were not for us. They weren't about growth. They were about revealing who someone really was, and I honestly didn't like being the person to lure out the worst of someone and then serve it up like a gift. And we knew most of the time they wouldn't believe us anyway.

Tola loved it, spent hours designing bright pink business

cards and an aggressively shouty website. But we knew it had to be a secret – it was this woman-only club, a sudden recognition whenever we spoke to anyone. *Yes!* they told us, *that IS what's happening, that IS what I've had to deal with!* So we knew it couldn't be an ordinary website. We needed a level of anonymity, protection.

It was Eric's idea to hide the Fixer Upper in plain sight – a website designed to support busy women, with articles, counselling links, something basic and colourful with no hint of what we were really doing. You could only get to the booking platform if you clicked on a link for moon cups and filled out a form. Eric created an algorithm to scan for the words 'tired', 'exhausted', 'fed up'. Tola's new business cards simply said *Unhappy? Fix it* with a password for the website.

We barely needed them, word of mouth was enough.

People are unique, sure, but their problems are not. There were patterns to identify and things that always seemed to work, and backups for if those strategies weren't right. I filled notebooks with different 'plays', like I was an emotional con artist and, though I'd never tell the others, I loved the pretence of it all. There were wigs and outfits to wear, and characters to become. Eric tried to do accents but he was terrible at them, so we vetoed that immediately. We were creating chance encounters that changed people's perspectives. And that felt pretty powerful, even if they were orchestrated.

My evenings were suddenly full, scheming with Tola, shopping with Eric. Staking out a bar, trying out that perfect opening line.

'You're still thinking too small,' Tola would say. 'We need

to be helping women help themselves, not just their partners. We could do big things here, Aly!'

'I like small,' I would reply, 'small is manageable. And this way we get to have fun with no risks. We get to play.'

Then she'd get that serious look that she got when she was frustrated with me, one eyebrow curving into a deep groove at the top of her nose, but she wouldn't say anything.

I knew she thought I was a chicken. She'd have huge ideas, big plans to launch the Fixer Upper as a lifestyle brand, a company, a twelve-step programme, and I'd pop the bubble, always finding a problem. I'd bring her back down to earth. But eventually, people start resenting you being the anchor, even if you are keeping them steady. Tola wanted to set the world on fire, and I was dousing every spark before it could flame.

So we agreed to let her factor in a few repeat clients – people who needed more of a nudge. A chance encounter and then a surprise follow-up, a reminder of the things you'd discovered to help the message sink in. After all, a pub conversation can be fleeting. We were creating the illusion of fated interactions. The universe was sending you a message, so you better listen up.

But the truth was, the more we did this (and did it well), the angrier I became at myself. Every time another woman sent us a bottle of champagne or a thank you card, I wanted to bash my head against a wall. I could control everyone else's life but my own.

But Tola didn't see it that way.

Which was why seven months and twelve days after our first experiment, she strode over to my desk and threw a business card down on the table like she was straight out of a gangster movie.

'We have a new client.'

I blinked. 'What?'

'The FU,' Tola grinned. She loved shortening Fixer Upper and watching me wince. I picked up the card and did a double take on the name, looking up at her.

'This is for real?'

She leaned against my desk and let her beautiful smile beam at full wattage. It was almost blinding. 'It is one hundred per cent legit. I spoke to her and her posse. It was mad.'

'How did she find us?' I frowned. 'Surely she has people for this sort of thing?'

Tola grinned. 'Babe, we *are* the people for this sort of thing. Her assistant heard about us from a friend and applied through the Moon Portal. I called to see if it was for real, and it is! Can you *believe* even the rich and famous need our skills?'

I looked at the spiky font, declaring *Nicolette Wetherington Smythe: content creator, producer, innovator, entrepreneur and influencer.*

'God, she's a busy one.'

'She must have run out of room for "social climber", "contestant on absolutely any reality TV show that'll take her" and "heiress to a kitty litter empire",' Eric said, leaning on the divider for my desk area, chomping on an apple. 'We've gotta do it though, right? If only for the shits and giggles. What kind of beefcake is she dating? Last thing I read, she was dating the captain of the England rugby team!'

'Nah,' Tola exhaled, 'that was years ago. It *used* to be

54

that posh Chelsea wanker off the TV show they were in? You know, on-again, off-again, drama for the sake of it? But I think this is like . . . a normal guy? Her assistant was pretty cagey. Said she wants to have a proper meeting if we're going to go for it. She wants . . .' Tola dropped her voice and lifted her fingers into quote marks, 'an *intensive series of occurrences.*'

Eric and I looked at each other, frowning in confusion.

'Is it me, or does that sound like some sort of horrible obstacle course?'

'Or a really scary summer camp.'

Tola placed both her hands on the desk, super dramatic, and paused to make sure she had our full attention. She was loving this.

'She wants full exclusivity for a month.'

'Jesus Christ, what's wrong with the guy? Bathe him in holy water or something.'

Eric had a point, and I tilted my head at Tola, requesting more information, but she threw up her hands.

'I know nothing. Except that I *really* want to go to this meeting. Because when the rich and famous come calling and demanding ridiculous things, you can be certain it's going to be interesting. And that there'll be expensive champagne.' She grinned and looked between the two of us like we were the rigid parents who could snatch away her dream of staying up till midnight. 'So we're going to do this, right? At least hear her out? I am so *intrigued.*'

'You guys go and report back,' Eric said, then mimed hiding his face behind his hands. 'I get all flustered around celebrities.'

'You *barely* knew who she was.'

'It doesn't matter. If *they* think they're famous, I get tongue-tied. Plus anytime I go to Fixer Upper meetings, they wait for me to say something and then go: *Oh, it's so interesting to have a male perspective*,' he moaned, and Tola looked at me.

'Um, welcome to our world,' I snorted, 'at least you get pockets.'

'Fine, me and Aly will meet the Kitty Litter Princess and see what kind of Peter Pan type she's dating and decide if it's worth the stress. Plan?'

'Plan,' I agreed, then paused, 'um, can I get back to work now?'

Tola rolled her eyes, and stalked off, throwing an 'if you must' over her shoulder.

'Do you ever feel like we're just along for the ride here?' Eric asked me with a little laugh, shaking his head.

'I'd feel more trusting in this scenario if there was some sort of makeover montage and Tola suddenly made me cool,' I replied.

'Maybe she's harnessing our potential, the same way we're doing with those guys. We were the ones who needed to be fixed all along!' He made a dorky *oh my God I can't believe it* face and I laughed.

'Too scary to contemplate. Go! I'll see you later!'

I had a nanosecond to watch Eric's eyeline as it switched to over my left shoulder and his lip twitched. Oh crap.

I turned in my seat, knowing exactly who I'd see.

'Hunter. How can I help you this morning?'

*

Nicolette Wetherington Smythe was not someone accustomed to having to wait for what she wanted. So when she replied to Tola's message with an invitation to The Royale for drinks that evening, I was intrigued to see how difficult one man could be that he needed our total attention for a whole month. I also wondered what kind of man would be worth putting in the work for, when it came to someone like Nicolette. She was beautiful in that way rich girls in reality shows were: painfully skinny and bronzed, and vaguely ethereal, like someone had brought a mannequin to life. So I wondered why, especially if she was dating someone non-famous, she didn't simply go out there and get herself a new model.

Tola met me outside the office and looked at my work outfit in dismay.

'Don't start with me,' I held my hand up to her, and then threw it out for the black cab coming up towards us. We jumped in, and when I gave the cabbie the address, only a few minutes away, he huffed. But we were not walking in heels down Oxford Street, I didn't care how famous she was.

'It's just so . . . black. What's with the war on colour, Aly? There is so much beauty to be worn in the world!'

'Black is professional, it's slimming, it doesn't show dirt. It's always chic,' I said, before digging into my handbag for my lipstick. 'Besides, look, colour!'

I applied my signature orange-red using my phone camera and pressed my lips together in satisfaction.

'One of these days you're gonna trust me enough to let me shop for you, and it's going to change your life,' Tola sighed, but smiled to show she wasn't serious. 'So, do we need to do any prep?'

'Like what?' I felt my phone vibrate in my bag, and rifled around until I grabbed it. Mama. Of course. I sent her to voicemail, wincing as I did, then rattled off a quick apology text, already worried about how she was going to react.

Tola was looking at me like I was about to mess this whole thing up. I put down my phone. 'What kind of research do you want to do?' I repeated, showing I was listening.

'Like . . . read up about Nicolette?' She narrowed her eyes at me. 'What is this? You love research!'

I nodded. 'Sure, but we don't know anything about the situation yet. This *is* the research part. We go, we listen, we ask questions and, Tola, this part is very important: *We do not commit to anything on the spot.* OK?'

She saluted, 'No worries. You're the boss.'

I don't think I am, somehow.

Whenever I meet famous people I'm always shocked by how normal they look. How inconspicuous, in their ratty jeans and scuffed Converse. If Tola hadn't made a beeline for Nicolette, I would have spent ages scanning the low-lit bar for the influencer, searching for someone who looked like they did behind a filter.

Nicolette sat in a one-shoulder top and ripped jeans with calf-skin boots, her long blond hair flowing over her shoulder. Her only really distinctive feature was her eyebrows, full and permanently arched like she was waiting for you to tell her a joke. She smiled and waved as we arrived, and it was like a magnet, reeling us in.

'Hello hello!' She grabbed our hands and air-kissed us both, before gesturing opposite her. 'Sit! Sit! I am *so* excited to meet you guys! I have heard *such* things!'

I could almost see the italics in her speech, but she was much warmer than I'd expected.

'It's so great to meet you too, Nicolette—' I started, but she shrieked.

'—Nicki! Please! You *must* call me Nicki!'

'Nicki,' I nodded, and she immediately jumped in.

'I ordered you cocktails.' She pushed the neon pink drinks across to us. 'My boyfriend says you've got to let bartenders do their thing, but I like being the creator, telling them what to put in. It makes it a really personal experience. So this is my creation: the Love Drunk Flamingo!'

Tola reached for hers, and I took a sip, plastering a smile on my face. It tasted like someone had blended a Barbie doll with a My Little Pony. And then stuck a grapefruit on top.

'Refreshing!' I blinked, smacking my lips.

'I always think it's so nice when you arrive somewhere and have something waiting for you, don't you?' Nicki grinned at me. 'There's too many decisions to make in life; I love it when someone takes control.' *Like a bartender . . . ?*

'So,' I assumed my bright-eyed look of enthusiasm and that voice that craved the gossip, 'tell us about *The Boy.*'

I always phrased it like that, like we were teenagers sharing secrets over a bottle of Bacardi Breezer at a house party. Like they could mention all the things they loved about him before they finally got to the stubborn parts they wanted to change. Before they allowed themselves to admit that things weren't quite right.

'Oh, he's so *amazing*, he's—' she started, before stopping herself. 'Oh, sorry, got a bit ahead of myself there. First I need you both to sign a *teensy* bit of paperwork – you know how it is. The tabloids and all that.'

She slid over two fairly basic NDAs, which Tola and I scanned before signing. Though I wondered if offering us a drink beforehand might have invalidated them. It didn't really matter, I had no interest in telling anyone who Nicki was dating. I just wanted to know what her problem was. And a tiny, stubborn part of me wanted to prove that I, Alyssa Aresti, could change a man who was too difficult even for a famous, beautiful heiress to conquer.

We slid the paperwork back, and she folded it away into her huge handbag.

'Wonderful! So, you want me to tell you about him?' Nicki asked, expecting a chorus of enthused yeses, but we simply nodded.

'We met in a restaurant a few years ago, he actually spilled a drink on me, and when I accused him of doing it on purpose, he told me to get over myself!' Nicki's laugh was high-pitched, like someone gently rattling a tin cup. 'I'd assumed he knew who I was, but he had no idea. But I like a bad boy and this gruff, not-out-to-impress-me thing was different to anyone else I knew at the time.' She rolled her eyes, as if realising how ridiculous it was that everyone around her catered to her every whim. But I had a feeling she was rolling her eyes at something else.

'Of course, once I got to know him, I realised he wasn't like that at all. He's warm and friendly and gets on with everyone. We went out a few times and it was all ... so normal. We didn't go anywhere fancy. I mean, one night we went to Nando's!' She put her hand to her chest as if the idea was outrageous. 'And then gradually I started showing him *my* world, we went on some great trips and spent time in nicer places and he met some of the guys on my shows...'

And he liked it. Of course. How could you not, seeing the privilege and glamour that came with Nicki's lifestyle? How easy it would be to get used to the free drinks and fancy holidays.

'And he understands, now, the life that I lead, what I'm accustomed to. We go on holidays, he plans dates, he gets what comes with dating someone like me. I'm not really a *dinner at Nando's* girl, right? And he learned that. But ... I get the feeling he doesn't really believe in what I do.'

What do you actually do?

'What part of your career doesn't he get?' Tola asked, perfectly phrased, and I wanted to squeeze her in relief.

'The influencer thing. He thinks ...' Nicki took an unsteady breath, 'he says it's like I'm always performing to an invisible audience. That I'm never myself, I'm never OK about leaving the fans outside my personal life.'

'Ahh,' Tola nodded, 'but that's the job, is it? You've gotta be completely vulnerable, completely authentic. Share every sob and every triumph.'

Nicki pointed at her aggressively. 'Exactly! Exactly! You get it, of course you get it! My fans are my bread and butter. They need to stay interested for me to get any work. My numbers, follows and engagement need to be up there. But he doesn't get that.'

'What does your boyfriend do for work, Nicki?' I asked.

You couldn't expect everyone to understand digital marketing and the way the money worked. Especially if

Nicki's boyfriend was someone who had a more traditional career. We would have to find a way to make him see the value. See the trade-off for those fancy holidays. It wouldn't take a month.

'He's an app developer.'

I almost spat Nicki's Barbie monstrosity cocktail across the table.

'An app developer who doesn't see the value of social media as a marketing platform for developing a brand?' Tola said, so scandalised I almost laughed.

'He's a start-up entrepreneur, really innovative and creative. He sees the value of it, he just wants me to step back.' She tilted her head. 'And I want him to step *up*.' *Ah, and now we were getting somewhere.*

'In what way, Nicki?' I leaned forward, willing her to trust us, to use exactly the right words so I could identify her problem. Diagnose her relationship.

'Well, there's the professional side. He's been a start-up for a while and he hasn't actually *started up*, you know? He's too cautious. He's been burnt before and I get it, but the whole point of start-ups is that they move quickly. You get a backer and you get going, right?'

'Right,' I nodded. 'But he's taking his time. Have you funded his business?'

'No, he wouldn't let me. He says it's his thing, his responsibility. I would have, though, it's really good. He's literally a genius.'

She pronounced it the way posh people did – *jeen-yus.*

OK, so it's not the money. He's got honour, wants to do it on his own terms. He maybe needs a little hand-holding?

My phone buzzed and I looked down at it, dismayed. Mama, again. I sent it to voicemail and plastered a look of apology on my face, but Nicki didn't even notice.

'I feel like I'm really focused on building my brand and he's ... not. I'm dragging him along behind me, and I'm tired. I don't have the time for that.'

Tola smiled and I had to give it to Nicki, she was doing exactly what Tola said. Putting herself first. The papers might call her a selfish, spoiled princess, but I kind of loved it.

'He's got a big meeting at the end of the month, pitching to investors, and I think he needs some help.'

I frowned. 'I mean, that absolutely aligns with our mission, but why wouldn't you use a business coach for that? Why use a relationship one?'

'Because *I've* got a big meeting at the end of the month too ...' She looked around, searching for the words as if they were hovering in the air next to the faux stained-glass windows or on the velvet lining of the booth. 'I don't have enough energy for the both of us.' *Oh, love.*

I'd felt that, so many times before. Like you were carrying a friend with a twisted ankle across the marathon finish line. But the reality was that a lot of the time they hadn't done the training and they weren't wearing the right shoes and they would rather you'd pushed them along in a wheelbarrow right from the beginning to save them the bother of having to run at all.

Tola reached over and put her hand over Nicki's, who looked up from beneath her lashes and exhaled shakily. It sounded like relief.

'I'm so glad you guys exist! I didn't know what to do. And of course, with my profile, it's important that I date someone who can be successful on their own, you know? Someone who's willing to be part of it all but will also bring something of his own to the table.'

Trying to follow Nicki's thought process was like chasing a butterfly around a sauna. I wondered how much editing they'd had to do on that TV show.

'So . . . it's important that your boyfriend be successful?' I ventured.

'Oh, it's *so* important. It's social equity, you know? My agent was desperate for me to move on to another reality star, or maybe an up-and-coming singer, someone who would really boost my brand, introduce me to a whole new audience. But, it's love, it can't be helped.' She shrugged. 'What *can* be helped is his anti-social-media thing. If he's successful and a bit more vocal about it by the end of the month . . .'

'His pitch to the investors will be better received?'

'Sure. But it will also look good for *my* meeting. I've got a chance at something really big, but I need him by my side. Him at his sparkliest, most impressive, social-media friendly best.'

I felt Tola look at me out of the corner of my eye and tried not to grind my teeth. 'Nicki, if we work together, it's really important we know exactly what you want, so we can manage expectations. Can you tell us about this potential project you're hoping to get?'

She looked at us with wide eyes, clearly loving every moment of the drama. 'You can't tell a *soul*.'

I made a zipping motion across my mouth.

'It's a new show called *Celebrity Wedding Wars*,' she squealed and clapped her hands. 'They have three celebs on, and they each go to each others' weddings and judge them, and the best one wins money for charity. If I win, they're talking about launching a wedding dress line with a respected designer. My own wedding dress designs, can you imagine?'

'I really, really can't.'

'So you can see why I'd need you for the whole month! That's a lot to do! A life overhaul and a proposal!' She laughed again, and the tinny noise made my molars twinge.

I was gobsmacked. Not only did she want her un-motivated, social-media-phobe, app developer boyfriend to finally reach his start-up potential, she wanted him presented with influencer-level followers, a changed attitude, and a proposal by the end of the month? What was this woman *on*?

'Nicki, no offence but have you considered just … getting rid of him and starting with a blank canvas?' I said, completely serious.

She laughed.

'Oh you're *hilarious*,' she turned to Tola. 'Isn't she hilarious? I can't, I love him.'

'But … nothing you've said about him matches what you *want*. You are asking us to change him into an entirely different person. In a month. Have you guys talked about marriage? How long have you been together?'

Nicki waved away my concerns like I was a doddering aunt. 'About a year. And of course we have, we've been to so many of my friends' weddings. It always comes up.'

'And . . . ?' Tola ventured, that serene smile now wiped off her face.

'He says when the time is right, it'll be right. So that's your job. To convince him the time is right. Perhaps he'll be so thrilled with his success with the investors that it'll be an immediate impulse anyway!'

'Is he expected to pick the ring, or would you like our help with that too?' I said drily, and Nicki chuckled.

'I've already picked it out. Goodness, you'd let a man pick the jewellery you have to wear for the rest of your life? You're brave!'

I'd never been a romantic, but I thought again of my grandparents. The way they danced together at the end of the night, the way his eyes softened as he looked at her across a room. The hand she put on his cheek sometimes when she was passing by. Love.

Listening to Nicki was like pouring a bucket of warm piss over every beautiful romantic gesture I'd ever seen. *This is what happens when influencers get endless attention and have no limit on resources. This is narcissism at its most extreme.*

I looked at Tola, who gave me a hopeless sort of smile. Well, we'd come, we'd drunk the awful drink and heard the famous lady with her crazy plan. It would be a fun story to tell. Plus, I loved The Royale, it was like standing on the deck of the *Titanic*, all the art deco features and fancy little tables. Maybe Tola and I could get dinner and laugh about how ridiculous this all was . . .

'Nicki, I've got to be honest, I don't know that we could pull this off,' Tola said gently.

'Oh, you're just being modest!' Nicki flapped her hands as

if dispelling our arguments. 'I'd do it myself if I had the time, but I've got so much else on. My last boyfriend proposed and he wasn't that into the idea either at first.' *The reality TV guy?*

'But he understood the benefit to both your brands, right?' Tola nudged. 'He was part of that world.'

Nicki sighed, clearly irritated. 'Look, why not start by meeting him? That's what you do, right, you meet him to assess the damage? And then if you really think it's hopeless, that's fine.'

Tola and I hovered, not saying yes or no, so Nicki took it as an affirmative and nodded, picking up her phone. 'Good. Also, we should talk fees.'

'Fees?'

We'd only been covering our bar tabs so far, like a hobby that produced champagne. That's why I'd been confident that this wouldn't turn into a full-time business, wouldn't get in the way of my career. The Fixer Upper had been three friends playing dress-up and having fun helping people. This felt . . . like a full-on legal nightmare.

'For your time, darling, if you took the project on? I understand it's obviously a lot of work, what with the business coaching and the social goals and the romance stuff, it's like a full-on life coach for a month.'

'Well, yes, we'd have to go away and crunch some numbers, based on how many hours . . .' Tola started, but Nicki fluttered her hands again.

'Well, I had a think about an average month's work, and then the travel and everything, so I thought ten thousand would be fair, what do you think? Though, obviously, if there are extra services along the way, I get that.'

She looked at us, wide-eyed and unblinking, and Tola squeezed my knee under the table, as if telling me not to screw this up. *Ten grand* to gradually wear down a guy's personality for a month? *Ten grand*.

I took a breath. 'Nicki, you do understand we can't *guarantee* a proposal, right?'

She smiled like a Cheshire cat. 'Of course, darling. Legally, that would be a nightmare. We could always set up a slightly more ... encouraging payment structure? Like five thousand for the month of coaching and the rest as a bonus *if* he proposes?'

I tried not to freak out. Why was this so different to the other women moaning about their boyfriends not committing? Why did it feel so much worse this time? I couldn't tell if it was the money or that I felt sorry for the poor guy.

I looked to Tola in panic, and she patted my hand.

'Nicki—'

'Just meet him, OK? Don't be so negative!' She grinned again, that wide, perfect smile that somehow seemed to take up too much of her face, like she'd transformed into a piranha after masquerading as a dolphin. And then her gaze shifted into the distance. 'Perfect timing!'

Nicki stood up and waved behind us, and I knew exactly what she'd done. She'd hired people to manipulate her boyfriend, and she'd manipulated us into meeting him. Of course. This was a woman who got shit done. I'd admire her if I wasn't so irritated.

I widened my eyes at Tola, who raised an eyebrow, unimpressed. We weren't taking on this crazy job anyway, so it didn't matter. We'd say hello, make our apologies, and leave to laugh about this somewhere more affordable. Tola nodded, as if she knew exactly what I was thinking.

And then I saw him.

The man walking across the bar to Nicki was tall, his dark hair pushed back almost artfully, and his blue eyes zeroed in on her. He had a lazy smile on his face. One I'd have recognised anywhere.

He wore a dark suit with an open-necked white shirt, and I knew without looking that he'd have a silver St Christopher around his neck and that one of his front teeth was a fake. I knew it the same way I knew he was afraid of horses and had broken his ankle when he was thirteen and that he pressed his thumb and forefinger together when he was thinking.

Dylan James.

He had been my whole childhood, my best friend, my first love. And I hadn't seen him in fifteen years.

Chapter Six

I was going to be sick, I was going to be so sick. How was I even meant to play this? Cool and reserved? Act like nothing had happened and hope he'd do the same? I had to pretend in that way that everyone pretends when they see someone from their past. I had to be the charming, plucky girl I was when Jason bumped into me in line at that restaurant: *Look how well I'm doing.*

But Dylan could always see through my fake smiles.

When he got to the table, I stood up, waiting for him to recognise me.

'Oh my God,' I started, and he looked at me.

'Well, that's quite the greeting!' Dylan held out a hand, laughing as he met my eyes. 'Dylan James, good to meet you.'

I felt my face drop. I stood there, still holding his hand, inwardly shrivelling. I wanted to yell, *Dyl, you idiot, it's me!* But the way his eyes met mine stopped me. This wasn't accidental. He was pretending on purpose.

Somehow that was worse than fake niceties.

I felt suddenly weak, and sat down.

'This is Aly and Tola,' Nicki trilled, focused on her phone in her hand, not even looking up. 'They're business coaches. I've been talking to them about a couple of my projects, but I actually think they'd be really good to help you ahead of your big meeting. What do you think, baby?'

She looked back up at him, clearly expecting an enthused response. Dylan rubbed the back of his neck and winced a little. 'I think I've been here thirty seconds and you're already trying to fix my life.' He kissed her temple to take the sting from his words, and took the phone from her hands, placing it on the table. Nicki raised an eyebrow, but said nothing.

God, you have no idea.

'So . . .' His eyes met mine, and I could feel myself glaring. *Say something, go on, say something.* 'If I hired you, I could depend on you to be there when I needed, right? You'll be around for the whole month? Wouldn't want to end up needing you only to find you'd disappeared.' He looked away and took a sip of the beer that a waiter brought over, nodding his thanks to him. 'That wouldn't be very . . . professional.'

Oh, so that was how it was going to be.

I wanted to let out a stream of excuses and arguments – *I left for uni, you had a girlfriend, and also, fuck you* – but I stopped myself.

I let Tola respond with how we worked in London and had met a few years ago, that we still worked at an agency while starting up our own business.

He sat back in the booth, relaxed as anything, smiling and nodding, completely pleasant. And then those blue eyes met mine like they were a dare.

'And what about you – Aly, was it?' *You know my name, you bastard. You know my middle name and my mum's name and the name of the bunny rabbit I had when I was twelve.*

'Alyssa.' I turned on my work smile, though it felt like chewing glass. 'What about me?'

'You can be trusted? If we hired you, you'd be there?'

Somehow, this arrogant man smirking at me was the boy who'd held my hand when my parents got divorced. The boy who'd cried on my shoulder when his mum died. The person I'd shared my first cigarette with, my first beer with. All my secrets with. Up until there was one I couldn't share.

'If people tell me the truth, I'm loyal until the end.' I smiled tightly, meeting his eyes. I got the satisfaction of watching them flash with irritation. There was no getting away from history. Dylan James could pretend all he liked, but knowing who someone used to be is a peculiar power.

I don't think I'd realised we'd been staring at each other for so long, until Tola narrowed her eyes at me, and said, 'We're open books, what other information can we provide?'

The whole time, Nicki watched us with interest, her chin resting on her hand. Like we were a TV show she couldn't stop watching. Maybe she thought this was all part of our spiel, that our act included me growling at the mark until he stopped acting like an arsehole. Still, her eyes kept flicking to her phone on the table, like she was waiting for an opportunity to steal it back. As interesting as we were, we couldn't compete with hundreds of thousands of loyal followers, validating her every thought.

Dylan focused on Tola, thinking about his question carefully. 'You two are business experts?'

'We're experts at helping people reach their potential,' I replied before Tola could, and tilted my head slightly. *Don't you remember? You were the first, after all.*

He laughed derisively. 'How sweet. Hand-holding and cheerleading then, is it?'

'Babe!' Nicki yelped, amusement surfacing alongside the embarrassment. 'Don't be rude!'

'Well, we won't be doing your maths homework for you, if that's what you mean,' I bit back, outwardly hostile now. Even my smile didn't hide it. He smirked like he'd won a point.

I'd been so excited to see him, even through my mortification. He could have greeted me with that same smile, that same shrug, and everything would have been fine. Instead, I felt like a fool for that brief jump of delight when he appeared. A child who should have known better.

'Well, leave me your business card, it's getting rather exhausting harnessing all this potential on my own,' he laughed, more genuinely that time, and winked at me. *Winked at me.* I bristled, but he'd already moved on, asking Tola about her customised leather jacket and getting Nicki's input on fashion, generally coordinating a conversation that completely bypassed me altogether.

Dylan had always been charming, even as a gawky teenager. He had a way of getting you to smile, no matter how annoyed you were at him. He knew that once he had you smiling – didn't matter if you were a girl with a crush or a teacher looking for geography homework – you were a goner. I always wondered whether that charisma and friendliness would grow into untempered narcissism without me around to make fun of him, to remind him to be real. And it seemed I was right. But it was unfair that he got to be handsome, too.

Nicki had picked well. She acknowledged every waitress who glanced his way, every woman who turned her head as they walked by, and no doubt she loved it. It was a fraction of the attention she would have gotten when dating that reality TV star, but still a little recognition that, yes, this one was special.

Dylan had filled out, he was solid and broad-shouldered, and his shirtsleeves tightened around his biceps as he reclined against the booth. I supposed that wasn't a surprise; his dad used to be in the army, he always made him do drills on Sunday mornings to keep fit. Some things were the same, though. Those dark eyelashes were still lush and curly. I'd spent endless minutes complaining about how unfair it was that he got Bambi lashes while I had to near blind myself with curling contraptions and mascara wands. He would flutter his lashes and grin at me. '*Why'd you bother with any of that crap anyway, Aly? It's only us, no one cares.*' I'd been the best friend, never a girl.

I knew Dylan could feel my eyes on him because his gaze kept flitting back to me, before refocusing. I wanted him to wonder what I thought of him, whether I was measuring him up and finding him wanting all these years later. I just didn't want to wonder what he thought of me.

When we said our goodbyes ten eternal minutes later, Dylan didn't meet my eyes. Instead he focused on my left earlobe as he raised a hand in farewell, still relaxed in the booth.

'Really *lovely* to meet you,' he said, stony-faced and thin-lipped.

'Yeah, Mr James,' I said, over-enunciating, 'really *illuminating*.'

I watched as the irritation appeared again and knew I'd won. Which would have meant something if I didn't have the strange desire to burst into tears.

When we finally escaped out onto the busy street, Tola grabbed my hand. 'What the hell was *that*?'

'*Unfuckingbelievable*, that's what that was.'

I felt like I'd been hit by a car, and the bright greys of a London sky and the people milling about us on the pavement weren't helping. I must have looked as faint as I felt, because Tola took charge.

She led me to a bar around the corner, sat me down, marched up to the bar and ordered us two Martinis and a shared platter of fried goodies, because as she often said, onion rings are good for the soul.

By the time she returned, I'd started to feel a little more normal. Tola placed the drink in front of me and gestured for me to sip, like it was a ceremonial beginning to our conversation.

'Good?' she asked, and I sipped and nodded.

'OK,' she splayed her hands, 'spill.'

It was hard to know where to start, or how much to reveal. Whether I should leave the embarrassing stuff out, downplay how much he'd been a part of my life. Keep it simple.

'Dylan James is my best friend.'

Tola frowned. 'Didn't *look* like that.'

I winced. *Idiot*.

'Was. Was my best friend.' Though he hadn't had much competition over the years. My last real friend before I'd met Tola and Eric, which was more embarrassing than I wanted to admit. I wasn't easy to get to know.

The years after Dylan I had been head down, focused on my studies, not wanting to get hurt again, dating a guy who barely even noticed I was around most of the time. *You make it difficult to like you, Aly,* he used to say. Three wasted years with someone who didn't even like me very much. Someone who took the place of friends and hobbies and all those experiences you're meant to have when you're away from home for the first time.

Which was why I left university with a first-class degree, and no one to hug goodbye at graduation.

'I met him on the first day of secondary school. We were the only ones who really got each other . . .'

I kept trying to place the image of a teenage Dylan onto the man I'd just seen, but it was almost impossible. The Dylan I knew smiled all the time, and not that tight, fake smile, but real and wide. He had the loudest laugh I'd ever heard.

'And you had a huge argument and never spoke again?' Tola filled in the details, 'because that was what that looked like. Except for the weird "pretending not to know you" thing.'

'It was a bit more complicated than that . . .' I sighed, trying to figure out how vulnerable to make myself. But Tola smiled and patted my hand.

'Tell me.'

'I developed a crush. It was the last year of school and I

76

thought if I could only get to uni and meet someone new, it would pass, you know?' I pressed my lips together. 'I'd start my whole new life, and he'd still be my friend and everything would be perfect.'

'But . . .'

'We were at this party, playing truth or dare, and one of the guys dared Dylan to kiss me. As if it was the worst, most ridiculous punishment they could think of for him.' I evened my voice out, tapping my fingertips on the tabletop. 'I don't know if you've ever been kissed by someone you have a crush on in front of a room full of people who think it's hilarious, but it broke me. It was like everything I'd wanted and the worst humiliation I could imagine, all at once.'

He'd smiled down at me after, thumbed my cheek with affection in his eyes, and for the smallest moment my heart had leapt with hope. Maybe it *had* meant something. Then he turned round to everyone else and said, 'All right, you've had your fun, you weirdos, next person!'

'I got absolutely hammered. Like, half-a-bottle-of-tequila-and-a-whole-freaking-lemon hammered. I was completely gone.' I blinked to stop myself cringing.

'Hey, it happens, you were a teenager,' Tola shrugged one shoulder and nudged me gently, as if reminding me she was right there next to me.

'But you know when you look back and realise how fucking dangerous it was, to be so out of control? How you treated yourself with so little care?'

Tola tilted her head and gave me a look, as if to say: '*You still do*.' She didn't speak for a few seconds, and then said, 'Babe, is this story about to get super dark?'

I shook my head, and she nodded, just once. I knew in that moment, no matter how dark the story might have become, she would have responded the same way: taking a sip of her Martini, smiling gently and encouraging me to continue in my own time.

'Dylan found me, took me home, and looked after me. I don't remember much, I don't remember what I said. I know I was sick, I know he gave me his T-shirt. I must have given myself away somehow because I said something and all I remember is his eyes widening in shock. He was horrified.'

God, telling this to Tola, even so many years later, was hard.

'And then it was morning, and I was under the covers and he was on top of them, and his phone buzzed. Messages from his girlfriend, annoyed that he'd looked after me instead of "*deflowering*" her as they had previously arranged.' I tried to laugh it off, but Tola didn't laugh with me. She looked sad, as if she could see where this was going. 'And the messages he'd sent back while I was asleep ... about having to look after me, about what a burden I was and how he wouldn't have to worry about it any more when I was across the country at a different uni ... well, I'd always felt a bit like a hanger on, him being so popular and fitting in so easily everywhere, but I'd never thought he'd seen me that way too.'

He made me into the sad little pathetic sidekick, embarrassingly in love with him. Always hanging on, always hoping.

'So I snuck out, and went home and asked my mum if I could go spend the summer with my grandparents in Crete until I went to uni. I blocked his number and I disappeared, and we never saw each other again.' I splayed my hands.

'Until today. Oh, Aly,' Tola said. 'But that still doesn't explain why he thinks he has the moral high ground here. Or why he pretended he doesn't know you.'

'I guess I ghosted him instead of having the big argument. I wasn't great at confrontation back then.' I shrugged, and sipped my drink. OK, I'd bared my soul. That wasn't too bad.

'Oh yeah, because you're brilliant at it now, doing Hunter's homework and constantly waiting for Felix to give you that promotion instead of just demanding it.'

'I have been demanding it! Anyway, it's not the same . . . I'd trusted him and been proven wrong. All those years of friendship felt like a lie. I thought I'd seen the real him and he'd seen the real me, but I was wrong. I was too embarrassed to have a big argument about it.'

I got on a flight that night. In a small village in Crete, I let my cousins stroke my hair and talk about broken hearts, and I drank coffee with my grandmother. In the evenings, I watched as she and my grandfather danced together under the awning on the stone veranda, huge bunches of juicy red grapes hanging above their heads as they swayed. And I remembered that there was someone for everyone, provided you were patient enough. I had a whole life ahead of me, I would go to university and find my people. It felt like hope.

And then of course, I went off to uni and I didn't fit there, either. I didn't make those friendships everyone always talks about. I was still on the phone every evening with my mother, who'd somehow gotten worse now that I wasn't there to play the grouchy teenager and keep my dad at arm's length. I threw myself into my studies, because that was what I was there for.

And then I'd met Timothy and I'd built a world around him, because I hadn't found friends and it seemed so very hard to trust someone again. And by the time I'd realised Timothy had been a bad idea, that I was a lonely, homesick little husk, I only had a few months left before graduating, and everyone was busy in the library anyway. I didn't have time for friends. I only had time for my plans: a first-class degree, a master's course I could do from home – where I could keep Mama safe – and a job that would lead me straight to a corner office.

That had been the plan for years, and I was *so nearly there* . . .

Tola picked at a mozzarella stick, frowning at it as she used it to make her point. 'Why wouldn't he admit he knew you? It's so weird. Nicki clearly noticed something was up.'

I shrugged. 'He was always good at pretending to be OK.'

'Well, at least you have that in common,' Tola snorted, and I nudged her. 'He wasn't what I was expecting from Nicki though. From the way she spoke I thought we'd have a socially awkward guy rocking up in board shorts and video game T-shirts.'

I tried to forget what I knew of Dylan and assess the guy we met. 'Well, the suit wasn't cheap, but that could be Nicki's doing. He walked and talked with confidence, he didn't seem like someone who needed help preparing for a pitch. He looked like someone who could stand next to her on a red carpet.'

Tola laughed, 'Yep, can't argue, he's a pretty boy. One who won't be taking her for chicken dinners any more, apparently. Seems like she's done a decent job of crafting him into what she wants already.'

'He was always good at that. He likes to be liked. A chameleon, fitting in with any crowd, any situation. When we were teens, he used to completely change himself for whatever girl he fancied, you know? He'd be the sporty one, or the sensitive type, or the romantic one. He'd know exactly what to do to make them fall for him.'

'Why do I get the sense you were involved here?'

I shrugged. 'I guess I used to help him, with school, with girls.'

'You taught him to hustle?' Tola laughed.

'I taught him how to be the perfect boyfriend. If anything, it's funny to hear him tell Nicki that she's playing a part. He's been doing that since we were kids. If she told him what she wanted, he'd do it. That's who he is. I don't think Nicki even needs us.'

'Apart from needing to fix the fact that he doesn't have enough followers to make it worth her while. I know the guy might have been a bit of a dick to you, but I do kinda feel sorry for him. He has no idea what he's in for.'

'Well, good luck to them both,' I snorted, holding up my glass. 'May we never have to deal with either of them again.'

'A month to get him to propose so she could be on a wedding show . . .' Tola shook her head, raising her glass to clink it against mine. 'I've dealt with some social media divas but really, she was off the charts.'

'Well, at least the evening ended well,' I gestured at our table. 'Good food, good company, and a good story to tell.'

'Cheers to that. Aren't you curious, though? Don't you

want to go back there and shake him and ask him why he's pretending and have it all out? I'd be dying.'

'That man is not my friend. He might have been once, but there's no point searching for the future in graveyards.'

'Damn, you're stone cold,' Tola laughed.

'I don't have time for stuff that hurts,' I said softly. 'That's all.'

We paid the bill and I wondered what kind of story Tola was going to build this adventure into for Eric tomorrow. We laughed on the tube on the way home and moved on to other stories, silly things people did in the office, the plans for the next Fixer Upper client, the drama that was going on in Tola's (infinitely younger and cooler) friendship circle. When we went our separate ways at King's Cross, she hugged me fiercely before turning with no warning and almost vaulting for her train.

But that night, when I was curled up in bed, warm and comfortable, I couldn't sleep. I kept seeing Dylan's eyes looking at me with a challenge, daring me to break first, to throw the game and ask him what the hell he thought he was doing. I redid our first meeting over and over again in my imagination, trying to find one where it didn't hurt. Where we greeted each other warmly, and left as friends. How would it have gone if we'd bumped into each other without Nicki, if I'd been having dinner with Tola, or had seen him in the street?

I was ashamed of that thrilled delight which hit me when I first saw him, that my first thought had been, *yay, my friend is here!* I was angry at myself. But the incredible irritation didn't stop me from finally giving in when the clock read one a.m., picking up my phone, and googling Dylan James.

I'd held out for a decade, on a strict diet of denial – no Dylan news. The most I got was when my mother mentioned seeing his dad at the local shops, and even then I changed the subject, not wanting to wonder if his relationship with his dad had improved, or if he ever came back to visit.

Because I knew, I knew I'd be like this. Addicted to knowing more. Once I finally stopped ignoring that shadow in the corner of my vision, I'd want to see *everything*.

Which was why I was still awake at four in the morning, scouring the internet and devouring the tiny breadcrumbs of history and achievement of the boy that I'd once loved.

Chapter Seven

'Alyssa, can you come over after work today?' My mother's voice was strained when she called the next morning. I yawned into my cup of coffee and tried to cover it. I needed Mama to stop calling on my work line. I didn't even remember giving it to her.

My brain was still buzzing with Dylan and everything I'd learned, my internet research making me feel a little icky, like a stalker.

Some part of me hoped he'd been as perturbed as I had by our sudden encounter, that he'd gone and hunted me down too, trying to find out if I turned out the way he thought I would, if I'd achieved my dreams and proven my worth. He'd probably only find my carefully curated professional bio and my LinkedIn profile. After all, it was easier to stay anonymous when you weren't dating a low-level celebrity. Once I looked for him, it was like he was everywhere. At one point, he'd worked at a company three roads over from my office. It didn't seem possible ...

I screwed up my eyes and blinked, trying to focus on

the tasks ahead. Talk to my mother, go to work, get that promotion.

'Sure, Mama,' I sighed, pinching the bridge of my nose, then scanning my desk for painkillers, 'you OK?'

There was a moment of silence, before a very quiet, 'Yes.'

My mother was a terrible liar. I tried to damp down my irritation. What was it now? What would I have to sort out?

'Mama,' I repeated, a hint of warning in my voice.

'We'll discuss when you come, darling. Don't worry.'

I wasn't going to push, it was only ten a.m. and I'd have to make it through the whole day before I saw her.

'OK, but you're healthy, right?'

She laughed, and I sighed in relief. 'My little worrier. Fit as a fiddle. All will be well, I just want my clever daughter's opinions on things. I'll order pizza.'

Uh-oh. Comfort food. Definitely Dad drama. When I was a kid I used to wish for siblings, so I'd have someone to share the burden with. Knowing my luck, I'd probably have ended up looking after them too.

I never knew how to fix this thing between them. They were divorced. Dad had remarried. And still, *still*, I was having the same conversations every week with my mother, like *Groundhog Day*. I just didn't know how to put a stop to any of it.

When my grandmother lived with us, after my grandfather died and I'd graduated, we had a good few years where my dad didn't come near. Mama had her support system, and my grandmother was a wolf. She'd shoo him away when he started turning up. One time she even chased him with a broom. I had howled with laughter: this tiny little old lady running out there with her broom held high, only realising she'd forgotten to put her teeth in when she tried to yell. She was brilliant. The kind of no-nonsense woman I wanted to be.

But after she died, Dad came back, saying he wanted to be there for Mama in her grief, that even if they weren't married any more, it was the right thing to do. Which sounds admirable, if you don't know him. And so she got tangled up all over again. In a way he made her the mistress this time, and I'd never forgiven him for that. Honestly, I wasn't sure I forgave her either.

When my father wasn't around, Mama was the best. She worked at the hospital, she went to pottery classes and danced salsa on Friday nights. She had a loud bunch of good friends who threw really excellent dinner parties, and she sang while she watered her garden. She grew these beautiful, colourful plants in her little garden that seemed to bloom the minute spring arrived. She had a good life. And then he'd come around and tear it down again. Sometimes, she wanted me to tell her it was all right, that he loved her really. Or else she wanted to hear that she deserved better, to build her up so she had the strength to turn him away.

It had been years, and I was tired of saying the same things when nothing ever got better.

The day dragged on, and I focused on my work, sleepy but determined. I asked how everyone's day was and what their families were up to, showing my enthusiasm to Felix or grinding my teeth to dust when Hunter appeared at my desk like a gremlin.

I wanted that job more than anything. Getting that

promotion would mean every other part of my life would be fine. So I kept a smile on my face, wrote my reports, ran my meetings and pretended. I ordered a retirement cake for one of the sales guys and reminded Felix that it was his wife's birthday this weekend.

'Shit! Aly, you're a lifesaver!' he said as he scoured the internet, frowning. 'What do you think she'd like?'

What do I, a woman who's met Marilyn three times, compared to you, her husband of twelve years, think she'd like for her birthday?

I offered a few options, and said I wanted to run a team-building day at the end of the month because I was worried the newer team members weren't feeling part of everything. Felix smiled and nodded and didn't really hear me. But I booked it in, sent round the email and figured he'd find it clever when it was happening. I felt like he kept telling me I needed to show up, step up, prove myself. He kept telling me to jump, but he wouldn't tell me how high.

So I just focused on jumping higher than anyone else, in all directions. I would be noticed soon enough. And nothing, not even the freakish reappearance of her erstwhile best friend, could throw Alyssa Aresti off her game.

'Hey, Aly, have you got a minute?' Matthew smiled, all nervous hopefulness, and I nodded, gesturing at the wheelie chair at the empty desk behind me, even as I felt the exhaustion making me waver.

'Of course! Pull up a seat, how can I help?'

Matthew's look of relief was sweet; he always had the look of a boy on his first day of school. I wasn't sure if he was wearing the wrong-sized shirts, or if he genuinely liked really colourful ties, but it made me want to take him under my wing. I'd been the first to help him get his bearings when he started at the company about a year ago, and, unlike Hunter, I didn't mind because he was always so damn grateful. Eric insisted it was an act, but I didn't think so.

'Oh, I so appreciate it, Aly, you have no idea,' he exhaled, that funny little furrow in between his eyebrows appearing again. I liked his curly dark hair and how easily he smiled. Which was probably why I'd briefly ended up kissing him in an abandoned stairwell at his first office Christmas party. It was an underwhelming, nervous drunken fumble, and we'd been a bit awkward for a while, but now he had a girlfriend and we were back to a very clear mentor–mentee dynamic again.

Besides, I'd learnt the day after that he was only twenty-four, which didn't feel great to me. Like I'd accidentally abused a position of power. So I helped him out, and he gushed and thanked me, and that was how we worked now. A nice, friendly thing.

'What do you think of this pitch for the new Velvet Touch moisturiser? Something's not right and I can't put my finger on what it is.' He slid the file across my desk, keeping an appropriate distance, and I focused, scanning the pages.

'Hmm, you're right.' I clicked my wrists, thinking, then reached for a pen. 'Do you mind?'

'You kidding? Go nuts. Your ideas are golden,' he smiled, gesturing at the page.

'You're sweet,' I said, eyes still on the papers. 'Is the company briefing document in here?'

He pulled it out from the back, and I frowned. 'Ah, OK,

see it doesn't align with their target audience, right? Design have gone young and fresh, but average consumer is thirty-five plus.'

'Yeah, but they want—'

'The younger market?' I nodded. 'Sure, but how much is a pot of their face cream?'

He made a face. 'About eighty quid.'

I held up my hands. 'It's your job to convince the client what's possible, Matt. Manage their expectations, redirect them to something achievable. You've got this. Shoulders back, talk with authority. You know this industry, you know what's good for their business, right?'

He smiled at me, so grateful, and nodded. 'Right. Thanks, Aly. Really. Don't know what I'd do without you.'

I waved it off as he got up and neatly put the chair back.

'Oh, and Matt?' He turned back. 'Change that godawful font, OK? Felix will have your head on a platter for even making a mock-up with Comic Sans.'

He snorted and saluted. 'You got it, boss.'

Hunter walked past my desk and did a double take, looking back at Matt walking off with a spring in his step. Then he gave me that smarmy grin. 'Why you playing favourites, Aly? You're never that nice to me when I need help.'

I bared my teeth in an approximation of a smile. 'Because he asks politely. And not five minutes before the end of the working day.'

Hunter pouted, 'Oh, don't be like that, you know you love the power, all of us in thrall to you, unable to do anything without you.'

I took a deep breath, and chucked my stuff into my bag,

pausing as I walked past Hunter to pat him on the shoulder. 'You're right. It must just be that he's prettier than you.'

I walked off before he could get another cheap shot in, and caught Tola's look of joy as I stepped into the lift. She marked a 'one' in the air like she was keeping a scoreboard. Knowing Tola and Eric's infamous office sweepstakes, she may have been.

Work had been a glorious distraction, but the minute I got on the train that would take me to my mother's house, I fell back into my googling hole yet again, going over everything I'd learned about Dylan last night. I found a web page for his firm, EasterEgg Development, but it didn't have much beyond a team page filled with young smiling faces oozing potential. He could be spotted in the background of a few of Nicki's social media images, but nothing distinctive. No social media profiles. I looked up the University of Portsmouth alumni page to see if he was in the graduation photo but I couldn't see him. The man nearly didn't exist.

I wondered again if he'd done the same search for me last night. Whether our surprise encounter had disturbed him too. Or maybe he'd spent the evening drinking expensive drinks and eating fancy food with his high-flying girlfriend and ignoring the fact that she wanted to change almost everything about him. Just like every girlfriend he'd had when we were teenagers. They liked his pretty face and his easy smile, but there was always something that needed fixing. And he was all too happy to be who they wanted him to be.

And I had been the only one who saw the gaffer tape and tears holding it together behind the scenes.

God, going home wouldn't help with this at all; every part of my journey was stamped with Dylan memories. The station where we'd spent ages waiting for the always-delayed trains in and out of London, going to see gigs at Electric Ballroom or Barfly, drinking pints in the World's End.

I walked down the high street, where we always used to get our pick'n'mix before going to the cinema or up to the peak in the park, looking out over everyone and making up stories about them. There was our school and the pub we drank in when we reached eighteen (or near enough) and the turning for Dylan's road. I imagined his dad still lived there, making their home a shrine to his wife, refusing to change a thing. She'd been on her way to pick us up from a birthday party when it happened. She was there, and then suddenly gone.

When I finally made it home, I stood outside for a moment, just looking. It was a beautiful house, always had been. Mama's lush garden in the front, that magnolia tree right in the middle, obscuring the full view of the building. In the summers, my grandmother used to put her little chair out under that tree and watch people go by. It was such a Mediterranean thing to do, but people on this street didn't mind. She'd be out there ten minutes and someone would offer her apples from their tree, or introduce their dog, or ask her where she was from in Greece.

This house was home. After Dad left, we painted the whole place bright colours. Dylan had come over while we were patting paint on the walls with my art paintbrushes and slapped a hand to his forehead in comedic horror, then went down to the little hardware shop on the high street, returning with tape and rollers and proper brushes. He made sure we did it properly, even if he let loose that loud laugh at the shade of bright orange we chose. He couldn't get over the idea of an orange living room, like it was the strangest, most wonderful thing he'd ever heard. We painted and sang, and Mama ordered pizza and didn't cry at all that day. It had felt like a new beginning.

I unlocked the front door and inhaled the smell of incense and fresh coffee and laundry powder. As I wandered through the hallway, I could hear music playing – she had set up her tablet on the counter, and it was playing their wedding video. I felt irritation climb up my throat like a gecko, settling in, ready for a fight.

'Mama.'

She turned around, and of course she'd been crying.

'Is this helpful?' I gestured at the tablet, and she wiped her eyes.

'I only wanted to see my parents again for a little while. Look at them dancing together, so beautiful.'

It occurred to me how hard it must be to watch your marriage fall apart when your parents were the perfect example of love. When they'd loved each other without limitation, unchanging, for half a century. Poor Mama, she'd wanted what they had, and she'd ended up with my bum of a father.

'Wine?' she offered, pouring me a glass of Prosecco before I had the chance to answer.

I blinked, accepting it. 'Is it a special dinner? We … we're not having *guests*, are we?'

Dread clutched at my chest. Another evening of

convincing my mother she was lovable and deserving of good things? Sure, I was used to that. An evening where my father sat at the head of the table and asked me questions as if he knew anything about my life? No way. Even a perfect daughter had limits.

Mama shook her head. 'I've been missing your *yiayia* lately. She was a firm believer in cocktail hour. And the sun was shining, so I thought, why not?'

She poured herself a glass, and we held them up to each other.

My mother scanned me, putting a hand to my cheek. 'You look pale, darling, you're working too hard.'

I shrugged. 'It's fine.'

'You meet anyone nice?'

I hated seeing how she lit up with hope. My mother was such a romantic, even after all this time. All she wanted was for me to settle down with someone, to adore and be adored. I felt like I was letting her down.

'I meet lots of nice people, Mama,' I smiled widely and sipped my drink.

'You know I mean a nice man, cheeky girl,' she turned back to the stove.

'No, I'm too busy with work, you know that.' I paused, wondering whether I should give anything else away. Somehow I didn't think the Fixer Upper would make her proud. She wanted me head over heels, stupid in love. And even the thought of that terrified me. I'd seen what it had done to her. 'But ... I did see Dylan yesterday.'

She gasped, entirely too dramatically, and I immediately regretted telling her.

'Dylan James? Lovely Dylan! It's been so long! How is he, what's he doing?' *Pretending I never existed, apparently.*

My mother clapped her hands in delight, and I felt my mood disintegrate. She never knew why we fell out. I was too embarrassed to tell her, to admit that I loved a boy who didn't love me back. Like mother, like daughter. So I let her think we'd simply lost touch, the way people did. No biggie. No heartbreak, no loss.

'He works in computers and he's dating a celebrity. You know the girl from that reality TV show, the Kitty Litter Princess?'

Mama wrinkled her nose. 'With the big mouth? She seems like a very silly woman. That said, Dylan didn't always pick the smart ones.'

'Mama, I'm pretty sure that's anti-feminist,' I snorted.

'But is it wrong? I don't think so.' She threw up her hands. 'Some men just are that way. They want an easy life. They want their partner to always be smiles and *everything's fine* all the time. Nothing real.'

I could sense the direction this conversation was going, my memories of the way my parents used to scream at each other firmly in my mind. How he would cheat, and Mama would smash plates, and then a day later I'd find them curled up together on the sofa like the perfect image of married love. I gulped down the last of my wine and held my glass up again.

'It's still cocktail hour, right?'

She raised an eyebrow at me but topped up my glass. When she returned to the subject of Dylan, I sighed, relieved that I'd distracted her for a little longer. At some point this evening, we were going to talk about Dad, the same way we did on my lunch breaks and at the weekends. The man took up all the air in the room even when he wasn't in it. And I was such a broken record, the words were starting to warp from repetition:

You deserve better, he's not good enough, this isn't love, start over, you can do it.

Mama smiled. 'I remember Dylan helping us paint. Whenever I clean the bookcase and see that smudge on the plug socket, I hear him looking at us in panic and saying, "Oh, Mrs Aresti, please let me go get some proper paintbrushes, trust me." And he was right! Is he getting on with his dad OK now? I still see him in the supermarket sometimes. Sad, sad man.'

'We didn't . . . it was a business meeting, we didn't get a chance to catch up much.'

'I bet he's very handsome now, isn't he?' Mama wiggled her eyebrows. 'You could tell he was going to be a heartbreaker.'

I thought of those bright blue eyes, how they'd looked me over and dismissed me immediately. How his hand squeezed mine for a second before he let go.

'Yeah, you could,' I said softly, and went to set the table.

By the time we finally sat down to eat, we'd run through every other topic of conversation, and it was clear that no one was sick or dying, and my mother was still employed. Our family in Crete were OK, all of Mama's friends were happy, and I'd had a full rundown of the next-door neighbour's cat's surgery. Which left the one possibility I had expected all along.

'Are you going to tell me why I'm here now? I can't enjoy my food until I can stop worrying,' I said.

'You're here to see your mother, who loves and misses you. And to eat good food and drink good wine. You're looking a little gaunt. I'll send you home with a doggy bag.' She was rambling.

'Mama, come on.'

She took a breath. 'Your father wants to sell the house.'

I frowned. '*Our* house? *This* house? What the hell has it got to do with him?'

She half shrugged. 'He still owns half of it, darling.'

I clenched my fists and then released them. 'Why now?'

'He's struggling financially, the three kids ... he wants to take a step back at work, spend some more time with his children before they grow up.'

'Oh, how nice for them.' I could feel the bitterness foaming over like a disappointing pint and I tried to reign it in. 'You're divorced, this is *your* house. Besides, didn't your parents give you the money for the deposit as a wedding present?'

'Yes, but both our names are still on the deeds.'

'He hasn't paid the mortgage for nearly twenty years!'

My mother closed her eyes, took a breath, and placed a hand on mine. 'Now, I didn't want you to get upset.'

'Well, I am upset! You should be upset! The man destroys your life and now he wants your home too!'

She twitched her mouth, attempting to smile. But I didn't want smiles, I wanted her to get *mad*. I wanted her to see that this man had taken too much. But it never ended well for me, that line of enquiry. It was always *Poor Aly, I've*

96

made you so angry and bitter, this must be my fault, I'm a bad mother. So I'd comfort her, and then that was it, over and done with so he could come around another day and start it all over again.

'He can't have this home. This is our home. He can downsize or move out of London if he wants his demon spawn to grow up with more space.'

Mama made a face. 'They're your siblings, darling. And they're younger than you. I don't need to be rattling around this big house.'

'So you're planning to give him what he wants, no matter what?' I threw back the remainder of my wine, hands shaking with anger. 'If he comes to you asking for a kidney next week, are you going to give it to him, Mama?'

She looked at me, and I knew she probably would. She loved him, beyond all reasoning, despite the type of man he was. My mother believed in having one true love, even if it didn't go both ways, it seemed.

'Look, my darling, legally he owns half of this house. And we can sell it and split the money, or I can buy him out. He said I can give him a smaller lump sum for him to sign over the deeds. Maybe we'll do that.'

'Oh, how *thoughtful* of him. How understanding. And where are we going to get that money from?'

It seemed that she had the exact same thought because she shook her head and picked up her drink.

'Days like this, I miss my parents,' Mama sighed.

Yiayia wouldn't let this happen. She'd build you up and tear him down and scare the crap out of him. So maybe that needed to be my role now.

'Let me talk to him,' I said.

'No.'

'Mama, this is ridiculous. He can't come in—'

'He *can*, Alyssa. Legally.'

'No, *not* legally. You got divorced. He agreed it's yours.'

'We never changed the deeds, we were always going to come to an arrangement when you were older.'

Well, that was news to me. And considering I'd had a front-row seat to the car wreck that was my parent's marriage, I wasn't just surprised – I was pissed.

'Is it not enough you worked to put him through university, that you gave up your career for his? Now you want to give up your home too? You know you don't get a prize for being the most selfless, right, Mama?'

'It is *my* marriage, Alyssa, *mine*,' she almost growled at me, and I wanted to shake her and cry for her all at the same time.

'It's not though, is it? It's not your marriage any more.' I stood up, shaking my head. 'Look, do you want to stay in this house, yes or no?'

'Of course I—'

'Then I'll find the money,' I said, taking my plate to the side, untouched. 'Tell him I'll take care of it.'

I had always taken care of it. When he used to leave for days at a time, and she'd hide herself away in bed, silently staring at the ceiling, I took care of her. I ushered her into the shower, I made her tea and toast. I opened the dusty recipe books to try and figure out how to make a meal. Even now jacket potatoes tasted like long, sad evenings.

I could fix this. I couldn't fix them, couldn't pull her away or make her wake up, but money wasn't the hardest thing in the world.

The gall of it, though. I'd been there, I knew what it was like when my dad shone that light of approval on you, when he smiled and called you a marvel. But I'd grown tired of pretending that fleeting interest was love. She never had.

I sat checking my accounts on my phone on the train home, wondering how much he'd ask for. That house was easily worth half a million. How much of a lump sum would get him off my back, how much would make him leave her alone for good? Mama was an administrator at the hospital, I knew she'd never had much in savings. 'I only need enough for my garden and to throw a good dinner party,' that's what she'd always said. And I'd nag her, and she'd tell me *she was the mother* and we'd laugh and leave it at that.

I had almost twenty grand that I'd saved for a decade, hoping to one day get my own little flat, but every year it became more impossible, so I kept saving, kept working, and time passed. I would use it if I needed to.

I wanted Mama to fight, I wanted her to say *No, of course you can't give your father your hard-earned savings, darling*. I wanted her to put me first. But she wouldn't, she couldn't. He always came first, even after all this time. Another family, another home, another wife, and still Mama was like a dragonfly stuck in amber. I tried not to resent her for it.

My father would get his way. Just like the Hunters of the world – getting what they want so easily they wonder why everyone else struggles so much. Just like Nicki, demanding people fit in with her expectations.

I wondered how different that was to what I was doing

with Tola and Eric. Manipulating, adjusting, adapting. Nicki and Hunter expected the best from other people right away. I didn't expect the best of people, but I knew how to plant a seed and grow potential. I knew how to get my own way, but it was a slightly longer game.

By the time I got back to my little studio, I was ready to have a good cry and a long bath. But I had one more thing to do. And if I thought about it for too long, I'd lose my nerve.

I called Nicki.

'Hello! I wasn't sure I'd be hearing from you.'

'A hundred grand,' I said, no preamble. No chance for me to chicken out.

There was no way she'd go for it. That was stupid money. I was only doing this because I needed to tell myself I'd tried everything, done everything I could.

'What?'

I gritted my jaw to hide the tremble in my voice.

'You saw how he was with me, you know how difficult this is going to be, and you know how much your TV show and dress deal is going to be worth to you.'

Nicki paused. 'Why *was* he like that? I've never seen Dylan be rude to anyone before. He's the sweetest guy I know. I'm not even sure I've seen him get properly mad.'

Well, I couldn't tell the truth.

'I must remind him of someone he dislikes,' I tried to shrug it off, 'or he's under intense pressure with this pitch and doesn't want to accept help. Either way, it's going to make it harder. What's it worth to you?'

What's he worth to you?

Silence at the end of the line. I wondered if I'd pushed

100

too hard. All I could think about was my mother, sitting in a damp little flat, calling up every day to ask me why she'd had to sell her home. Sitting and waiting for my father to visit. Not singing as she watered her plants. My mama would wilt without her garden.

'For that you've got to guarantee the proposal,' Nicki said suddenly, and I wondered if she'd thought this was how it would go all along. 'Otherwise it's meaningless.' *Nice way to talk about your relationship*.

And then I realised what she was saying. A hundred grand. She'd agreed to a hundred grand. The answer to my problems.

I paused, thinking of all those years of friendship that I was betraying. But then I visualised Dylan's face as he saw me again, that blank look of dismissal. I thought of those text messages that told me I was nothing but a hanger-on, a loser, a pathetic girl who looked at him with hearts in her eyes. Someone who never meant anything at all.

And then I thought of my mother's face.

'You've got a deal,' I said.

Chapter Eight

'You said yes,' Tola blinked at me. 'Without even talking to us?'

'There were extenuating circumstances,' I said, pushing down my guilt as I clicked the kettle and got out our usual mugs. She sat on the office kitchen counter even though she'd been told not to hundreds of times.

Eric leaned next to her, and they shared a look. That *Aly's being weird again* look.

I hated that look.

'Which are ... ?'

'Personal.' I closed the cupboard firmly and focused on spooning coffee, measuring it carefully. Anything to avoid looking at them. Tola's lime green fingernails tapped the cupboard door.

I should have been more prepared with my plan. I was the Fixer Upper after all, I should be able to use this situation to my advantage.

But if I told them about the money, I had to tell them about why I needed it. I'd have to explain that all the energy

I'd spent on fixing men was nothing compared to the lifetime I'd spent trying to fix my parents. And they'd look at me in the way people did when you opened up your chest and let them see your fragile heart – *Oh, that's why you're like this, of course.*

Only one person knew how my parents were, and ridiculously, that was Dylan. He'd helped forge apology notes, calculate 'accidental' meetings, cook dinner when she was too sad to eat. He'd seen it all. And now if I could fix him, I could fix them for good.

Eric looked at me. 'We're sure it's not just that Aly wants to get back at the boy she fancied when she was a teenager?'

I raised an eyebrow at Tola. 'Thanks for that.'

'He's our business partner! He had to know some of the situation!'

I put my hands down on the counter and prepared myself to argue.

'Look, you wanted a challenge, right? Well, here it is, right before us. The biggest challenge we could have asked for. So let's prove we're the best. That we can do this.' I tried to rally *go team* enthusiasm, but they knew it was a front.

They were waiting for more, and I panicked. 'She offered us more money.' I paused. 'Twenty grand,' I sang the number jokily, trying to lure them in like I was sitting in my gingerbread house waving lollipops, and hating myself for the deceit, 'split three ways?'

Eric let out a low whistle. 'Nice chunk of change there . . .'

He looked hopeful, but Tola was unconvinced. She frowned at me, narrowing her eyes. 'She doubled her offer. And you're interested? You said it was manipulative and ridiculous and . . . kind of gross. It's your friend.'

'My ex-friend,' I corrected. 'And sure, it feels a little . . . icky. But that's probably because of Nicki's personality. When she called back, she was much more vulnerable. Is it really so different from the other women we've helped coax proposals for? Is it different to how people pretend to be completely different for the first month of a relationship until that good behaviour wears off?' I argued.

'Yes,' Tola said, 'absolutely.'

'Of course it is,' Eric added. He tilted his head in concern. 'What's going on with you?'

I shrugged, irritated, as I poured the hot water and stirred each drink more aggressively than I needed to. 'I don't know what to tell you. I need to do this. So if you don't want to be involved, that's fine. But I'm in.'

Tola clenched her hands in front of her face like she wanted to strangle me. 'One of these days I'm going to crack your head open and see what the hell is happening in there. Because something isn't right.' *You're telling me*.

'But what with it being such a *huge* task, I could really use your help with this . . .' I tried smiling, wheedling, fluttering my eyelashes. Make them laugh; as long as I could make them laugh it would be fine. I handed them their coffee cups, all innocent and full of hope.

'Oh, *now* she bothers to turn on the charm.' Eric rolled his eyes, taking his rainbow mug, his one nod to his sexuality in the office, where everything else remained lad jokes and banter.

'Please?' I pouted, widening my eyes, looking between the two of them. 'We are going to turn Dylan James into her dream boyfriend and prime him for a proposal. I know him, and we can absolutely do this.'

'Ah, the opposite of a fairy godmother. That poor guy.'

'Believe me,' I said, 'Dylan's a pleaser, he'll appreciate the direction.'

'From a woman he couldn't even make direct eye contact with?' Tola raised an eyebrow. 'Come on.'

I had to redirect her. It wasn't about me. It wasn't about Dylan. It was about keeping Mama's house. About not letting my father win, again.

'You keep saying we're thinking too small, right? So let's think big. At the end of this experiment, we'll have a girl with a TV deal, a guy with a successful company, and a proposal on the way! We already know we can do it when the stakes are lower. Let's see how far we can take this thing!'

Tola and Eric looked at each other. There we go. They knew that we could do this. They knew that I hadn't been fired up about something outside of work in years. While they ran their team bingo betting ring and went to Disney-themed spin classes, I was here, working late, proving my worth.

And now I was begging them to try something risky with me.

'Come on,' I grinned, wiggling my eyebrows, my final attempt. 'Aren't you at least intrigued that *I'm* the one suggesting we take a chance? Me. The responsible one.'

'That's what scares me,' Tola snorted, and held up her coffee cup in a toast, waiting for us to raise our own. 'OK, babe, let's work some magic.'

The next day, I took the afternoon off from work and strode into the reception of Dylan's office space, wearing my power jacket and my favourite black boots with the metal studs all over them. Tola called them 'punky stegosaurus' and they were one of the few items of clothing of mine she deemed interesting.

I knew I had to break him down quickly, before he had a chance to say no. My hope was that he would really want to please his girlfriend (true to form) or that he'd admit that he really did need the help (much more unlikely). The third option, that he actually might be curious enough to want me around, didn't even merit consideration.

He was renting a painfully modern office space by the river, one of those places where young, start-up hipsters tried to claw back the fees in fancy coffee and free pastries, while looking out over the city and dreaming of success. It had energy, and it wasn't surprising he'd chosen it. Dylan loved the look of things. He'd always wanted the fancy gyms and the attractive bars. He wanted the good life. He'd fit in with Nicki's life just fine.

Of course, he hadn't been shallow when we were teenagers; back then he was hungry for experiences and places and people. He lived in a grey house with a former soldier who wanted routine, structure and diligence. There was no space for colour or frivolity in Dylan's home life.

I remembered when we were applying for our university courses I asked him to dream of his future life, and he said, 'We're eating steak and lobster in a super-fancy restaurant, and I've ordered a fifty-quid bottle of wine and no one thinks we're out of place at all.'

'That's it?' I'd replied, amused, but secretly thrilled that I was in this future he'd dreamed up. 'Money?'

He wrinkled his nose. 'No, *fitting in. Having adventures. Tasting everything!* You need money to make that happen. It's gonna be great!'

And now he didn't even need money for that, he had Nicki. Maybe my nudges would be a gift to him, offering him a life of fitting in with beautiful people in fabulous places. All the adventures he could ask for.

When I exited the lift on the second floor, a young guy with horn-rimmed glasses and slicked-back blond hair was waiting for me, eyebrows raised, ready to impress.

'Hello there! Apparently you're here for EasterEgg Development! We rarely get unexpected visitors! Can I help?'

'Well, I sure hope so!' I smiled at the gatekeeper. I had my power boots and my orange-red lipstick. I was a force of nature, and no one was going to stop me. 'I'm here to see Dylan James.'

The guy frowned slightly. 'Is that right?'

I beamed at him and held out my hand. When you can't get them with force, get them with enthusiasm.

'I'm Aly, I'm a business and branding consultant hired by Miss Wetherington Smythe. I'm here to help you guys prep for the presentation at the end of the month.'

The man's face changed immediately, and he looked suddenly young, reaching out to take my hand and shaking it vigorously. 'Well, hallelujah. We need you, desperately. I'm Ben.'

'A pleasure.' I was taken aback by how quickly he warmed up. 'You work with Mr James?'

'I was one of the first to join the team. Dylan's a brilliant ideas man and he wants the best for all of us, but … if we don't get this investment, I'm going to have to go back to bartending, and honestly, all the booze is terrible for my skin.'

I frowned at him. 'You're a bartender who's allergic to booze?'

'No, I'm a bartender who has to drink to deal with how stupid drunk people are,' he grinned, leading me towards the office.

Maybe that was my in: if his team wanted me around, Dylan would have to keep me, I was sure of it.

'Ben.' I put a hand on his arm to slow him down before we entered the room. 'Dylan is not likely to be happy to see me. He kind of rejected my services when Nicki offered before. How, in your eyes, can I get him to accept my help?'

Ben took a second to think about it. 'Dyl is everyone's best friend, he'll take your advice if he thinks it'll make you happy to give it.' Ben shrugged, and I nodded. That sounded about right. 'But I think deep down he knows he needs help. He knows that if we don't do this, we're toast. We've already come back from the dead once. We joke that we're phoenixes.'

'Phoenixes?'

'Yeah, but our wings are a bit singed right now, you know? Can't take another house fire. Hell, can't even take another back garden barbecue.' He gripped my hand and looked into my eyes. 'I am very relieved you're here. Normally Nicki's pushiness is unbearable, but this is exactly what we needed. Honestly, I'd send her a gift basket, but it would only get lost amongst all the other free crap she gets.'

I laughed. Clearly Ben was the person who knew everything here.

As he turned towards the office, he threw a look over his shoulder, raising an eyebrow. 'Don't let him charm you into thinking we don't need help.'

'Believe me, he has no intention of charming me.'

Ben frowned, but shrugged and walked through the door, into a small room with a couple of desks. The walls were floor-to-ceiling glass with a lovely view of a crisp grey London skyline, but something didn't add up. The motivational posters framed on the walls, the expensive watch on Dylan's wrist. The number of fancy computers when there were only three people in there.

They were dressing up in their dad's suit and pretending this was a real business. And God knew how much they'd spent on this facade. *Oh Dylan, what have you done?*

He sat with his back to us, hunched over a laptop, while a dark-haired woman sat opposite, typing away at speed, headphones on and completely unbothered by his huffing.

He was at least in jeans and a T-shirt this time, so apparently he'd only been playing *successful businessman* for his girlfriend. Interesting. I could see the stress in the line of his shoulders. Panic had started to set in, and I was about to trigger an avalanche. And a small part of me – a tiny, insignificant splinter – wanted to see him panic, so I could be the one who had all the answers. Just like old times. *Try forgetting me now, Dylan.*

'Hey, Dyl, you've got a guest.'

He turned and for a beautiful moment his face only showed shock, before it morphed into displeasure.

'Aly,' he started, frowning at me as he stood.

'Oh, you *do* remember,' I said brightly. 'I wasn't sure

I'd made such a good first impression the other night.' *You wanted to play this game, Dyl, you've got it.*

But he didn't want to play. 'What are you doing here?'

I shrugged, walking across the room to put down my bag. 'Nicki said you needed help. She has acquired my services for you. So I'm here to help.'

He laughed, sharp and unpleasant as he crossed his arms, leaning back against the table. 'No way.'

I caught Ben's jaw drop and watched as the woman at the table looked between us. Apparently they hadn't seen their boss be rude before. I could well believe it. When he found out his mum died, he'd waited until he was safely at home, with no one to see him, to cry. Even at thirteen he didn't give anything away. He'd let me squeeze his hand in the car ride home, though. But the Dylan in front of me wasn't my one-time confidante, he was a project. One who was going to make my life very difficult.

'So you're willing to risk your chance at investment and make life harder for yourself because … you don't want to accept help from your girlfriend?' I tilted my head slightly, daring him to break eye contact. 'I wonder how your colleagues feel about that?'

'You can't come in here and start telling me what to do, it's not …' *It's not like we're at school any more. Go on, say it, Dylan.*

'It's not what, Mr James?' I smiled politely, daring him to break.

'It's not appropriate, *Miss Aresti.*'

Ben looked between us, eyes widening. He shared a look with the woman on the other side of the table, who had taken her headphones off to listen to the conversation and seemed to be struggling to hide her laughter. She ran a hand through her shoulder-length black hair, untangling it from the silver hoops in her ears and then fiddling with her nose ring as she watched us both. I noted the black and white delicate line tattoos forming a sleeve on her arm and had that brief pang I sometimes had where I desperately wanted to make friends with someone who seemed oh-so-cool.

'This is Priya,' Ben said, 'our other team member.'

Priya nodded at me, the curve of her mouth shifting as if she found everything a little too amusing. I felt like she was rooting for me.

'It's just you three?' I asked, confirming my suspicions. 'Your website . . .'

'Needs updating,' Ben said quickly, and I watched as two embarrassed red patches appeared on Dylan's cheeks. He'd lost staff along the way. A fair few, depending on when that website was set up.

He looked desperate, his dark hair mussed up and almost falling into his eyes from where he'd been running his fingers through it. There was a stubble shadow around his jaw, perfectly messy, in need of someone to fix it for him. He tugged at the neck of his white T-shirt.

'Look, either you're willing to accept help from an expert, or you're willing to jeopardise the livelihoods of your team members.' I shrugged, turning towards the door. 'I'll go get myself a coffee. Come and find me when you've decided.'

It was a power move, but the best way to get the decision you wanted from someone was to give them the tools to make it. Dylan didn't want Nicki's help. He certainly didn't want *my* help. But did he hate me more than he loved his company? I had to hope not.

I caught Ben's impressed look, like he was pleasantly surprised, as I turned around and walked out, so that was something. He'd fight for me, at least.

I spent a little time fiddling with the fancy coffee machine in the lobby, looking out at the view of the city. I checked my emails and saw another request from Hunter. Then an email from Felix, noting my holiday request had been approved, but asking if I was all right. I usually had to be forced to take my holiday, so no wonder he was shocked. But at the end of that email enquiring after my well-being, there was a line: *We'll be discussing internal candidates for the head of brand development role shortly – make sure you're showing your dedication.*

I felt a wave of panic and took a deep breath, closing my eyes. When I opened them, Dylan was standing in front of me, glowering. He'd attempted to push his hair into place, and he stood ramrod straight like he refused to be intimidated. That silver chain was visible at his throat, the St Christopher pendant creating a clear indentation under his T-shirt. I looked away, as if even acknowledging it would give him some sort of power. I focused on sipping my coffee, looking out at the view, and waited for him to say something.

'Haven't even hired you, and you're sleeping on the job?'

I smiled my shark smile that I'd learned from Nicki. 'Well, when you've got to wait an age for someone to make a sensible decision ... you get sleepy.'

He rolled his eyes upwards, as if asking for strength,

and even that was so familiar I felt something in my chest tug a little.

'I guess you know what I'm here to say?' he said, like a fifteen-year-old wheeled out to a great aunt to say thank you for their birthday presents.

'Well, you're intelligent and you care about your team, so I think I do.' I nodded, and stood up. 'Shall we get started?'

'Wait.' He tapped my elbow briefly to stop me. 'First I need to know why you're doing this.'

I creased my brow in mock confusion and shrugged, smiling at him. 'I don't know what you mean, Mr James. It's a job. Nicki hired me, and I think I can help. That's it.'

He looked at me with suspicion, tracing all my features for any sign of a lie. I stood and regarded him calmly while he scrutinised me.

'I don't care that Nicki hired you,' he said suddenly. 'If you're working for me, you're working for me.'

'I'd prefer to think of it as working *with* you.'

'Whatever helps you sleep at night,' he said, and walked off, pausing by the door. 'You coming, or do you need a few moments for your grand entrance, oh wise business sage?'

Oh, well, wasn't this going to be just fantastic?

As long as I wasn't talking to Dylan, looking at Dylan, or listening to Dylan, it was absolutely fine. Ben was a dream, full of ideas, support and context, and Priya was wry, quick and had no time for bullshit. I often found that with women in male-dominated industries. She'd probably had to work twice as hard to get where she was, and she wasn't going to be ignored. But on the balance, she had a kid, so she worked her hours and she went home. She wasn't getting pulled into anything by anyone's ego. I was shocked by how impressive her boundaries were. Maybe that was how you got to have a family and a kid, by making that space for them. I wanted to be her.

'OK, so pitch me the app,' I said, hands splayed, leaning back in the chair.

'What, like the official presentation?' Ben said, frowning. 'We haven't really . . .'

'No,' I smiled. 'I want you to tell me what you made and why it's important.'

Dylan took a breath, and I held up a hand. 'Without any of the tech stuff.'

He huffed at me, 'Brilliant, a technologically illiterate business expert. Just what we need.'

Ben and Priya shared a concerned look, as if their happy-go-lucky boss had been taken over by an ogre.

'Actually I specialise in digital, but that's irrelevant. Focus on what the app does and why it matters, how it will impact people. The code may be really clever, but it doesn't matter if the app doesn't connect with an audience.'

'Yeah,' Priya nodded, 'only other nerds care about how clean the code is. Which is why my husband begs me to shut up when I talk about it.'

'Not a nerd?' I asked, and she made a face and half shrugged.

'Accountant.'

'Ah, different strain of nerd. Gotcha,' I quipped, and Priya laughed.

'If you're not taking this seriously, Miss Aresti, then I

think it's a waste of everybody's time,' Dylan said roughly, and I couldn't help it. I looked at him, trying to be all serious when most of our childhood he'd be the one disrupting lessons, trying to bunk off, finding ways to get the teacher laughing so we couldn't be given homework. His lips were a thin line and his brow was furrowed, and I couldn't help myself.

I burst out laughing.

'Really?' he asked, crossing his arms as I gasped for breath, trying to suppress my giggles.

Priya and Ben looked at each other again.

'Hey, Dyl, can I grab you for a minute?' Ben asked, tilting his head to outside the room. I imagined he was going to ask his boss why the hell he was acting like such an arsehole to the nice lady offering the free business support. It would serve him right.

Priya waited for me to stop laughing and pushed a glass of water across the table.

'Thanks,' I said, gulping it down. 'Sorry, don't know what happened there.'

'I imagine you're not usually berated for being friendly,' Priya said. 'Are you friends with Nicolette?'

I shook my head. 'She approached us for some other work, but mentioned Dylan and wanted to support him. She said the start-up's been a bit slow at ... starting up?'

Priya nodded slowly, as if wondering how much to reveal. 'I haven't been here as long as Ben has, but ... Dylan likes things to be perfect. He doesn't want to rush ahead and miss his shot. But, you know, until we get the investment, we're not getting paid, so ...'

I blinked, 'You're not getting paid?'

'We work in four- to six-month sprints, usually,' she replied, tapping her nose ring like she was guilty for revealing too much. 'Then we go get short-term contracts with other companies for a few months, save up enough, then come back. We've been doing that for three years.'

'Isn't that exhausting?'

She laughed, 'Yes! And when you've got a kid and you've gotta send her to nursery to afford coming to work ... but I believe in what we're doing. And apart from today, when he's being super weird, I believe in Dylan. He's a problem-solver, an eternal-pain-in-the-arse optimist. But doesn't do pressure well.'

'*Don't you find it exhausting?*' I'd asked him once, '*being the life of the party, being Mr Perfect?*'

'*If you're gonna be the life of something, might as well be the party,*' he'd shrugged, with that perfect, affected grin that worked on all the girls.

Some things didn't change.

'This has been really helpful,' I said as I made a few notes, and Priya looked concerned. I shook my head. 'Don't look worried. Nicki gave me no information beyond app development and a meeting at the end of the month, so I need all the info I can get.'

'Did she warn you Dylan was going to be like that?'

I pressed my lips together, trying to find the right way to phrase it. 'I anticipated some resistance. But I'm like a pitbull, I'll be fine.'

She looked out to the corridor where Ben was clearly giving Dylan an absolute earful. His face was red, and he was pointing and gesturing and tapping his toe. It was satisfying.

When they returned five minutes later, Dylan sat down again, and gestured towards me.

'I'm sorry if I've been a bit ... short. Obviously we're under a lot of pressure at the moment, and I wasn't expecting you today. I'd be grateful for your feedback.'

His voice was sincere, but when I met his eyes there was a challenge there. 'For as long as you're willing to give it.'

I simply smiled as if I bought what he was saying and splayed my hands. 'OK then, let's fix you right up.'

Chapter Nine

Suddenly, my life was incredibly full. Or rather, incredibly busy. There was no time to be the shoulder to cry on at work or the problem-solver to my mum. There were no third Thursdays out for fancy dinners and personal growth. There was work, and when there wasn't work, there was Dylan, with Priya and Ben running interference trying to keep things friendly, or at the very least civil.

Tola had wanted us to continue doing our other Fixer Upper activities. After all, we'd been booked in months in advance, but she was mostly taking the lead on that, which was a relief.

'I'm not as good at pretending to be someone else,' she sighed on the phone to me on a Wednesday evening, as I folded my laundry and wondered whether to buy another dehumidifier for the peeling paint on the walls. God, I hated my flat.

'That's because you're so excellent at being you,' I replied, mobile in the crook of my neck. Watching Tola try to wear nude makeup and dress conventionally was almost heartbreaking. It was like all the life was sucked out of her.

'Well, hopefully things will calm down soon, they've been easy plays anyway. More career motivation and more thoughtfulness. The last one was super easy. The wife sent a bottle of champers, I'll keep it to share with you.'

I laughed, giving up on the laundry and heading over to my kitchenette, filling a pan with water and setting it on to boil. I'd been in my little studio for years now, and I knew I was lucky because it was rare to be able to afford to live alone in London. But still, the more I thought about Jason and all those exes with their houses and spouses, the lower I felt when I came home every day. The Artex ceilings and lack of natural light were the worst features, along with the damp. I'd tried to make it homey, a bright squashy blue sofa with yellow cushions, a multicoloured tapestry I'd found in a charity shop that hid the big crack along the back wall.

But it was only meant to be temporary, and that's how it felt. I hadn't made a home, I'd made a place to sleep in between workdays. I got my single wine glass out of the cupboard and narrowed my eyes. I was thirty-three, and I was still living like a student. And not in the fun way.

Tola's voice pulled me from my irritation.

'And how's things with the Boy Wonder? Were you terrorised today?'

'I sent an email with creative templates for presentations and some research I did on the firm they're pitching to,' I said lightly. 'Dylan sent an email that said thanks, so I guess that's a win.'

'What did the email actually say?' she probed, and I laughed.

'Literally just the word "thanks", no greeting, no sign-off. No full stop.'

'Man knows how to hold a grudge, apparently. He still pretending he doesn't know you?'

'Yep. I've got a full day with them day after tomorrow, so I guess we'll see how well that holds up. Felix is pissed about my time off. Says it could affect my chances of the promotion.'

I could almost hear her frown. 'I'm pretty sure that's illegal, babe. I'll have a chat with Irene in HR, she's partial to a caramel macchiato and a bit of office goss. But apart from that, the work itself is going OK?'

'You know,' I said, almost incredulous, 'it's shockingly easy to prep them for the presentation. I'm loving it. Is that bad? Am I, like, some evil power-mad master manipulator or something?'

'You've got years of experience in a high-pressure environment, you practically run this place without getting any of the credit, and you still deal with Hunter's bullshit with a smile on your face,' Tola said, before pausing dramatically. 'So obviously, you're a psychopath.'

I snorted, 'Good thing I've got you to keep me grounded.'

'You kidding? You're a goddess in my eyes, all hail Aly, queen of the long game. We will be toasting your promotion and Hunter's demise by the end of the month.'

'If there is any justice in the world,' I sighed, suddenly unsure. 'They like him.'

'They're idiots. You are a *ball-buster* and a *go-getter* and whatever other stupid shit they say about ambitious women.

If being paid to turn your ex-best friend into a proposal Ken doll for a social-media socialite was what it took for you to finally recognise you're a goddess, I'm on board.'

Tola was a one-woman cheer squad. She was also sensitive to caffeine and I could tell it had clearly been a 'three Redbulls' sort of day.

I snorted, 'OK, well, thank you for the support. Let's see how the next meeting goes. Dylan might push me over the edge. Either figuratively or literally off the building, the way these calls have been going.'

'Call me if you need backup,' she said seriously, then paused. 'But not tonight, because I am going dancing, and I'm gonna pull someone fit who won't remember my name in the morning. Just the way I like it.'

I laughed, and we said our goodbyes. I considered pouring myself a glass of wine in my sad single glass. God, going out to dance and kiss someone because you wanted to. What would that even feel like?

I needed to be more like Tola, even if tonight that meant eating twice the recommended portion of pasta, just because I wanted to. But no sooner had I started crawling through my cupboards in search of carbohydrates than my phone rang. A number I didn't know always made me nervous.

'Hello?'

'Do you always answer your phone like an axe murderer might be on the other end?' a male voice asked, and I struggled to place it, heart suddenly racing.

'Who is this?'

'It's Ben! From EasterEgg Development? Good to know I made an impression.'

'Hi, sorry! I just wasn't expecting a call!' I went into problem-solving mode: 'Is everything OK? We're still booked in for our session this week?'

'Yeah, that's kind of what I was calling about. I thought it might be good if we got together and did some prep beforehand. Maybe tonight? With some really toxic cocktails?'

Oh. That was unexpected.

'Um, Ben, that really sounds lovely but I'm not sure it would be professional—'

He burst out laughing. 'Oh God, no, that wasn't—'

'Oh, sorry, I didn't mean to—' I could feel my whole body erupting into a blush, and I cringed. Damn Tola and her pep talks.

'Aly,' Ben cut in, 'you are a beautiful and interesting woman, and were I ever to stray to the dark side, it would be an honour. But I like men. This was more of a dastardly scheme for me to give you some of that important information that I don't think Dylan's going to mention.'

'Tonight?'

'Have you got plans?' he asked, and I looked at my saucepan of boiling water on the stove, visualised eating alone at the breakfast bar again.

'Could there be some food included in these drinks plans?' I asked, and heard him chuckle.

'My kinda gal. Meet you at seven.'

It is terribly important to make friends with people who know the best places in the city, and it was clear straight away that Ben was one of those people. La Bamba was hidden down the backstreets from Embankment, a cute

Mexican affair, with outdoor seating and lights strung up across the courtyard. A warm breeze promised summer was on the way, and Ben stood up from the table when I arrived.

'I always think tapas is the friendliest way to eat while you're drinking,' he said in greeting and kissed me on both cheeks. 'What do you think?'

Two huge margaritas arrived at the table, and I half closed my eyes as I sipped at mine – perfect.

'I think you're in the running for my new favourite person. Thank you for this, definitely beats my sad bowl of pasta in front of old *Friends* reruns.'

'Hey, sometimes those nights can be good too,' he raised his drink and clinked it against mine, 'downtime is important. Most people never figure out how to be on their own, so when they're in a couple that's all they are.'

I raised an eyebrow. 'Are you talking about Dylan?'

'*However* did you guess?' he snorted, pretending to be looking at the menu. 'I've been with him a while, and before Nicki it was Delilah, and before Delilah it was Nadia, and before that ...'

'OK, I get the picture,' I frowned, wondering why that made my stomach hurt a little.

'He just doesn't know how to be by himself. He attaches himself to women who look at him and see ... I don't know, not him, but ...'

'They see potential,' I said sadly. *Oh, you have no idea.* 'I've been there myself.'

'On which side?'

'Both,' I tried to smile. 'It's a powerful drug.'

'That's why I don't date casually.'

I laughed, 'Then how do you get to date seriously?'

'I take my time and pick the right person. I've got my life almost exactly how I want it. I've got my lovely flat and amazing friends. With your help, my sometimes great job is about to become absolutely fantastic all the damn time. I've got my puppy and my pottery class, and I've finally found an eye cream I'm happy with.' Ben winked and tucked a strand of hair back into place. 'I need to find a person who complements that. Someone who wants to be a part of it.'

'You sound like my friend Tola. But as brilliant as that sounds, all self-love and self-worth, I've gotta wonder, do you ever meet anyone? Does anyone ever seem worth bringing home?'

Ben laughed and made a face. 'No, not really.'

Talk turned to the menu and we ordered, with Ben chatting to the waitress and choosing the wine to follow our too-soon-finished cocktails. It was nice to be taken care of.

'So what's your first impression of Dylan?'

Tread carefully, Aly.

'He is clearly someone who cares about his company and his team. And he's proud and wants to protect what he's built. And maybe he doesn't want someone his girlfriend hired messing around in his business. Or knowing that he's not quite the big success story he's let her think he is ...?' I raised my voice in a question, but Ben fought a smile and looked away, coy. 'I can get that. We want the people we love to be impressed by us. But I also think he's scared.'

Ben picked at the tortilla chips on the table, munching one thoughtfully. 'Nicki's never really gotten what we're about. She sees everything as an opportunity for either money or recognition. But the app is about connecting teens with mental health support in a variety of formats. It's about doing something good. Sure, we want to get paid, so we can keep making stuff, but we didn't get into this to get rich and famous. But the longer Dylan's around her . . .'

'He forgets?' I offered, and Ben shook his head.

'No, it's not that, he just . . . he ties himself up in knots trying to make it seem like he's exactly what she wants.'

Apparently he's not doing a good enough job.

'How do you mean?'

Ben cringed, and I almost felt bad watching the war wage across his features. Was he betraying his friend to a near stranger, or helping their business get the support it needed?

'It wasn't too bad with the others,' he started, swirling his wine around his glass. 'They were normal. He was perfect with their parents, sent flowers for no reason. It was like he'd been given a user manual, but the truth is, Dylan just likes making people happy. And obviously, eventually he couldn't keep it up, or they'd push for more, or he'd have a bad day and they didn't know how to deal with it, and then the cycle would start again.

'But Nicki, with her family, her upbringing, her influencer lifestyle? The fifty-quid flowers weren't going to impress someone like Nicki. So things got more expensive, holidays went on credit cards, and suddenly we moved from our basic basement office to a swanky place by the river and he's wearing designer suits and talking about being a tech entrepreneur.'

I winced. 'He's in debt.'

Ben looked down at the table. 'I think so. I'm worried

about him. The guy's been my friend for years, and I'm worried he's losing himself. Until you turned up, I'd never seen him snap at anyone, ever.'

'I ... clearly bring up some stuff for him,' I said. *Understatement of the decade.* 'And that's OK, I can handle it.'

Ben nodded and tapped the table again.

'Was that what you wanted to tell me? About the people-pleasing and the debt?'

Ben looked guilty, raising his eyes to the sky. 'Nope, I'm just giving up secrets left, right and centre this evening. What a good friend.'

'Hey,' I said, getting his attention, 'you seem like a great friend, one who wants to look out for his mate and his business. It's your livelihood too, after all. Whatever you say will be kept in complete confidence.'

'He won't want me telling you.'

'Is it going to make a difference to how you approach the big business deal?'

'It might explain Dylan's ... hesitance?' Ben paused, 'and attitude.'

I gestured for him to continue, and then rested my chin on my hand as I sipped my red wine, giving Ben my full attention.

'In the early days, EasterEgg was Dylan and one other guy, Peter. Peter got Dylan into coding, helped train him up. Dyl had this idea for an app, something he'd been fiddling with since he dropped out of uni—'

'—dropped out of uni?!' I yelped, then winced. 'Sorry, that sounded judgemental. I'm surprised, that's all.'

I'd spent months helping him choose where to go, what to

study. When he got his acceptance, he'd grabbed me round the waist and spun me round in the school library, yelling in celebration. Even the librarian had smiled, despite the noise. He'd been so excited for his future.

And he hadn't even stuck it out?

'He said he lasted a few weeks, but his heart wasn't in it. He ended up moving to a flatshare, living off his loan and volunteering at the library to teach old people how to use computers. I imagine he was pretty good at it, he's quite patient. Most of the time. With most people.'

'I can see that,' I said politely. 'So what happened?'

'He and Peter started working on this app, and I joined them soon after. It was called HomeSafe. It was a way for parents to stay connected to their kids, track their phones but with permission. It wouldn't show you exactly where they were, but it would give you an approximation and ping off of registered safe spaces. Like a friend's or a relative's.'

'Cool,' I said, immediately thinking of promotions. I could sell something like that, no problem.

'Yeah, Dylan was super passionate about it. He said it was something from his school days that prompted the idea. Something about calling a friend's mum when she got too drunk, the shame and embarrassment of it. The fear in the mother's voice. He didn't want parents to have to worry any more. He had this idea that if parents could see where their kids were, safe at the party, or still within the school gates, maybe they wouldn't rush to pick them up in a panic. It would be safer for everyone.'

My heart clenched a little at that. I wondered if he knew about Dylan's mother's accident. Probably not. And that mother out of her mind with worry when her daughter didn't come home? That was my mama. Dylan had been righting wrongs after I'd disappeared.

'That's ... that's brilliant,' I said softly. 'It sounds like a wonderful idea.'

'It was, and the app was so good,' Ben said. 'We were killing it, honestly. We were all in our twenties, full of energy, pulling all-nighters. Living on energy drinks and frozen pizzas. We wanted this thing to be the best it could be, Dylan most of all.

'We took on more developers, and it really felt like we were on to a winner, you know? It was like when you're a teenager, hanging out with your friends and laughing and creating something. Having fun.'

He paused, as if trying to figure out how to tell the rest of the story without getting anyone in trouble.

'So what went wrong?'

'Peter was really desperate for us to properly pitch the app. Or even get it up on the store and charge for it, make changes as we went. But Dylan wanted it to be perfect. Every time we got close to being ready, he'd find something else to work on or want to add another feature. He was just never ready to let it go.'

Ben shook his head, 'We were all exhausted, stressed, no money coming in. He and Peter had this huge argument and they parted ways. A few of the other developers went with him, tired of working and never seeing anything come of it. And about two weeks later we realised Peter had gone and sold the app to one of the bigger developers. Got himself a job out of it, too.'

'Did you guys sue him for breach of contract, intellectual rights? Copyright? Non-compete?' I asked, thinking *Oh, poor Dylan*.

'We would have … if we'd had contracts or anything official. There was nothing to stop him. Whoever hadn't left at that point quit. There was no money, no project and no hope. It was only me and Dyl at that point.'

'Why didn't you leave, too?' I asked. 'Clearly you're talented. You got screwed over.'

'We got screwed because Dylan cared too much and trusted too much.' Ben shrugged. 'I'd rather work for someone like that than someone who'd use me without a second thought. He made a mistake but he deserved my loyalty. So I went back to bartending, and he went back to helping out on the building site during the day, and a few months later we turned up again and started pitching ideas. Starting from scratch. That's where the teenage mental health app came from.'

'I can see why you wanted me to know,' I said, tapping the rim of my glass.

'He may pretend everything's all right, but that's because he can't afford to be seen as a failure. He can't afford to let being afraid stop him from making this work. And I don't think he will …' Ben said, but trailed off, his eyes softening slightly.

'But?'

Ben looked torn, taking a moment to clean his glasses on the bottom of his shirt, and then taking a huge bite of the last taquito so he didn't have to talk, focusing on chewing. The poor guy looked miserable. I waited.

'The Nicki thing worries me. He's so busy playing Mr Businessman, he forgets to make the choices that don't look good. The boring, unsexy stuff. We didn't need to be in that office, we could update our website so we don't look like a huge company. He could stop walking around with a smile on his face like he hasn't got a worry in the world. He needs to be honest.'

'Sometimes you need that smoke and mirrors when you're making a deal. Make them think you're bigger fish, get a bigger payday?'

Ben shrugged. 'I guess.'

I frowned, trying to figure it out. 'Is he trying to build an online brand, like Nicki? Influencer stuff?'

'No, at least that would be useful!' Ben exclaimed, then laughed at himself. 'He completely takes a back seat when it comes to her life. Like he's afraid of the limelight.'

'He loves her, right?' I asked before I could stop myself, and then noticed Ben's raised eyebrow.

'Why?'

'Because ... a lot of men would find it helpful to have a famous girlfriend when they're pitching for the deal of their career.' *Switch it around, take the pressure off you.*

'He's not like that, he doesn't use people. He's a good man. I know you haven't seen much of that ...'

'I've seen enough.' I patted his hand. 'If I judged every man on how he reacted when I came in to point out his flaws, I'd never date anyone.' *Well, that joke was a little too close to the bone.* 'Tell me: you guys all have contracts now, right?' I crossed my fingers and smiled widely, hoping to distract him.

'We do.'

I exhaled. 'Good.'

'But only because I wrote them and me and Priya signed them. Dyl doesn't have one.' *So close.*

'Why the hell not?'

'He says he trusts us.'

'So he wants to play the part without having any semblance of a real business?' I put my head in my hands. 'Ben, I'm glad we did this, don't get me wrong, but you're ruining my life.'

Or rather, Dylan is.

I lifted my head. 'Real talk – is there anything else you think I need to know, about this situation, about Nicki, about Dylan?'

'Only that . . . well, he's a really good guy. I know he's not acting like it right now but I promise you, he is.'

'I know,' I said gently. 'And believe me, I am just as motivated as he is that this works out. Maybe more so.'

Ben held his glass up in a cheers to my dedication and to our success. To being phoenixes, singed wings and all.

Chapter Ten

For every problem I solved at EasterEgg, every moment I felt like a winner, there was always Dylan glaring at me across a conference room to bring me back to earth. At every opportunity, he would make things unpleasant. I asked a question, he'd scowl. I'd sit quietly and he'd wonder aloud if they were getting their money's worth. But I wasn't going to let him win. And sometimes, just sometimes, I'd catch that look before he rearranged his features into something unpleasant, where he looked at me with intrigue, as if he'd forgotten to play his part.

I lived for those moments. But I wasn't sure what to do with them when I got them.

At one point, while Priya was explaining the functionality of the app, my phone rang: Felix. I winced and sent him to voicemail, but Dylan raised an eyebrow.

'Are we having an impact at all, Miss Aresti?'

'Yep, you're making me think I should have upped my prices for consultation,' I said roughly, before turning back to Priya with a sweet smile. 'Sorry about that, could you tell me more about the journaling feature?'

She grinned back. 'There is a journal, that's for notes, but what I'm super proud of is this.' She sent the image up to the whiteboard behind her, a video she'd made using the app. She was scrolling through different words, moving them about and sorting them into piles on the screen.

'It's like that fridge magnet poetry, you know?' she said. 'Sometimes kids find it hard to find the words. And you don't want to feed them thoughts because they won't connect, they'll probably latch on to the easiest one that feels the least painful. But this allows them to find the words that resonate and spend a few moments playing, sorting through feelings and images, identifying or categorising them. It's calming, but it also makes them feel in control. This tested really well in our demographic as a sweet extra that set us apart. Play is important.'

I tapped my nose and then pointed at her. 'That, right there. That's it. That's how you pitch it. With that warmth and care and innovation and playfulness.'

Priya looked briefly proud of herself, then sat down.

I caught Dylan watching me, head tilted, and I didn't pause to give him time to get his next barb in.

'OK, so we've covered features, I'll make a few notes and send them over. But it's such a strong product, you should be really proud.' I paused, preparing myself. Time to start bringing in a little more fixer-upper flavour to this situation. 'Seeing as you can't load it up to the app store and show sales, my recommendation is to find other forms of social proof.'

Dylan ran a hand through his hair, tugging at the ends, 'What does that even *mean*?'

'It *means*, Mr James, get a freaking social media account. I don't even particularly care which one. Show people are interested in your app, that it fits with what you stand for and what the kids these days are using. You can't sell a piece of tech without acknowledging how they use their devices.'

'Yeah you can, because the mental health of both adults and children is significantly damaged by social media.' He crossed his arms and properly glowered at me.

'Maybe so. But they're going to keep using it, right? It's their way of feeling connected, less alone. It gives them a roadmap towards happiness, even if it's wrong. If you go out there shouting it down, if you make them choose between feeling popular and their own self-care, they're going to pick popularity. If anything, you should harness it with a share feature to connect communities, show them looking after their mental health is something to be proud of.'

Priya started scribbling furiously, nodding her head, and Ben grinned at me. But Dylan was still scowling. What a shame, he'd always had such a pretty smile. I wanted to say it, if only to piss him off even more, but I resisted.

'Treat it as an adventure,' I said, smiling broadly, 'try something new and see where it takes you.'

Dylan looked at me in confusion, narrowing his eyes as if he was looking for a hidden message in my choice of words. We stared at each other for a moment, trying to figure each other out. *What had I said?* Finally, he blinked and shrugged.

'You're just saying that because you work with Nicki.' It was so close to the truth, in some way, that I gathered up all the energy to argue, but he turned to Ben before I could say anything. 'Yesterday she spent ten minutes talking to her fans about what kind of cheese she eats. Who cares?'

'But they *did*, right?' I laughed, and he whirled round, glaring at me. 'They *did* care. That's what drives you nuts.'

'Fifteen thousand people listening to my girlfriend list types of cheese. *Fifteen thousand*, commenting with different types of cheese so she could say if she'd eat them or not. What the hell is that?!' he snorted, and I laughed, and for the briefest moment, we were smiling together. Until he met my eyes and stopped abruptly, looking at the floor as that frown re-emerged.

'You know why, though, right?' I turned to the others. 'Connection. She's giving them something of herself.'

'Her views on dairy?' Ben laughed.

'It doesn't matter. She's consistent, she's there. She's sharing something. That's what a brand is. You can know exactly if something is "Nicki" or not. If she posted up a picture of her bedroom with a dinosaur duvet cover, you'd immediately know she'd been hacked. Consistency gives people something to depend on.'

Priya and Ben nodded, and I turned to see Dylan leaning against one of the desks, legs stretched out in front of him, scanning me. I could feel his eyes on me but couldn't tell what he was doing. His brow was furrowed but not with that same look of displeasure he seemed to always be giving me these days.

'You know much about giving people something to depend on, Aly?' he asked, and it should have been pointed and sharp, but he just sounded sad.

Something tightened in my chest, so I started packing up my bag and kept my eyes down. What a weird dance this was; he'd press and I'd retreat. He'd back up and I'd push forward again. Always on edge with no one winning.

'Not really. I stay for a while, fix what I need to fix and then I'm gone and on to the next,' I said lightly, sliding my laptop into my bag and putting it over my shoulder. It was mostly the truth. I walked away before he could say anything else.

'Aly, get in here!' Felix yelled across the office as I went in the next morning, and I felt my cheeks colour. I carefully placed my jacket over my chair and picked up a notebook.

'Good morning, boss!' I said, cheerful and channelling efficiency as I closed the door behind me. 'What do you need?'

'I need you to stop taking days off!' Felix stroked his little moustache and pouted. Felix looked like an actor in a silent film. Unfortunately he sounded like someone filming one through a foghorn. 'You tell me you want this job, you want to step up to the next level, yet you're not here!'

I wanted to make excuses; *I'm sorry I need to turn my ex-best friend into a Prince Charming for the Kitty Litter Princess or my mother will lose her home. Otherwise I'd be here, promise.*

'Felix,' I tried to sound as confident as I had with Dylan the day before, 'I haven't taken time off properly in years. And it's odd days, I'm not off for weeks!'

'I need you dedicated, I need you hungry. Showing leadership ...' He tapped his fingers on the table in irritation, eyes on the door. *Oh crap.*

I dropped into the seat opposite him. 'What happened?'

'Can I trust you with this?'

'If you want me to fix it, sure,' I replied, and he didn't blink at how forthright I was. I was clearly the only one who could fix whatever this issue was. If I wasn't, it would have already been dealt with.

'The BigScreen account . . .' he started.

'Teddy Bell. He's coming in next week to talk strategy,' I supplied, trying to keep myself from rolling my eyes. Teddy Bell booked in to talk strategy every quarter, and every time he came in, listened to our presentation, told us it was all a bit too 'modern' and insisted we carry on doing exactly the same thing we'd been doing for the last ten years. Which was very little.

'I need you to go and talk to him before then. He's giving a talk at Tech X-change tomorrow.'

'The same as every year.'

'Probably the same talk as last year too,' Felix snorted, softening slightly. 'I need you to convince him to stay with us.'

'He's being poached?' I was silently relieved. Letting go of a client with no vision freed us up to do bigger, better things. And make more money. 'Maybe it's for the best.'

'He's not being poached. And it's not for the best,' Felix tugged on one side of his moustache, the same side he always did when he was frustrated, which was why he continually looked lopsided. 'Teddy Bell is a close friend of the Big Boss, has been for years. It's the reason we put up with him. And Teddy is looking for a new firm due to an . . . indiscretion from one of our staff members.'

I frowned in confusion. 'Someone propositioned him? Isn't he in his seventies?'

Felix rolled his eyes. 'Not him, his wife. His thirty-six-year-old, very pretty wife.'

I watched as Felix tilted his head to the left of his office, and I almost didn't need to follow his gaze.

'Hunter,' I sighed.

'He and Teddy play golf sometimes. He became ... *acquainted* with Teddy's wife through the club.'

Ah, to be young, posh and free of any of the consequences of your actions.

'So send Hunter, make him grovel. The end.'

Felix huffed, 'Teddy doesn't want to see him. But he wants someone on their knees promising him the world and it'll go down easier if it comes from you.'

'From me? Hunter's apology should come from me?' I searched for a logical conclusion, but the best I could come up with was: 'Because ... I'll be his manager?'

Felix grinned at me. 'There's that hunger! Aly, I've seen you talk people into things I could never have believed if I hadn't seen it with my own eyes. You suggest something, ever so gently, and forty-five minutes later they're acting like it was their idea all along.'

'So you *are* paying attention when people steal my ideas?' I asked, eyebrow raised, but he shook his head.

'Not the point. Look, go and get Teddy back onside. You're great at making people feel important. Take him for dinner, promise him whatever he wants, apologise for us hiring a shithead who can't keep it in his pants. Just make sure he promises to stay with us. Take it as a task to prove you're capable of the responsibilities of the new role.'

'So I *will* be Hunter's manager?'

Felix held up his hands, and then made a little zipping motion across his mouth. 'I guess we'll have to see, won't we?'

I gripped the arms of the chair and sat up. 'So, just to confirm, you want me to go to Birmingham tomorrow morning, sit through his *stupid* talk about how great his rapidly failing company is, beg for forgiveness on behalf of Hunter, and flirt with the old guy to make sure he stays in contract?'

'Yes.'

'And what will Hunter be doing while I'm doing all that?'

'Ruminating on his own stupidity,' Felix frowned. 'Do it for the job, Aly. Forget Hunter. Do it to prove you can, while you've got an audience.' He smiled encouragingly, and something flickered within me, a semblance of that fighting spirit, I supposed.

And then an idea sparked.

'I want extra tickets to the conference. And I'm getting a first-class train ticket. *And* I expect my expenses to cover an incredibly indulgent lunch. With drinks.'

He looked amused and slightly proud. 'Whatever you say, kid. You're the boss.'

Time to push my luck.

'Last thing: I need Tola and Eric with me; they're leading on a few projects for our other clients who will be there ...' I started formulating excuses, but Felix waved it away, as if he didn't have time for me to make the case and win. It was easier just to say yes. Even that felt like success.

As I left Felix's office, I noticed Matthew hovering, and he tilted his head. 'Everything OK? He was in a *foul* mood this morning.'

I waved it away. As much as Hunter was a thorn in my side, I didn't want the office gossip to be traced back to me. 'It's fine, I've got to go do a little client retention offsite tomorrow.'

'Can I help at all?' Matthew asked, and I blinked, surprised. 'I mean, I'd probably only get in the way, but . . . if I can, let me know.'

I nodded. 'Thanks, I appreciate it. Were you—' I gestured at Felix's door, 'were you waiting to go in?'

'No, I was waiting for you actually.' Matthew scratched the back of his neck, embarrassed. 'I wanted to see what you thought of this tagline. The copy guys think it's perfect, but I'm not sure it's hitting the right tone . . .'

I looked back over across the office to see Tola raising her eyebrows at me, wondering what the hell was going on. 'Do you need it now, Matthew?'

'It'll only take a second,' he said, thrusting the file in my face, and watching me, wide-eyed and anxious. I withheld a sigh, gave in, and scanned the document. I pressed my lips together.

'Try changing it to present tense, see if that gives it more urgency,' I shrugged, handing it back with a smile. 'But in general, trust the copywriters. They know what they're doing.'

Matthew's smile was so wide that I felt a bit embarrassed for him. 'Thanks, Aly! I knew you'd be able to help!'

When I finally made it to my corner of the office, Tola

was in my chair. 'What's going on? And could that boy stop looking at you like an adoring puppy? It's distracting.'

'He's not adoring, he's grateful,' I corrected, poking her until she stopped spinning and got up from my seat. 'Can you and Eric be free tomorrow to come to Tech X? I've got a rubbish assignment and a dastardly plan.' I stroked my chin dramatically.

'Oh, can do, I'm always down for a bit of scheming.'

The next thing I had to do was get Dylan onside. And I didn't really have time for niceties. I rang his number and didn't bother with a greeting. 'I need you guys to be available tomorrow.'

'Well, obviously we're only here for your amusement, it's not as if we—'

I huffed and rolled my eyes, phone in the crook of my neck as I looked up train times on my computer.

'Kill the attitude for a moment, would you?' I sighed. 'I've got you tickets to the Tech X-change.'

'The conference?' In his shock, he briefly forgot to be cold.

'Yeah. Birmingham, tomorrow. Can you make it?'

'Wait a second . . .' I heard muffled voices. 'Priya's gotta see if her parents can watch her kid, but me and Ben can definitely come.'

'OK, I'll see you both at Euston station at nine a.m. Dress the part, you're going to be networking.'

'I know how to dress, Aly,' he huffed, and if I closed my eyes it was like we were seventeen again.

'Sure. Well . . . I'll see you then.'

'I guess we're going on a bit of an adventure,' he said

141

quietly, and I smiled to myself, feeling a little sad. *Oh, that's why he looked like that earlier.*

'I haven't been on an adventure in quite a while,' I replied, barely daring to hope we might have reached an impasse.

Dylan had always had this thing he picked up from his mum, this saying.

'Stop what you're doing,' he'd say, 'and tell me five things you're excited about today.'

Five Wonderful Things was what his mum called it. She said that she couldn't bear to live one day without finding five things to be grateful for. Joyce was great at finding things to delight over: the sound of the wind through the trees, a hug from her son, the cat making her laugh. And if she couldn't find something, she'd conjure it. A perfect piece of cake, or dancing in the kitchen to her favourite songs.

I had this really clear memory of her asking me, and I just couldn't answer. My parents had been fighting again, and Mama had been crying and I was dreading going home. 'You can't think of one thing, pet?' she'd said. 'Well, we can't have that, can we?'

She drove us out to get ice cream before we'd even had our dinner. 'If you can't think of five things, you've gotta take yourself off on an adventure, sweetheart, those are the rules.'

She'd seemed so infinitely cool in her stripy red-and-white jumper, eating her chocolate ice cream and stealing some of Dylan's scoop of strawberry. She was like someone who could conjure all the wonderful things out of thin air.

After she died, we didn't talk about it any more. Until the

day after my dad left. The next morning Dylan called me up and asked me for five wonderful things.

'I can't think of anything, Dyl. Seriously.'

'Then we've got to go on an adventure.'

We jumped on a train to Brighton and spent the day at the seaside, eating candy floss and sticking our toes in the water. We browsed the shops and went to the movies, spent pennies in the arcade and ate burgers on the train home.

'Can you think of five things, Aly?' he'd asked again.

'I can think of a hundred.'

His smile had been unbelievable.

That was who he'd been back then, my instigator. Dragging me along by the hand and refusing to let me be unhappy. He knew I always needed to be busy, to be distracted. That I loved facts and stories, nuggets of trivia. Dylan kept a list in the back pocket of his jeans. I saw it once: *True Things for Aly*. We had our routines, our sacred rituals, that way that kids know how to look after each other.

When that perfect Brighton day came to an end, and we had to get on the train home, I was dreading it. Dreading walking back into that house and seeing the carnage, and worse, letting him see it. But Dylan was unfazed, as always. He walked me home, poked his head in and saw my mother, a barely coherent lump on the sofa, and then he said, 'You and me are gonna cook dinner, Aly. Let's see what we've got to work with.' He opened the fridge, made it a game, and even my mother took a seat at the table, painting on a ghost of a smile as she ate dinner and listened to us talk about our day of adventure. It was like he'd worked magic.

The man on the phone now, making snarky comments

about late notice and last minute, who hadn't even thanked me, he wasn't the same boy who kept that list of facts in his back pocket. The one who knew exactly the right thing to say.

But maybe that little exhale at the other end of the line was some sort of acknowledgement? Maybe that mention of adventure meant he thought about those moments, too? Shared history was a secret language, and I was surprised to find how much of ours I still remembered.

'Dylan . . .' I started, hopeful, but he cut me off.

'Try not to be late,' he said, suddenly gruff, and I half laughed in outrage.

'I've never been late a day in my—'

He hung up.

It's easier to miss a ghost, to build up these moments and memories into something that had meaning. A history. But when that ghost turns up every day and is so different to how they used to be, it makes you wonder if any of it was ever real at all.

Chapter Eleven

'So, I've gotta tell you, I think Ben is perfect for you,' I said that morning to a sleepy Eric as we got coffee in Euston station.

'Nuh uh, don't do that shit. You're better than this,' he took a large bite of his muffin, sunglasses on, looking both effortlessly cool and incredibly hungover. 'Every straight girl wants the only two gays she knows to get together. The fact that we both sleep with men is not enough of a connection.'

'Good enough for your usual hook-ups,' Tola quipped, reapplying her lipstick using the camera on her phone. Today it was a lavender colour, blocky like a crayon. It matched the lilac bumbag worn over her denim dungaree mini dress. She looked like she was off to a festival, and yet the minute she handed anyone a card with the words *Social Media Expert*, they'd get it. I, of course, was in my usual black with my usual lipstick. I'd added a pair of gold lightning-bolt earrings for a bit of boldness. Teddy Bell needed to know I wasn't messing around.

If I could convince the old dinosaur to stay, even though I thought he was an uninspired husk, it would be a triumph. I wanted to return like a conqueror, throwing down his business card on Felix's desk tomorrow morning and say, *'See, didn't even break a sweat. Give me the branding role, you know I deserve it. Let me run the team! I've got this!'*

But I was glad I had the guys with me for support. Teddy Bell was not an easy man to have a conversation with. There was a reason Hunter always met him on the golf course, half-cut and willing to pay for flattery. But I could handle it, I knew I could.

'It's not like that. I really do think he's wonderful,' I said, turning the conversation back to Ben. 'And seeing as you're going to meet him in a few minutes, I thought I'd pre-warn you.'

'Fine,' Eric flicked his hand at me, 'go ahead, pitch him.'

'What?'

'He's a product you think will change my life, pitch him.'

'Great hair, horn-rimmed glasses, fit, like if the class nerd suddenly started putting in time at the gym. Knows great places to eat and is funny without being bitchy.'

Eric raised an eyebrow. 'Why does that last bit feel like a pointed attack?'

'Because it is,' I laughed. 'He's really nice, and he has his life together. He loves his flat and he's got a sweet little beagle, and he knows how to make a great cocktail.'

'So what's wrong with him? Why's he single?'

Tola raised a perfect eyebrow and looked unimpressed. 'What, so every single person is damaged goods?'

'Um, yes,' Eric huffed, 'obviously. Look at us. Except you, Tola, you're just young and living your life.'

Tola nodded, and resumed fixing her makeup. 'Thanks, babe.'

'Hey!' I half laughed. 'Excuse me!'

Eric looked, pushing his sunglasses down his nose. 'Do you really want me to start on you?'

I sighed, 'The only thing that might be wrong with him is that he's so loyal to Dylan, even when the company is a shambles.'

He snorted, 'Ah, one of those fake weaknesses that's actually a positive trait. You are too much, Aly, really. Leave me to my meaningless sex and let me get my own dog. I'll be my own happy ever after, thank you very much. I don't need some sad set-up.'

That was when I saw Dylan across the concourse. He was wearing a similar suit to that first time I saw him with Nicki. Blue with a striped shirt, but this time his collar was done up, he wore a navy tie and an anxious frown. He looked professional, and I didn't let my thoughts stray any further than that. Though I liked that he wasn't completely clean-shaven, it gave him a little edge.

Next to him, Ben looked stylish in his own way, subtle brown tweed trousers and waistcoat, a cream shirt and his hands in his pockets as he walked along. Simply handsome, like he'd just walked out of a 1940s movie. Timeless. I waited for Eric's response, and I wasn't disappointed.

His jaw dropped. '*That* was who you were talking about? The fair one?'

I nodded, and he grasped my hand.

'I want him.'

'He's not a pony,' Tola snorted, but peered over her own shades, 'cute though.'

They paused and waved across the concourse, and I was thrilled to see Priya hurrying through the crowds, looking effortlessly cool in blue flared linen trousers, white trainers and cream shirt, huge sunglasses on her head. I waved and grinned, so pleased she'd be with us after all.

'I apologise for every stupid thing I said before,' Eric rambled as they approached, 'please be nice!'

'Not that you deserve it,' I said out of the corner of my mouth, through a gritted-teeth smile, turning to face them. 'Hi! Excited for a day of geeking out over tech stuff?'

'You have no idea.' Ben kissed my cheek and gave me a warm smile. 'I've wanted to go every year and we never quite got round to it, did we, Dyl?'

Dylan nodded, that nervous look on his face as he squared his shoulders. 'Should be good.' He paused and looked at me, taking in my sixties-style black dress with the Peter Pan collar. Tola called it 'Boss Bitch with a dash of whimsy'.

'You look nice,' he said, and the surprise in his voice made it clear he hadn't intended to say anything at all. I waited for a punchline, but there was none, so my silence sort of hung there, making it awkward.

I recovered and gave him a sarcastic salute. 'Only the best for you, boss.'

Dylan frowned at me as Ben guffawed, and I realised I'd just snapped his olive branch in half. Oops. I turned to Priya, desperate to shift the focus elsewhere.

'You made it! You look fantastic!' I grinned, and she twirled, hands raised like a princess.

'Amazing what you can do when you haven't got a little shit monster spitting sweet potato all over you.' She smiled back, and nudged the boys with her elbows. 'Besides, these guys get to do all the fun stuff. I didn't want to miss out this time.'

'I'm glad! This is Tola, that's Eric,' I gestured, 'my colleagues.'

'Her lackeys,' Eric corrected as he looked at Ben, a slight drawl around his lips I'd never seen before.

I noticed Ben consider him, before pointing out Tola's bumbag. 'I love it, it reminds me of clubbing in my twenties. Only the essentials.'

'Exactly,' Tola said, seamlessly opening it and reaching in. 'Gum, anyone?'

'Oooh, me!' Priya held her hand up, and stepped towards Tola. 'You look like a woman who has all the answers.'

Tola grinned, 'I like that *a lot.*'

We took over an area of the train, and I tried to stop my leg twitching. I was going through my notes on Teddy Bell, what to say, how to play it. I'd made flash cards to remember all the points, so I knew I could change tack if he didn't go for my first approach. The others all sat at the table opposite, and I gave myself space, saying I needed some time to focus and prepare. They all seemed to be having fun, even Dylan. Watching him with my friends and his, I could forget the tension between us. Like he could be the old him, as long as I wasn't involved.

'Is that BigScreen?' I heard a voice and looked up to see

Dylan sliding into the chair opposite me and picking up one of my flashcards. 'Teddy Bell.'

'You know him?'

'They call him "Dinosaurus Tech",' he shrugged, eyes focused on the table, hands splayed over the cards, as if when he looked up the truce would be broken. 'Most companies fall away when they don't adapt, and his will too, eventually. It's too expensive to produce the machinery, so he hasn't got many competitors. No need to be innovative or creative. No one snapping at his heels, or making him wonder if he's making the right decisions.'

'No, not unless you count my colleague who came on to his wife,' I said lightly, tapping the cards with my forefinger.

'Ah, you're on damage control. Of course.'

'Of course?'

'Fixing other people's messes,' he said. 'Classic Aly.'

He lounged back in his chair, arms stretched above his head. It was so odd to see him look so young, dressed like a grown-up but slouching like a teenager.

'Teddy's known for his ego. He wants what other people have. Sounds like him and your colleague have that in common,' he said. 'You want to dangle something exclusive in front of him.'

I wondered if Nicki knew how astute her boyfriend really was. I nodded my thanks, desperate not to breathe the wrong way and screw it all up. The last few moments had felt like a balm.

'Will you take my advice?' he asked, and I nodded.

'Thanks.'

He tapped the table twice and went to move, but paused. 'I took your advice, too.'

I saw Tola and Priya watching us carefully. 'About what?'

'You said Nicki uses social media as a form of connection. She gives people something, even if it's only her opinions.'

He slid his phone across to me, and there was his first social media post: A photo of him making a face, holding a giant block of cheese. *Hi, my name is Dylan James, and I really like gouda.*

I snorted, but by the time I'd looked up, the phone was whipped away, and he was down the aisle in search of coffee. But it felt like a tiny moment of progress, and I let it warm me. Tola tilted her head and raised an eyebrow, and I shook the smile from my face. Dylan was a project, he was taking my advice, and we were going in the right direction. That was all I needed to focus on. Well, that and *Dinosaurus Tech*.

Priya rested her chin on her hand and looked at me, as if she was trying to figure me out.

'What?'

'Absolutely nothing,' she grinned. 'Just pleased to see my boss taking some much-needed direction, that's all.'

You and me both, I wanted to say, but didn't want to jinx it.

When we got to the conference, it was a messy free-for-all over croissants and coffee until the talks started. I beckoned Tola and Eric over to me, speaking quietly.

'We're throwing them in at the deep end. They don't know how to talk about what they've got. Keep an eye on them and send them a life jacket when necessary.'

Tola paused. 'What about the other side of this deal?' She

hummed the wedding march. 'Business first, relationship chat with booze on the way home?'

Eric perked up, his gaze on Ben. 'Well, that sounds like a brilliant plan.'

'Put your tongue back in your mouth. I thought you wanted real connections? You were tired of the hook-ups,' I reminded him.

'I am. I can still nurture a crush. They're few and far between these days. Let me enjoy something!' Eric whined.

'Be a professional.' I nudged him with my elbow, then walked past Dylan, Priya and Ben over to someone I recognised. 'Laney, hi! How's it going? Have you met EasterEgg Development? They're working on a counselling app for teens I think is going to fit so well into the self-care and resilience through tech market – zeitgeist for this year, right? Guys, why don't you tell Laney a little more about it?' I turned back to them with a wide-eyed smile. 'I've gotta run, but I'll catch you later!'

'Knock 'em dead,' I said quietly to Dylan as I walked past and gave Tola a look. *Don't let them drown, but don't jump in until they're going under.* In the meantime, I had a dinosaur to find.

Of course, Teddy Bell had one of the last slots of the day, and so I had a lot of time to get nervous in between pivoting Dylan, Priya and Ben throughout the crowds and trying to actually do some work.

Felix called me, frustrated and wanting an update. 'He won't turn up until his slot, never watches anyone else's talks, so you'll have to get him after.'

'As I've discovered,' I said. 'How's our Prince Charming?'

152

Felix laughed, 'Happy as a lamb. Although he's sad he's missing out on a golf buddy. I've taken him off the BigScreen account. He's working with Matthew on the hair gel stuff. You'll run BigScreen from now on.' *Yes. Take that, you lazy, philandering posh git with your too perfect hair and your terrible spelling.* 'You can handle that, right?'

'Of course,' I said, confident. *I was pretty much redoing all Hunter's work anyway.*

'On a trial basis, Aly. After all, we don't want you so busy you can't take on further responsibilities, do we?' Felix said, and I could hear the smile in his voice.

'Absolutely,' I grinned. 'Is there anything else you want from me while I'm up here? I'm just checking in with our clients when I see them.'

'You're a star. That's all. Call me when you've spoken to Teddy.'

Felix was being entirely too nice to me, but I supposed that if I fixed this situation with Teddy before the Big Boss found out, I'd be saving his bacon too.

I took a moment to check my work emails, for some reason hoping there might be some apology or appreciation from Hunter, but no. There were two emails from Matthew, asking what I thought of the print visuals and if I thought his tweet would go viral. The problem with some people was that they thought too small, too detailed. I was a fan of worrying, but sometimes you had to use your instincts. I'd been telling Matthew that since he joined, but he still didn't trust himself.

I walked back over to see Tola watching from the coffee station as Dylan, Ben and Priya chatted to someone from Google.

'How're they doing?' I said as I sidled up, pouring myself a coffee.

'I think they might have actually perfected it. First one this morning was a rambling mess. Now they're natural, calm, know what makes their thing cool.' Tola nodded with approval. 'Good job.'

'That part isn't the hard part,' I sighed, looking at Dylan.

He did look more relaxed, a smile on his face, a curl from his hair falling into his forehead. His jacket hung over a chair, his sleeves rolled up and I watched as he spoke with his hands, explaining with enthusiasm. It was nice to see.

'Too much,' Tola said suddenly, 'the staring, I mean.'

I blinked and looked at her in shock. 'What?'

Her mouth curled into a smile. 'Eric? Looking at Ben like he's an ice cream that's about to melt? Why, who did you think I was talking about?'

She knew exactly what she was doing.

'Don't be mean. You're not the one walking around with a ghost from your childhood who refuses to acknowledge you.'

'Oh, he does, babe. Just not when you're looking. He has known where you are this entire time. The boy would make a good private detective. Maybe that's why he hates social media, too much attention.' I tried to follow what she was saying, but the announcement came over the tannoy for the next speaker, and I wanted to see what Teddy had to say. Plus I had to catch him after his talk.

I signalled to the guys that I was going into the talk, but they seemed to take it that they had to follow me. And of course, as we were sliding into the aisles, Tola held back, forcing Dylan to sit next to me. He immediately crossed his arms, eyes focused on the stage. Great.

If that's how he was going to be, I wasn't going to acknowledge him either. I sat up straight, hands folded delicately on top of the notebook in my lap, attentive even as the stage was empty.

'Of course, star pupil,' he said under his breath, still not looking at me.

'Paying attention is polite,' I replied.

'There's no one even up there yet,' Dylan said.

'Well, clearly I didn't think I was going to get any riveting conversation from *you*,' I hissed. *Because you won't look at me. You won't let me exist.*

'Stop getting your knickers in a twist for a second, I can tell you exactly how this thing is going to go,' Dylan said, and turned towards me.

'What thing?' I breathed, hopeful.

We're going to do this back and forth we do, Aly, and then we're going to go back on the train and drink a bunch of stolen beers and laugh because we've both been so pig-headed. And then we're going to be friends again, because I've missed you and you've missed me.

'Teddy Bell. He does this same talk every year,' Dylan whispered. I tried to stamp down on the disappointment.

'I thought you'd never been?'

'I haven't, but you don't need to, it's legendary. Look around, the room is half empty and the only people in here are the newbies to the industry. They don't know what they're in for. Someone uploads the video every year to YouTube. The only thing that changes is the colour of his shirts.'

I snorted, turning my head towards Dylan. 'Doesn't surprise me. He's not a man who likes change.'

Our eyes briefly met, as if in talking we'd forgotten we were meant to be angry at each other. I started turning away and could feel myself starting to blush. I'd forgotten how blue his eyes were.

He carried on talking, eyes back on the stage. As if he could pretend he was talking to himself.

'He'll open with how he started the company, even though it's not a good story, then he'll brag about how much money they've made, talk about how no one in the industry does what they do – which isn't true, use the word "innovator" a bunch of times and then compare himself to Churchill and Steve Jobs in a truly awful double whammy to finish.'

'You guys really didn't need my help at all, did you? You know what you're doing.'

He paused and I saw him press his lips together, like he was trying to stop himself. 'Sometimes you play a part for so long you forget it's acting.'

And before I could ask anything else, darkness fell and the stage lit up.

Dylan was completely right. Teddy droned on using the same tired language he'd been using for years, even the exact same PowerPoint presentation I think someone in our office had designed for him over a decade ago. And as I watched this little man stand with his chest puffed out and his legs apart, talking about how successful he was, how much money he made, I wondered if I even wanted this account.

Maybe making Hunter deal with him would be punishment enough. But I deserved that promotion. Whether I wanted to or not, I was getting Teddy Bell onside.

He ran over by five minutes, and when everyone was squirming in their chairs because there were no questions, he asked himself some. When it finally ended to applause that could only be described as 'polite', I made a beeline for the front of the stage.

'Mr Bell,' I said warmly, hand outstretched. 'Great talk.'

'Why thank you, young lady,' he said. 'I think I know you from somewhere.'

'My name's Aly Aresti, I'm from Amora Digital, your marketing firm? I've been working on your account for a few years now.'

He raised an eyebrow. 'So I suppose you're here to give me a spiel about loyalty?'

'I'm just here to offer our sincere apologies.' I held my hands up to show I was unarmed, before launching into my prepared talking points. 'Personally, I'm embarrassed that we even need to have this conversation. What Hunter did was incredibly inappropriate, and the whole company is mortified.'

He frowned. 'Is that right? So you think it's terrible, what young Hunter did?'

I nodded. 'Of course.'

Bell gave me a shrewd look. 'I've been in business a long time, and forgive me for saying, but you seem a little naive.'

'I'm sorry?'

He made a gesture with his hands, like he was trying to find the words. 'The world is a complex place, Miss Aresti,

157

you can't always trust the people you expect. I like Hunter, he reminds me a lot of me at that age. How old are you, if you don't mind me asking?'

I raised an eyebrow. 'Old enough to know better than to give inappropriate attention to a client's spouse. So I take it you're not upset with the situation, and I've wasted my journey here to apologise?'

That rattled him, as I'd intended. But it also let him know he was *so special*. I'd made this trip *just for him*. He'd dine out on that story for a few days, about how important he was that I'd been sent up to hunt him down and fall on my sword.

'Of course I'm *upset*, I've been betrayed!'

Now was the time for the understanding nods and equivalent shushing noises.

'Of course, and we are incredibly sorry for the disrespect. I'll be taking over as your direct contact at the agency, and you won't have to see Hunter again.'

He looked at me with a new level of respect, vaguely impressed. 'Well, hasn't that worked out well for you, Miss Aresti? Perhaps you're not so green after all.'

'I'm not—'

'Nothing to be embarrassed about, my dear, it's important to be cut-throat in business. So often, women are the best at the machinations and backstabbing that are necessary. It's the way of the world.' He smiled at me, and I tried not to shudder, painting my face as serene and polite.

'That's a . . . unique take on it, Mr Bell.'

He waved away my words, and stepped forward, taking my arm. 'Teddy, please. Now, what are the agency willing to give me for the inconvenience and embarrassment?'

I smiled at him. Now we were talking my language. I launched into all the things I was already doing for his campaign, but framed it as if they were added. More advertising space, more print, more this, more that. He nodded and smiled, but I could tell he had no idea what we did for his company, he was only focused on the freebies. Funny how the ones with money always were.

'And, of course, Mr Bell, when you get back to your office tomorrow morning, you'll find a *really excellent* limited edition single malt sitting on your desk. I know you're a Glenfiddich man. Just a small thank you for seeing me today.'

I watched as he smiled and grinned my work grin. *You're so special, so important.* I had him. He thought he was the shark, but I was. I wanted to run a victory lap. Even as he shook my hand and told me he was looking forward to working together further, I was visualising striding into Felix's office tomorrow morning.

Bell was shaking my hand, his other hand on my arm, when I felt someone brush past, separating us. I turned in shock.

'Teddy! Teddy Bell, how fantastic.' Dylan arrived out of nowhere, leaning in to shake his hand, and somehow positioning himself between the two of us. 'I see you've met my branding consultant, isn't she brilliant?'

I wanted to tell Dylan none of this was necessary, but couldn't get a word in.

'Do I know you, son?' Bell peered at Dylan in distrust.

'Dylan James, EasterEgg Development,' he replied smoothly.

'I've been hearing that name a lot today.'

'Well, that's good news. But we actually met last year, at the polo, I think it was? You know my girlfriend, Nicki Wetherington Smythe.'

Bell's face relaxed, and he even looked sincere for a moment. It was an odd experience.

'Ah, little Nicolette, of course. She grew up into such a beautiful girl. And so successful.'

I nodded, about to try to remove us from the situation, but Dylan held his hand up behind his back, a silent warning to hold on.

'Yeah, you go way back with her uncle Artie, right?'

Bell's smile dropped and his voice took on a new tone. I didn't like it. 'We're acquainted.'

'Well, Artie loves our Aly here.' Dylan put an arm around my shoulders, and I squeaked in surprise, stiff as a board. 'Really invested in her personal happiness and her career. After all, she's so clever, so many great ideas.'

'Oh, lots of great ideas,' Bell said faintly and then recovered himself. 'She's going to be running my account from now on.'

'Well then, you're incredibly lucky! We've only managed to hire her for a few weeks, but her input has been invaluable. I can't imagine what a huge company like you could do with all that talent. We're small fry, but *you* guys, you could really dominate the market.'

'We already do,' Bell said stiffly, but I could tell he was bored of the conversation.

'For now, but you've always gotta be one step ahead, right?' Dylan said with a smile, then looked at his watch. 'Sorry, Teddy, was great to chat but I'm going to have to steal

Aly away. We've got a train to catch. Did you get everything you needed from her?'

Bell looked between the two of us, trying to understand the relationship, but eventually gave up.

'I look forward to our next meeting, Miss Aresti. You've impressed me.' He looked at Dylan, distrustful. 'Make sure you continue to make good choices.'

He walked off, and we watched silently until he'd exited the conference room. I pulled away from Dylan's arm.

'What the *hell* was that?' I huffed, marching away towards the exit.

'You clearly needed rescuing! You're a people-pleaser, and *that man* is ... not a good guy. Who knows what could have happened?' Dylan ran a hand through his hair, half yelling.

'I know what could have happened because *I* was the one running the situation,' I kept my voice low. 'You realise I'm a grown professional? I'm actually quite good at my job. Which you might notice if you weren't undermining me at every possible moment.'

Dylan shook his head, clenching his teeth. 'This isn't about me. I know that guy. I know *exactly* who that guy is. What he's capable of.'

I met his eyes. 'But you don't know me.' *Any more.* 'You don't know what I'm capable of.'

I took a breath and raised my chin. 'I am a valued and respected member of my team. I took this task because I thought I could get *you guys* something out of it. You're welcome, by the way.'

'What is happening right now? I thought I was helping!' Dylan threw his hands up. 'I don't get this.'

161

'*YOU* don't get this? You're the one playing whatever weird game this is!' I tried not to screech, but I saw him chuckle before he could hide it. Oh great. Now he'd won the game.

He took a breath, stepping back from me, hands up. *I'm retreating, don't shoot.*

'Look, Aly. I didn't mean to suggest you couldn't handle yourself.' He paused. 'The way he was crowding you, I assumed . . .'

I nodded, trying to regulate my breathing. We'd come so close to finally acknowledging everything, and the chance was passing us by. 'OK, fine. Let's move on. What was all that stuff about Uncle Artie?'

Dylan snorted and looked at the floor. 'Artie is a bookie Nicki's dad uses. I think he used to work in the stock market, an old Italian guy in a three-piece suit and bowler hat. Proper gent.'

I twirled my finger to say, *yeah, go on.*

'Rumour has it Artie's mafia, and he's very protective of the womenfolk. Doesn't like to hear of any scummy behaviour, *capiche*?'

Jeez, how did Nicki keep that connection from the reality TV shows and celeb mags?

'And *is* he mafia?'

Dylan shook his head, snorting, 'He's just watched *The Godfather* a few too many times. I think he started the rumour himself for a little bit of drama. It's really boring being retired, apparently.'

'OK, well, that's . . . interesting. But Bell was a perfect gentleman, he was completely professional.'

'Hmm,' Dylan clearly didn't believe me, 'just make sure your meetings are group ones, that's all I'm saying.'

I sighed, 'You really know how to make a girl feel like her work doesn't matter, you know?'

He snorted, 'What do you think I've been trying to do all week?'

I laughed, too surprised to respond, and he grinned at the look on my face.

'So are we good to go now?'

'Was there anything else you wanted from here?' I asked as we started walking, side by side, a tender peace negotiated.

'Well, now that you mention it, I think we should sneak some of the happy-hour complimentary beer for the train ride home.'

I laughed, desperate to say *classic Dylan* or *of course you do*.

But instead I nodded. 'Sounds exactly like what a good start-up would do. Shoestring budget and innovation.'

Something loosened between us after that. As if we didn't have to keep circling and growling at each other. We knew we were safe enough for the time being. As long as we didn't mention the past.

On the train journey home, I became part of the group, welcomed in amongst the laughter and teasing. Eric still had his eyes glued to Ben at all times, to the extent that I wanted to tell him he was getting a little creepy. Ben kept giving him these searching glances, as if he was trying to figure out who was underneath. Priya kept looking at them, and back to me, as if to confirm that something was *definitely* going on there.

'So how are we going to punish Hunter?' Tola asked, and I growled a little. Dylan popped the cap off another beer bottle and handed it to me. I was still getting used to him being polite. It was odd.

'Thanks,' I paused, 'Um. Well, obviously I need to get this promotion and then have the power to boss him around all the time. I might also shred all his cravats.'

Eric laughed, 'Aly, guys like Hunter ... he'll still be turning up asking you to do things and acting like he's doing you a favour, no matter your title. It's the level of privilege. It's inbuilt.'

'Oh,' I frowned, 'so I'm going to have to kill him?'

'Your best bet is placing some sort of heiress in front of him so he fucks off to Dubai to live the life he's always expected. One with minimal work, minimal consequences and lots of shopping,' Eric laughed.

'I'd watch that movie,' Priya said, then yawned. 'I mean, I'd fall asleep halfway through and miss the ending, but anything with a manipulative woman and an idiot man is a winner.'

'Does Nicki have any heiress friends?' Ben smiled and Dylan laughed.

'I think most of her friends are from TV, not the heiress circuit.'

'The KLP,' Tola said, almost wistful. 'It's amazing what she's done, becoming a name in and of herself. I did one of my college presentations on Nicki. It was called *From Cat Shit to Top Dog*.'

'You're kidding!' I turned to her, grinning. 'I didn't know that!'

164

'Well, it was a short course in social media, it wasn't like a whole uni thing.' Tola shrugged and smiled, before turning to the others. 'I focused more on life experience than grades. But now I kinda wish I'd had the chance for that. Everyone else always talks about uni like it's the best time.'

Nope. I shook my head. 'I don't think that's true for everyone. Besides, you went off to New York by yourself at eighteen and became a West End costume designer. Beats living on noodles and reading Kafka.'

Eric shook his head too. 'I liked the studying but ... I spent a lot of time trying to be what other people wanted. It wasn't what I imagined.'

'I dropped out,' Dylan said suddenly, making eye contact with me. 'I'd been excited at the beginning, but it became clear that I wasn't good enough and I wasn't as interested as other people. I didn't fit. I felt stupid all the time. So I dropped out and moved in with some random guys.' He paused, before laughing to the others. 'Which, if you'd seen the state of what was growing in that kitchen, wasn't exactly a prime choice either. But it was good, stopped me wallowing. Stopped me worrying that ... that I'd disappointed people who'd believed in me. I felt like I'd let them down.'

He waited for me to say something, and I offered half a smile. 'If you did the right thing for you, then no one has any right to be disappointed. Besides, I bet all those people had idealised views of university life anyway. Look how far you've come without it.'

Everyone else looked at us, falling silent.

Ben was the first one to break. 'OK, what's happening

here? You guys have been mortal enemies since you set eyes on each other, and now everything is friendly. What gives?'

Dylan shrugged. 'I guess I just needed to see Aly in action to trust she knew what she was doing.'

'And I just needed Dylan to trust I knew what I was doing,' I supplied, backing up the lie.

Priya and Ben exchanged a look but said nothing.

Tola raised an eyebrow at me, coughed. She was right, we needed to get on with the relationship stuff. Three weeks to perfect a business pitch was fine. Three weeks to ensure a proposal was harder.

'What's Nicki up to today?' I said, changing the subject so quickly I was surprised they didn't get whiplash. 'She seems like a busy woman.'

Dylan sighed, looking out of the window. 'Well, I woke up at six to her talking to her fans again, this time about her favourite pyjama brand for an ad. Then she videoed herself washing her face from a bunch of different angles, and I left as she was setting up her bedroom for some sort of photo-shoot including three hundred pounds' worth of rose-gold foil balloons and a puppy she rented for the day.'

Tola's eyes widened in alarm, but she tried to soften his clear derision. 'That must take so much effort.'

'You mean getting up at five to do her "natural" makeup so she can wash it off in her *ordinary morning routine*?' Dylan laughed, peeling at the label on the beer bottle. 'I didn't realise how much of social media was a lie before. People would say "Oh that's fake" and I'd think, "No, why would it be, who would go to all that effort?" And then I realised: *Nicki would.*'

Ben nudged him. 'Yes, poor you with your rich, famous, beautiful girlfriend who takes you to insane restaurants and on fancy holidays and provides you with wonderful branding consultants.'

Dylan suddenly looked at me, as if remembering I was on another team. God, if only he knew.

'It's not that I'm not grateful, it's . . . I thought even with influencers, even with someone who's a bit famous, there'd be parts of your relationship that weren't on display.'

'Yeah,' Ben clapped him on the shoulder, 'that thirty-minute Instagram story she did on your sex life last week was a bit harsh.' He grinned widely, laughing at Dylan's face. 'I'm joking! See, she has boundaries!'

'Maybe . . .' I started, then paused, biting my lip, as if I wasn't sure whether to share my idea. Whether we were there yet in our delicate truce. I waited for Dylan to push me, and of course he did.

'Maybe?'

'Maybe she would back off a bit if you give her a little of yourself in front of that audience? She's a woman in love, she's proud of you. Pop up and say hi in one of her videos, and maybe she'll step back with some of the other stuff. After all, you've made such good progress with your first post.'

I offered him a soft smile, and he didn't quite return it, but the hard set to his mouth wasn't there any more.

'And it might be good for the app, right?' Tola added, building on what I'd said. I smiled at her, grateful. 'Nicki's got millions of followers. It's easy to dismiss it when it's your girlfriend, but that's literally what influencer marketing is for. Get her to build a real buzz.'

Dylan looked to Ben, seeming to converse with him tele-pathically. Priya shrugged at me like she was used to this mind-melding during her workday.

'It's just . . . it's ours,' Dylan said eventually. 'It's our thing that we worked on. And we think it's going to help people. Nicki might make it . . . trivial.'

Priya winced a little, and I resisted doing the same.

Oh God, we had bigger problems than I realised. Most people weren't exactly on the road to proposing to partners they thought trivialised their life's work. Surely this couldn't be what Dylan wanted, that it wasn't fair of me to push and sculpt and scheme?

The question was, how far was I willing to go?

The last hour of the journey took on a different feeling, it was almost timeless. It had softened, from the laughter and excitement of free beer and a day well spent, into some-thing else. Ben and Eric spoke in soft tones, laughing and whispering. Eric looked lit up, like he'd never been so beau-tiful or alive. Even when I first met him, when he had that whole 'I'm the king of the world' vibe going on, he hadn't looked like this. He was glowing with possibility. Tola had walked off down the carriage, on the phone to one of her friends, arranging what club she'd meet them at. She'd rock up tomorrow, tell us she'd been partying till six a.m. and have no clue of how a real hangover could devastate you. Priya had her headphones in and looked more comfortable than anyone should curled up in a window seat on a train with their eyes closed. She said she'd take sleep wherever she could get it. Dylan was swiping through music choices.

I'd been frowning at my own phone, trying to make my

way through a theory-heavy marketing article when the battery died. I huffed, chucking it down on the table. I looked out of the window, then back at the table again. How did I forget a charger? My leg was already jittering at the idea of not having any way to be productive.

Then I saw an earphone on the table in front of me. I looked up at Dylan, and he nodded. When I heard what he was listening to, I couldn't help smiling. The same whiny teenage rock we'd loved years ago. This could have been a playlist we'd made back then, sitting on the school bus with one strand of the earphones each, listening on his Walkman, then my CD player, then his MP3 player. The music barely changing with the technology. Always one set of earphones, heads pulled together as we nodded along.

The nostalgia was so visceral it gave me a stomach ache.

Dylan slid his phone across to me. 'You choose the next track.'

Then he looked out of the window again, like it wasn't happening. Like he hadn't offered me the smallest way back to our past.

That was how we spent the final hour home, revisiting the music we used to love, smiling out of the window, and pretending it meant nothing at all.

Chapter Twelve

'Don't you think the wig is a bit much?' I tugged at my newly light brown bob as it brushed my shoulders. Tola and I were in the toilets of the bar, preparing for my big entrance, and I stood in front of the mirror, suddenly nervous.

'Hey, if I get to be the boss, I'm creating the vision. Seeing is believing.' Tola laughed at me and adjusted my silver dress, handing me some lipstick. We'd been limiting the Fixer Upper sessions, what with solving all of Nicki's problems taking up most of our time, but we had commitments, and Tola needed me.

She held up the phone with the photo of the latest project. Mark Jenkins, thirty-five, sales associate. His girlfriend Lucy had hired us for a motivation package. Those usually fell into three categories: career, commitment, or self-care. You'd be surprised how many grown men didn't shower regularly. It was horrifying.

That night's Fixer Upper was an easy one – encourage Mark to finally step up in terms of his career. He'd been talking about it for eight years, and Lucy was basically paying us so she never had to hear about it again.

Luckily, Mark seemed like a man of simple dreams – he wanted money, he just needed to know someone like him could do what he wanted to. It was a comfort thing. After all, people are afraid of failure. Especially in front of a partner. It's easy enough to keep saying you'll do something, because then you never have the chance to fail. And luckily enough, life will always find a way to get in the way.

But not any more.

Tola nodded at me. 'Eric's at the bar. You know what to do.'

I nodded, swishing my hips a little. Tola followed me out from the toilets, then set herself up at a table nearby. I didn't need her for this bit, but she liked to 'see the magic happen'.

Eric was already next to Mark at the bar when I stumbled over.

'Baby, baby, I want to drive the Jag home, please!' I threw my arms around Eric's neck, and he smiled indulgently.

'You think I worked this hard to finally buy my dream car, only to have you crash it? You're having a laugh, woman. I love ya, but you're mad.' He watched as Mark made eye contact, so they could share a '*women, honestly*' look. That was why I needed Eric. It didn't work without him. Turns out men don't listen to women they're not sleeping with. Shocker.

'Brand-new car I've been waiting half my life to buy, and she thinks I'm gonna let her drive it!' Eric exclaimed, having found his male audience. 'Can you believe it?'

'What've you got?'

'Jaguar F-Type,' Eric smiled, 'my pride and joy.'

I looked across and saw the bartender approaching Tola with a bright green cocktail on a tray. Someone had sent it to her. I never saw anyone do that in real life except for around Tola. And she always accepted them with a flirtatious smile and a thank you, but never drank them because you couldn't trust people.

I focused back on the conversation, waiting for my moment in our little play.

'You never would have been able to afford the car if I hadn't nagged you about that accountancy course,' I said petulantly, hand on hip like I was perpetually ignored and underestimated. 'If it wasn't for me pushing you and getting that discounted training course, you'd still be selling shoes for minimum wage.'

Eric softened. 'Aw, you're right, petal, I'm sorry.' He put an arm around me, turning to Mark. Time for the big sell. 'Been in retail all my life, no qualifications or anything, you know? And the missus is always nagging, *you can do more*, but I figure what can I do, really? But I started this accountancy course and now the money's rolling in!'

'That easy?' Mark raised an eyebrow.

'Well, ya gotta study, mate, I won't lie to you. But I'm not particularly book smart and I did OK! I like numbers, dealt with stocktakes and stuff in the old job.'

'I work in a shop,' Mark offered. 'Do you think I could do it? My missus has been on at me too.'

'Mate, you could definitely do it. In fact,' Eric produced a card from his pocket like a magician, 'I got a half-price course when I completed it, as a gift to pass on to someone else. Have it, I think it's fate.'

'Seriously?'

'Yeah, honestly. Spend a couple of months, stick it out, and get yourself a nice little number too. The car, I mean,' he grinned, and I elbowed him sharply. *Too much*.

'Cheers, man, I really appreciate that.' Mark held out his hand to shake Eric's, and the deal was done.

'Best of luck to you, every success, yeah?' Eric wrapped an arm around my waist and led me to the exit. I felt Tola following behind.

When we piled into Eric's car (most certainly *not* a Jaguar) we roared with success, the same way we always did.

'Are you *sure* that's all it took?' Eric said, the way he always did.

'Psshaw, he was an easy one, you could tell. Totally pliable. The girlfriend did a lot of the groundwork, all she needed was someone to finally tip him over the edge.' Tola grinned.

'It would probably work just as well if you'd been the one with the fancy car,' Eric said, with little conviction.

I rolled my eyes. 'Tola, what's the one thing that stops a man who is persistently trying to hit on you in a club?'

'If you say you have a boyfriend.'

'And why is that?'

'Because they have more respect for a man they've never met over a woman right in front of them?' she answered seamlessly.

I made a buzzer noise, and affected a show-host voice. 'You win the car, the cash and the holiday! Congratulations!'

Eric and I laughed, but Tola stayed silent.

'What's up? We killed it in there.'

She sighed, 'OK, real talk for a second. Where are we with Dylan? Because time is counting down and I am severely doubting our abilities right now.' I was surprised to see the anxiety in her expression.

'Are you OK?'

'We're off book, Aly! We're never off book! We always have an exact plan of who the man is and how he works and thinks. We don't have that.'

'Well, no, but . . .' I started, trying to figure it out.

'We have Aly's history with the guy,' Eric added, 'and he stopped hating her, it seems, so that's progress.'

'Two and a half weeks!' Tola said, 'two and a half weeks is all we've got!'

I turned around to look at her in the back seat. 'Tola, what's up? This isn't like you.'

Tola's dark lipstick had rubbed off, and she put a hand through her hair, looking suddenly so exhausted. 'We worked really hard to build something. And it's *going somewhere*. But if we fail with the biggest client we've ever had, because it was impossible . . . then we've shot ourselves in the face. We've just undone everything we've achieved so far.'

I reached back and squeezed her hand. 'I can do this, I promise. I need to find the right angle, that's all.'

'To get a guy who thinks his girlfriend is shallow to make a lifetime commitment,' she replied.

'Hey,' Eric shrugged, eyes still on the road, 'men have done stupider things for access to an easy life and a nice pair of boobs.'

'You realise you're allowed to get out of character now,' I bit back at him. 'They need to reconnect. There was real affection between them when we first met them, right? We just need her to put in boundaries, and him to step up. A balancing act.'

'So now we're couples counsellors too. Excellent.' Eric hit the indicator a little too aggressively.

'You're only annoyed because Ben didn't pick up the hint and ask you out,' Tola teased gently, looking a little more like herself.

'He gave me his number!' Eric argued, loudly buzzing his horn as another driver cut him up.

'Yeah, for *work stuff*.'

'Maybe he was being subtle.'

'A lot of that in the gay dating scene, babe?' Tola retorted, before turning to me. 'I'm sorry, it's not that I doubt you, but ... I don't want this to compromise what we've done. For you guys, working at the agency is the dream, and I respect that. But ... I think what we're doing here could be my dream. And I don't want it getting fucked up by an heiress and her grumpy boyfriend.'

'OK,' I said, in problem-solver mode, 'what do you need to feel confident?'

'A plan. And a promise that you really want this to succeed.'

Tola had this way of looking at you like she saw right down to the bone – X-ray vision.

'Believe me, you have no idea how much I need this to succeed,' I said, thinking of my mother's house, remembering my grandmother beneath that magnolia tree as a talisman.

'So you have no feelings about the boy you once loved

getting married to someone else, and being the one to make it happen?' Tola crossed her arms and arched a perfectly shaped eyebrow.

'Love,' I scoffed. 'I was a teenager, T. I loved Kurt Cobain and Barry M shimmer eyeliner and trousers with too many pockets. He was a boy I had a crush on once. And I knew him well enough to know he will want what this brings.' *Is that true, really?*

'Everybody wins. That's the plan,' I told her, grasping her hand. 'You've got to trust me.'

'OK, then tell me where we start,' she said, and I paused, scrolling through Nicki's social media feed.

I grinned as I turned the phone to her. 'We start with proof that we're on the right track.'

Because there Nicki was at the TV and Film Streaming awards, standing on a red carpet in Leicester Square. She looked every bit the perfect starlet, her blond hair with extensions in, flowing poker-straight down to her waist, a pale blue sparkly fitted mermaid dress catching the light of the photographer's flashes.

And right there next to her in a tuxedo was Dylan, smiling for the cameras.

Who's the babe in the suit?

Uh-oh, the KLPs got her claws into another one!

Is that guy an actor, I think I've seen him in something?

The tabloid mentions and captions had been carefully curated: Nicolette Wetherington Smythe in Givenchy, accompanied by tech entrepreneur boyfriend Dylan James.

'This is our shot,' I said to Tola. 'We need to keep building momentum.'

'I know exactly how to work this, we just need to get Dylan on board.'

As Tola detailed her plan for a live Q and A with the couple, I could see Dylan's scowl in my mind. Sure, he'd gotten all dressed up for a fancy night out and smiled in front of the cameras, but serve up his relationship online to be judged? It would be a hard sell. But we did have Ben on our side. Ben, who knew a few carefully timed questions about the name of the company and the projects they were working on could go a long way. And maybe, just maybe, if Dylan was the same Dylan I remembered, he'd paste on a smile, say 'of course!' and pretend he was fine with everything.

Which was how we ended up sitting in Nicki's palatial Chelsea flat the next evening, setting up a tripod and a light ring. The flat was expensive based on size and location alone, but it was beautifully decorated, dripping with luxury in the way influencer design always did. A five-hundred-pound throw, so artfully draped over the sofa, as if it was constantly being snuggled under. A collection of coffee table books that had never been opened. Art that looked pretty but said very little about the owner. It was beautiful, but it looked like a showroom. It felt empty, even with the flurry of activity of assistants, makeup artists and hairdressers.

'OK, tell me again how this is going to help the app?' Dylan asked me as a hairdresser attempted to smooth his hair down, his cowlick seemingly incapable of lying flat. She gave up and tried to tousle it instead.

'We're harnessing Nicki's fame to benefit your company. People were interested in who you were after your red carpet appearance last night. We've got to capitalise on that while they still care.'

He looked at me, long-suffering. 'It feels exploitative.'

I shrugged. 'Not to Nicki. She wants to help.'

He put his head in his hands, and the hairdresser looked at me questioningly. I made a sign for 'two minutes'. When she'd left, I took her seat opposite him.

'Why is this so hard?' I asked.

Dylan sighed and sat back in the chair, opening his eyes. 'Because it feels fake, Aly. Every day of Nicki's life, she takes photos and makes videos and arranges her living space and rents dogs and cooks food she won't eat. All for these nameless bozos on the internet who feel like they have a right to her. And now I'm going to be part of that.'

'You know how to do this, Dylan,' I said softly. 'You know how to be the most charming, affable person in the room, how to give people what they want, what they expect. How to make them love you.'

He gave me a look I couldn't decipher. 'Well, I learned from the best.'

I felt a sharp pain in my chest and tried not to let it show.

'It's just an extension of that. It's not a lie, it's ... presenting the parts of you they want to see.'

'Curating,' he said softly. 'All I wanted was to make an app that would help people. And for my team to be well paid for their time, so we can keep doing it. It's the first thing I've made that has any value, Aly. The only thing I'm putting out into the world. We worked really fucking hard on this, and all it's worth is a three-minute video as part of Nicki's life, because we're dating?'

I took a breath and looked at him, our knees almost touching as he ran a hand through his hair again and then winced at the texture of the gel they'd put in. I laughed.

'You know, that's the most honest you've been with me since we met again,' I said.

Dylan gave me a look, as if he thought I was trying to tell him something else. Whatever it was, he didn't seem to find it.

'Probably best not to go down that route right now,' he said quietly, staring at his hands.

'OK, so focusing on the here and now: You trust that I want this app to succeed, right? That I want every kid who needs access to counselling to reach it, in whatever form they prefer? That I believe in what you and Ben and Priya have built?'

'Sure,' he shrugged.

'And you trust that I'm good at my job and I know my shit?'

He laughed. 'Yes.'

'OK, so trust me when I tell you that this is just how it works. It's not a reflection on you, or Nicki, or your relationship. If you weren't with Nicki, we'd be looking at other options to get the word out, but you are and she wants to help. So let her. She believes in you.'

He almost laughed but not quite. Like I'd pressed on a bruise without meaning to.

'She believes in my potential. Same as they all did. Same as you did.' His eyes met mine, and for a moment I forgot how to breathe, then he looked away and it was gone. Dylan pulled at his shirtsleeves. 'When we first started dating, I tried to go along with it, all the social stuff. But her followers tore me apart. It was in some of the glossies too. *Who's Nicki slumming it with? A step down from her Chelsea roots.'*

I closed my eyes, wincing.

'They'd take these awful photos and compare me to the guys she dated before.' Dylan shrugged. 'That's why I ended up going to the gym so much, because I was terrified they'd keep judging me. Keep looking at her rich, business-owning, trust-fund exes with their South of France tans and six-packs, and keep reminding her that I'm not enough.'

I smiled gently. 'But Nicki doesn't think that. She adores you.' *And the bits she doesn't adore, she's paid me to fix.*

'She supported me stepping back on social media while we figured out where this went. So we could get to know each other. But I know she wants me to be that person, to bring *value to her brand.'*

'You bring value to her life, surely that's more important?'

He met my eyes. 'I think the two are so linked for her, she's not sure any more. I know we need to do this for the business, but … Nicki got us this meeting with Silicon Valley, she's promoting us today. She brought me you. It's like everything I did was meaningless without her.'

I had two options here, and I didn't like either of them. I could offer him empty platitudes. Or I could tell the truth. Make myself vulnerable like he had and hope for the best.

I took a breath. 'You remember when you failed history, and your dad said he wasn't disappointed because he hadn't expected you to pass?'

Dylan looked at me in surprise, his features softening slightly. 'Yes.'

'And you remember what you did?' I prompted.

'I studied, and I resat the exam and proved him wrong.'

'You got ninety-eight per cent. The highest in the year.'

'I did,' he grinned. 'I guess being a stubborn bastard paid off.'

'Exactly. That's the guy I need now. The guy who knows he has what it takes to prove them all wrong and is willing to do whatever he needs to do it. The guy who uses charm like a weapon.' I looked at him. 'Can you be that guy?'

The smile he gave me was blinding. Something about it was so pure, so grateful that it made me want to cry.

'I think I can do that, boss.'

'Hi, guys! We're on a *Hello* Insta takeover live, and we know after the awards you're all going to want to know two things from our special guest: What was the afterparty like and who was the gorgeous guy on her arm?'

Tola switched so easily into her work persona that I almost forgot it was her, talking into her phone, before switching it to Nicki and Dylan, sitting casually on the sofa, his arm trailing along the top of it, her snuggled into his side.

How much of all of this was a game, the way they looked at each other, curled around each other with adoration in their eyes? And yet, the way Nicki cupped his cheek with her hand, the way he tangled his fingers in her hair ... that had to be real. It had to be worth it.

'So, Dylan, why haven't we seen you online before now? You're a bit of a mystery man!' Tola intoned, following the script we'd come up with.

He waved his hand like the idea was preposterous. 'Honestly, I'm really boring. And I see how much effort Nicki puts into this, being here for her followers, answering their questions, it's a lot of work!' He smiled at her with affection, squeezing her shoulders.

'And what about your work?' *OK, here we go*.

'Well, I'm an app developer, my company is called EasterEgg Development and we're working on something big around mental health right now. We really want to help as many people as we can, otherwise what's the point of it all?'

I gave Dylan a thumbs up, and he nodded at me.

'And what's your favourite thing about Nicki?' Tola asked, and Dylan froze. He hid it pretty well, turning to look at her with a smile on his face, but I could sense the panic.

'I guess ... when she's having a bad day, she'll make pancakes and pile them up with whipped cream and not even take a photo before diving in. She just really enjoys this thing she's made. I love that. And I love pancakes!' He smiled winningly, and Tola 'awwed' appropriately, but I saw Nicki's face tighten.

'And what about you, Nicki? What do you love about Dylan?'

'Oh, he's so *fun*,' Nicki smiled at him, 'and he always puts me first. Booking weekends away and holidays and stuff to help me chill out. He's always looking after me. Whisked me away to Barbados last year!'

'And he's still paying it off,' Ben said quietly in my ear.

Tola moved on to Nicki's favourite trends right now, while Dylan sat and looked attentive. I could tell he was relieved.

Tola ended the chat, tagging a bunch of accounts for cross-promo. As Dylan was getting up, she said, 'Hold on, we need a photo for the grid. Look all cute and coupley!'

Dylan wrapped his arms around Nicki, pulling her in

close, and she looked at him with such adoration that I was left spinning. One thing couldn't be denied; they looked perfect together. A beautiful couple. Two shiny, sparkly people.

But when they got up, Nicki turned on him. 'I can't believe you said that about the pancakes!'

'What?' He half smiled, as if he thought she was joking. 'It *is* my favourite thing! It's the only thing you eat that you don't take a photo of!'

'That's because I'm meant to be on a dairy- and gluten-free diet! They are going to *skewer* me for this! I knew I should have given you a pre-approved list of answers!'

Dylan frowned. 'I thought we were being authentic?'

Nicki closed her eyes as if she was asking for strength. 'I have a multimillion-pound brand, Dylan. It depends on me hitting certain demographics. It's business.'

'Apologies, I should have chosen a more business-aligned thing to love about you,' he said stiffly and gave me a brief look before walking off.

Nicki turned to me and threw up her hands, as if to ask, *Shouldn't you be fixing this?*

Tola shot me a concerned look as Nicki walked off to get a green juice from her fridge, and I wondered if we were making a terrible mistake.

Chapter Thirteen

'And then I told him I didn't deserve this, and that he needed to apologise,' Mama said. I'd had an exhausting day and the last thing I needed right now was more parental drama. But at the moment, my mother was on a high from demanding even the most basic respect from my father.

'Good for you,' I said, then paused. 'And did you talk to him about the house?'

Silence.

'Mama, I don't want to push, but . . .'

'You're right, you're right, of course. You need to know if he agrees to the money you've offered, I know, sweetheart. And I so appreciate what you're doing for me. For us.'

Which 'us' was she talking about? Me and her, or her and him? She didn't want to ask me how I was getting the money, she didn't want to know if I was draining all my savings. She just wanted the problem solved.

'Oh, I saw Dylan in the magazines at the supermarket!' Mama said, redirecting the conversation somewhere less dangerous. 'Was that your work, clever girl? Surely they'll have to give you that promotion now.'

'Maybe,' I said lightly, 'it sounds like I'm nearly there.'

My mother paused. 'Do you think if you don't get it, it's worth looking somewhere else, darling? You've spent so many years of killing yourself for this company. Work is your whole life. How are you going to meet anyone? How are you going to get the chance to fall in love?'

My first thought was *if it looks like what you have, no thank you*. But I couldn't tell her that.

So I didn't say anything. Instead I called Tola, and drank a glass of red wine while she filled me in on the impact of the social takeover. Thousands of new followers, the updated website had new hits and Tola had even set up a way of signing up testers for the app, so they'd have real world data to take to the pitch. She was so good at this. And she was willing to take more risks than I was. She could be so much more than this.

'Have you given any more thought to us making the Fixer Upper a real business? Making it something *more*?' she asked.

'Yeah yeah,' I sighed.

'Look, I know you want your title and your pension and a pat on the head from a man at the top table.' I could hear her rolling her eyes, frustrated with my lack of vision. I didn't want to take a risk, that was all. I had a plan, I was sticking to it. 'But you could *be* the man at the top table.'

'I want to be head of branding.' I heard my mother's voice: *Work is your whole life*. But it was the only part of my life that was nicely ordered, that made me feel like I had everything together. I was good at work. Beyond the Fixer

Upper, the rest of my life didn't work like that. Love didn't work like that.

'You can be super-high sorceress of branding, for all I care,' she'd huffed at me. 'Think *bigger*.'

She'd hung up before I could argue any further, and I didn't blame her.

I'd had a very clear idea of what my life was going to look like – I was going to get the branding job and the money that came with it. I was going to be respected by my colleagues, I was going to push for creativity and I was going to bring up the other women in the company. The smart ones who got overlooked in the face of loud, ballsy incompetence. I was going to buy a cute little ground-floor flat with a garden and stick two fingers up to everyone who said you had to be a couple to buy. And then . . .

Well, after that it got a bit harder to see. That had been my goal for so many years, I wasn't really sure what came next. Putting the effort into meeting someone who didn't need fixing, I guess. Someone I could take home for my mother to fawn over. Someone I could trust to look at my fucked-up family and not judge them, or me.

I had a text from Eric, a blurry photo of some tapas on a table. *On a date!*

I laughed, and replied: *You're always on a date*.

The response was immediate.

Not like this one. This is the real thing. x

I smiled to myself.

As I was crawling into bed to watch TV and fall asleep with my face in a bowl of ice cream, the phone rang. I assumed it would be my mother again, but it wasn't her.

It was Dylan.

'Hi,' I said, surprised. 'Is everything OK?'

He coughed awkwardly, 'Hi, um, yeah. I just wanted to say thank you for today. I guess you saw all the numbers? Ben was losing his mind. Priya's spent the evening mocking up test environments and sending me text messages in all capitals. It's the happiest they've been in ages.'

'And how about you?' I asked, snuggling under the covers. Curled up in bed, Dylan on the other end of the phone: this was like a jump back in time.

'I'm pleased, obviously. It's all ... happening.'

'Hmm,' I said.

When we were fifteen, Dylan got accepted to a national art show, and he'd spent weeks working on his final piece, putting every spare minute into it. The day before he was meant to deliver it to the exhibition, it was found destroyed in the art room. The headteacher was horrified and gave Dylan such a heartfelt apology. They thought it was a bunch of younger-year kids messing around, but I knew. Dylan didn't handle pressure. And he'd rather miss out than risk failing. Which was probably why his start-up had been stalling for all these years.

'What, *hmm*?' he demanded, and I laughed.

'Might have fooled everyone else with that smile, but you don't fool me,' I said softly.

'I think that's my line,' he replied, tone matching mine. I didn't like how my stomach flipped when he whispered.

'How was everything with Nicki?' I switched tack before this got too messy, and heard him sigh.

'She got a journalist to give her a front page on one of the glossies revealing her emotional eating habits. They get a nutritionist to assess her diet and tell her what to eat instead. She'll be switching the pancakes for banana protein waffles. Or something.'

'Wow.' *Genius, really.*

'She said she's not mad at me, that it's her fault for not explaining how this all works.' He paused for so long that I wondered if he was still there. 'What does that say about me, that the thing I love most about someone is the thing they want to hide from the world?'

I snorted. 'Dylan, it wasn't about the pancakes. The pancakes were just something she did without pretence, not shown to her followers. Something real she shared only with you.'

He made a 'huh' sound that I took to mean our tentative truce was still in place.

'And I'm guessing you apologised, too?'

I could hear the smile in his voice. 'What do you think, Aresti?'

'I think you probably sent her a painfully huge bouquet of her favourite flowers, took her hand and looked into her eyes as you gave a heartfelt apology and then made the disgusting banana waffle things for her to show you understand her.' I waited. 'How many did I get?'

'Spot on,' he laughed, 'but I put whipped cream on the waffles.'

'Of course, rule breaker.'

'Well, I take my role as leading man very seriously,' he said, but as the laughter started to seep from his words, we stayed on the line, letting the silence sit between us.

'Dylan?' I whispered eventually. 'Are you still there?'

He replied in a whisper. 'Just trying to figure out if I fell through some sort of wormhole back to the early 2000s. This all feels very familiar.'

My chest tightened into a knot, tied with a bow.

If I didn't acknowledge it, we didn't have to have the conversation. He'd started this game of pretend, but it was easier that way. Because if he asked me why I left, I'd have to ask him about that night, I'd have to remember that he hadn't been who I thought he was. Right now, I needed him to be a project. He wasn't Dylan James, the boy I'd once loved. He was something I needed to sort out, so I could save my mother's home. That was the only way I could justify it to myself.

We stayed silent on the phone for what felt like an eternity, while I built that wall up, painfully putting each brick in place, stamping down on those memories.

'I'll speak to you tomorrow, Mr James.'

'Good night, Miss Aresti.'

I woke to my phone ringing at five a.m.

'Hello?' I croaked, my heart racing and already conjuring thoughts of the worst.

'How's my favourite little romance guru?' Nicki crowed, and I held the phone a bit further away from my ears. 'I didn't wake you, did I?'

'Oh no, I was up doing my sun salutation and drinking my green juice,' I said as I slipped on my ageing dressing gown with the crocodiles all over it and shuffled to put the kettle on. 'What's up?'

'Well, Dylan – obviously, it's Dylan.'

'I thought the Insta takeover went so well, didn't you? And it looks like the couples photo had great engagement. Your fans love him.' I kept my voice encouraging because it was clear the KLP was not a happy kitty.

'Yeah, that part all looks good. And he's agreed to smile into the camera when I'm doing my thing. He'll wave like a little nerd. He took a selfie in bed with me this morning. He's never done that before.'

I hadn't realised he'd been at hers last night on the phone. For some reason that made my stomach contract.

I tried to erase that vision, the two of them, curled up together laughing without any of the realities, like morning breath or cold feet or farting under the covers. Just picture perfect.

'So what's the problem? Sounds like he's trying really hard.' I put her on loudspeaker so I could stalk her social media feed.

'Yes, thankfully he made up for that debacle with the pancakes! Imagine, all the things I've achieved, and he liked that I used to stuff pancakes in my face when no one was looking!' Her laughter was high like one of those bells above shop entrances – *warning: attention needed*.

'Thankfully I've been working with Dr Karen, a nutritionist, to help me deal with my cravings and emotional eating. She's an absolute *genius*.'

It had been less than twenty-four hours and already she'd crafted this into a new narrative. Her team were impressive.

'It looks like he's really making an effort with the social

media thing, we're on the right track. And the prep for the presentation has come along so well,' I trilled, fearing some sort of issue was going to arise.

'Well, the thing is . . .' *There it is* '. . . he's so busy working on the presentation, I'm afraid he's not going to feel romantic enough to propose, you know? Men can't multitask like women can.'

'But we . . . *he's* literally doing everything you asked for. He's more involved on social media, he's working on pitching his business, being successful. He went to your event . . .' I trailed off. 'We're on track.'

'And what about the proposal?'

I cringed. Even hearing her say it sounded awful. So demanding, like I was refusing to sell her a pair of shoes she thought she deserved, even if they weren't in her size.

'Did you see that photo, how he looked at you, how he held you? That's romance! Most people would kill for that!' I trilled, all enthusiasm. *Give me a fucking chance, lady. I'm a hustler not a miracle worker.*

Nicki sighed. 'He . . . there's things he doesn't share. And I share everything!' *Except for the fact that you're paying to fix him.*

'Well, maybe that's part of it. He probably likes the parts that are only his, the parts of you he doesn't have to share . . . Nicki, we are getting shit done, OK? You don't have to worry about a thing, we are on this.'

'I know, I have complete faith. I just wish . . . I wish there was more time for romance in all of this.'

I was going to murder this woman. This was how my career ended, not with a burnout-induced breakdown, but shaking Nicolette Wetherington Smythe, yelling *what do you actually want?* until they locked me away.

'Didn't he send you flowers and make you food?' I asked, and her voice took on a hard tone.

'He told you?'

'He did.'

A weird silence hung in the air, and I felt the need to apologise but held my ground.

'Well, I know that sort of thing might impress the *average woman*, but for me, getting flowers is just another Tuesday, you know? I require a little more va-va-voom for my grand gestures. Maybe keep that in mind when it comes to the proposal.'

At this moment, I absolutely hated her.

'Nicki, if you'd rather take my original advice and organ-ise a proposal with someone who has their own team of assistants and agent and PR company to make it an event that'll sell papers, then let me know.'

'Don't be ridiculous.' Her tone was breezy again, and I started to wonder if I'd imagined that coldness altogether. 'Just ... encourage him to think big, right? A big public declaration of love.'

'With a decent Instagrammable backdrop?'

'You're getting it,' she said. 'I'll check in soon.' *Please don't.* 'I've got a preliminary meeting with *Celebrity Bride Wars* next week, and they already said they love our colour-ing together. They can really visualise like a winter-themed wedding, all cool colours and ice bars. A big sculpture of a polar bear, can you imagine?!'

For Dylan, who soaked up the sun like a battery, his skin

turning caramel at the first touch of sunshine? Who had booked up our summer weekends with camping trips, festivals and days on the beach with the sole aim of smiling at the sky and getting a tan, quietly begging summer to never end? A winter wedding for *that* man?

I downed the rest of my coffee, and thought only of my mother's drawn face, my father's smug grin.

'I'll see what I can do.'

Chapter Fourteen

I had to admit it to myself if no one else: the pressure was getting to me. Nicki, sending me photos of winter wedding themes, Dylan emailing about whether we needed to add two more slides to the presentation. Ben asking if Eric liked old movies. Eric asking if Ben had said anything about him. Felix asking why my reports weren't submitted early and why I hadn't brought him new ideas to support team morale, like I normally did every month even when they were ignored. Hunter asking why I looked tired. Matthew asking my opinion on every single tiny decision he made, like a dog afraid of the postman.

And then there was Tola, silently wondering why I was so obsessed with a job that clearly wasn't fulfilling me, every doubt she had showing on her face.

On top of it all, there was my mother. Who was texting and calling and finding every reason to check on me so she could ask me everything but the one big question: *Do you have the money to save my home?*

I sent Mama to voicemail for the second time that

morning as I tried to get on with my work. I couldn't hear about my father right now. I couldn't hear her make excuses as I made more and more questionable decisions to get this money for him.

'Aly baba! How's it going?' I closed my eyes and took a second to compose myself, then I swivelled in my chair, gripping the arms.

The great big galumphing moron was back again, with his styled hair and smooth voice. He wanted something. Again. I'd only just finished redoing his *last* brief.

'Hunter.' I painted a smile on. 'I'm fine. *Busy*, but fine. How are you?'

He swept a hand through his hair. 'Actually, I'm in a bit of a pickle, babe.'

No, no more. I saved your cheating arse, I've done enough, leave me be.

I saw Tola peer over her computer screen and give him a death glare, then a warning glance to me: *Don't you dare help him.*

I nodded at her.

'Well, I'm sorry to hear that. You should get a burger,' I said, not looking up from my screen.

He was silent for a moment. 'What?'

'You're in a pickle ... they're good in burgers.'

'Ahar, ahar har!'

Add Hunter's laugh to the list of terrible things.

'The thing is, Aly Cadabra ...' he tried again, leaning on the edge of my desk and towering over me, so that I had to stand up to even out the power balance.

'The thing is, Hunter's-actually-your-name-so-I-can't-

195

make-it-sillier, I'm afraid that this time, at this precise moment, I have reached my limit. I simply don't care.' I took a deep breath and met his eyes.

He frowned in confusion, his features seeming to crumple like his very expensive handkerchief.

Oh crap, this was happening. I'd broken. Once I'd started, I couldn't stop. 'I *don't care* that you didn't get around to analysing the data because your sister bought a puppy, or you were featured in *Guardian* Blind Dates, or you ended up winning a really intense game of high-stakes poker . . . I don't care. I just want you to do your job.'

He recoiled, all attempts at friendliness now retracted. 'Well, that's not very nice.'

'Neither is pawning your work off on your colleagues so you can go and have beers with the boys. Or *me* having to get a train to Birmingham to apologise for *you* coming on to the wrong woman.'

He briefly looked abashed, but it was gone in a flash, like his face didn't know how to wear shame. *Say thank you. Say sorry. Say something!*

'So you're . . . not going to help me?' he asked, as if he truly didn't understand.

'Nope, sorry, not this time.'

He wrinkled his forehead. 'What if Felix wants you to?'

'If Felix wants me to prioritise fixing your work above producing my own, then he's going to have to meet with me and reorganise my calendar so I can accommodate that on top of my clients. *Including* the meeting with Teddy Bell I've got next week because you were more interested in your dick than your career. Are we done here?'

I briefly stopped typing to look at him, and saw that scowl, that moment men turned on you. I'd almost forgotten it was coming.

'Well, there's no need to be such a bitch about it.'

I held up my hands and made a face. 'Apparently there is. Good luck with the report.'

As he trudged off, mumbling, Tola punched her fists in the air in silent triumph. I gave her a wink and settled back into my work. I might be collapsing under the pressure, but like hell was I going down without dragging him with me.

I watched as Hunter headed across the office to Felix's door, and my stomach sank. A brief moment of victory and it likely wouldn't matter anyway. God, I needed a run. Or a solo delicious meal. Or dancing all night where no one knew me, or could ask me for anything, or expected me to be Aly-with-the-answers.

But I didn't have time for that.

On my lunch break I replied to Dylan and Ben, ignored Nicki, and went for a walk to clear my head. I didn't call my mother back, but sent a text saying everything was being handled and not to worry. I wondered if she thought I was carrying out a bank heist or moonlighting as a call girl.

The fact that I hadn't told Tola and Eric the truth about the money was worrying me too. Sure, they'd get a cut, but not explaining the stakes felt so inherently unfair, like I was tricking them.

Surely they would understand, though, if I told them? But that would involve explaining about my dad and what he'd done to my mum, and they'd look at me with something like pity. This look would appear on their faces, *Daddy issues, of course!* The only path available to a grown woman with bad relationship history. And no one ever blamed the dads, only the girls who got screwed up by them.

By the time I reached the end of the day, I was exhausted, and ready to collapse into bed with a portion of garlic bread and an early noughties romcom. Heath Ledger, singing in front of the whole school. That was what I needed.

'You ready to go?' Eric said at five, looking particularly dashing in his suit and slightly ridiculous with a matching fedora.

'Where? Why?'

'Fixing up? Amy and the writer boy? In about half an hour at Hoxton Lounge?'

I sighed. Crap.

'You forgot?' Eric frowned. 'You never forget anything.'

Well, you try starting your day with a call from an heiress worried that your ex-best friend's romantic gestures aren't loud enough and see how you do.

'Even elephants have off days,' I said tiredly. 'Give me ten minutes to freshen up my makeup, and I'll be my sparkliest self.'

'I'll grab you an energy drink and meet you downstairs.'

'You're an angel.' I smiled as I grabbed my handbag.

'Yep, and then we have the whole journey there to talk about Ben. His likes, his interests, his taste in men. And what you think I can do to avoid fucking this up.'

I sighed, feeling that weary exhaustion settle around me like a cloak. 'Excellent. Can't wait.'

Tonight's client was Amy Leyton. She'd been with her boy-friend Adam for four years, all during uni, and they'd been living together for a year since then. Amy had been offered an internship abroad for three months, and Adam was feeling a bit sensitive about being left behind. He'd been hinting about going with her, but she wanted to do this for herself. Her big jump into her first career role. She wanted to stay together, it was only three months, but understood if he didn't want to wait for her.

I filled Eric in before we entered the bar, making sure we weren't overheard. 'They're both writers. Amy got a journalism internship. He's decided that if she was going to launch her career, he was going to launch his. By writing a novel.'

Eric shrugged. 'I mean, chance in a million, right? But good luck to him. What?'

'The plot is the story of a girl who leaves her boyfriend to go do a journalism internship abroad.'

He snorted. 'OK, fair enough, that's how he's processing. He can write whatever he wants, it's in his head.'

'It's not.'

'It's not what?'

'It's not in his head,' I winced. 'He types it out on yellow notecards and pins them up on the walls to keep the timeline in order . . .'

'Types as in . . .'

'Old-fashioned typewriter? Yup,' I sighed. 'And they live in a studio flat.' I pulled up the photo on my phone. Amy had sent it to me earlier. In the middle of the tiny room was a bed, and that was it. The walls were covered in yellow scraps of paper, their aggressive typed capitals yelling out a nonsensical story.

Currently, my opinion was that Adam was very likely to be a trash bag of a human being, but she loved him.

'Do you ever think maybe this shit should be dealt with by a professional? Someone with a degree, who has experience with narcissists?'

'I'm a single female in my thirties, working in a male-dominated industry. I have experience with narcissists.'

'You know what I mean.'

'I guess we'll see!' I pulled him by the arm and walked through the door. 'You remember the play?'

'Oh yeah, I've been practising my "pretty boy genius" vibe for this one.' He gave a pout, a strange mix of angry and bored.

I caught sight of Adam, slouched over a notebook at the edge of the bar, the way Amy said he always was in the evenings, since she'd almost thrown the typewriter across the room.

We took seats behind but to the left of him, close enough to grab his interest, but not so far back he'd have to swivel in his seat. Let him spy on us for a bit, let him think he was the one doing the chasing.

We ordered two drinks, and I launched into my spiel.

'Darling, I *adore* the new draft, adore it. We'll get it through copyedits, and I think it'll be out on the shelves by early next year,' I said, briefly referring to the notes on my phone.

Eric assumed a bored expression. 'And you're sure it's better than my last? I don't want to be embarrassed or seen to be ... derivative.'

I could almost *feel* Adam's ears prick up.

'You? Never!' I laughed. 'I think we'll have a good chance

at film or TV rights this time. It's so ... visceral, you know? Man, woman, betrayal. How she leaves him at the end, him in that little room, her out in the world, it was poignant, you know? Really heartfelt. I think people will get it.'

'Well, I just write what I know,' Eric looked up at the ceiling, 'heartbreak, being underestimated, misunderstood.' *God, dial it back, Eric, you're meant to be a successful writer, not a minor royal on stage at the Old Vic.*

I wiggled my eyebrows at him, and his lips pursed.

'Well, that certainly comes across ...' I said. 'You're an absolute genius, sweetheart. There's no way anyone who reads this could doubt that. And I think whoever she is who inspired it will regret having gone.'

'Eh,' Eric flicked an imaginary cigarette with his fingertips, and seemed to suddenly develop the rumblings of a French accent. 'She needed to grow, little flower that she was. I have roots here. Trees stay where they are. They grow upwards.'

'So *very* wise.' I gave him a hard stare, and Eric looked like he wanted to laugh.

I glanced at the mirrored back wall and noticed Adam watching from the bar, so I tapped my fingers three times on the table. Eric recognised his cue: 'I've just got to make a quick call. You don't mind, do you?'

'Of course not, I can catch up on my emails.'

I watched Eric reach the door, opened my phone and counted down in my head. *Four, three, two ...*

'Hi there.'

I turned with a look of calculated surprised delight to find Adam hovering at the edge of my table. 'Hello ...'

'Sorry to eavesdrop, but it sounded like you're in the book business?' He waited for me to nod and then slid into Eric's chair without asking. 'I only ask because I'm writing a book.' *You and everybody else, buddy.*

'I see, and you'd like my ... advice on how to submit it?' I tried to appear piqued. I knew I needed to be impressed, to say wonderful and encouraging things, but it was difficult. It felt like working with Hunter.

'I'd like you to publish it. It's very good.' He gave me what he clearly thought was a winning smile.

'Is that so?' I snorted.

'I know that I'm good at what I do,' he shrugged, 'when you've got the talent you've got to grab opportunities when they come along.'

'OK, pitch it then.' I looked at my watch and leaned my head on my hand, watching him. 'Sell me your story.'

'It's about a girl who has these huge dreams, and she wants to go off and see the world, but she leaves someone behind. Sort of a *grass is greener* thing. And then it's his journey in growing on his own, and her journey back to him.'

I smiled, sighing in relief. OK, that sounded like someone who was processing his relationship in a healthy way.

'So it's a love story?'

Adam looked at me as though I'd spat in his coffee. 'No, it's a story about justice and redemption.'

'How so?'

'The girl is working in Australia, and she gets her arm bitten off by a shark. And she comes home, realising she never should have left and the guy rejects her because she's so ugly and selfish. And she has to live alone with the weight of her mistakes for the rest of her life.' *OK, I take it back. Completely looney tunes.*

'And what happens to the guy?' *As if I even need to ask.*

'He becomes a very famous screenwriter and writes a movie about her.'

'Inspired,' I said. I was going to have to go off-piste with this one. 'Well, why don't you give me your email address, and I'll put you in touch with my assistant. So when you're ready you can submit your finished draft.'

He smiled like he was doing me a favour, writing his email address down. When Eric returned to find his seat still taken, he tilted his head at me. I smiled at Adam with faux regret.

'Pleasure talking with you . . .'

'Adam.'

I nodded as he scarpered back to the bar and Eric assessed me.

'I don't like that look,' he whispered.

'I don't like that man,' I whispered back through gritted teeth.

We finished our drinks, enjoying our time together, and when we escaped out into the street, taking in the last of the summer evening's warmth, I called Amy.

'Hello?'

'Amy, it's Alyssa here, we spoke yesterday. When does your internship start?'

'I leave in two months.'

I didn't mince my words, 'Can you leave earlier?'

'I'm sorry?'

'Leave earlier. Go live your life, have your adventures and do not waste a second's thought on that man.'

She paused, 'I ... uh ... really? So he's fine?'

'Oh no, he's a selfish arsehole who will forever resent you for putting your own dreams above his. Don't waste time, don't look back. Go.'

Eric grinned at me, shaking his head.

'That's very kind but ... I love him.'

'Of course you do, you wouldn't have contacted me otherwise,' I said gently. 'Obviously, it's your choice. But Adam's love for you depends on you putting him first. If you're still doubting, read all the way through those yellow cards, see how the story ends.'

She was silent for a moment, and I thought of all the moments my mother considered leaving. *Please, let this be it*.

'Thank you,' Amy said quietly. I knew in her voice then that she'd already read all the note cards. She just needed someone to tell her it was OK to go.

'You're welcome,' I said softly. 'Watch out for sharks, OK?'

Amy snorted, and I hung up the phone.

I smiled at Eric as we walked along, feeling a sense of relief.

'Aly, what the hell was that? That wasn't the goal of the Fixer Upper!' Eric laughed, and I waved away his concern.

I stopped walking and tried to find the words. 'You know how we're meant to make-do-and-mend? Like previous generations lose their shit at us because we want something shiny and new instead of something old? But think about an old toaster ...' I held up my hands as he pulled a face. 'Stick with me. You have this old toaster and you don't want to get rid of it, because it works fine, even though it burns the edges of your bread and you have to keep screwing the cover back on and it only works on alternate Tuesdays. But you feel guilty getting rid of that toaster, even though it's not giving you what you need? Like you're a failure.'

'Sure . . . ?'

'Adam is that shitty toaster. And I am tired of watching women stay with egotistical men just because they feel like they need a better reason to leave than their own happiness.'

'But aren't we meant to fix the fixer upper?'

'You can only fix decent raw materials. I don't fix up rubbish. We need to give them permission to leave – that being unhappy is enough of a reason to go.'

Eric grinned at me. 'I like this sassy girl-power version of you.'

'Thanks. Me too,' I smiled, linking my arm through his. 'Now tell me all about your guy problems.'

Chapter Fifteen

Finally, it felt like I was doing something *good*. Something useful. I'd stopped believing in our mission to fix partners. We needed to help them leave if they didn't get what they deserved. We needed to help their partners learn to be more active participants in a shared life. There was good we could do, without demonising men. I started to get what Tola was saying.

But with Nicki, I felt like we were being paid by a spoilt woman to carve Michelangelo's *David* out of an already perfectly lovely statue. It didn't feel like helping, it felt like destroying.

And every message she sent, every time I visualised Dylan standing in a designer tux, smiling out from a wedding shoot for *Hello!* or *OK!* I felt worse. I was starting to worry that I was actually the bad guy in this story.

The advantage of my blistering moral dilemma was that I kept my head down and worked my behind off. I'd had no more distractions or requests from Hunter, I had happy clients and one pitch in particular that I thought might win an award. Matthew kept up with his questions, but he was so appreciative – dropping off cups of coffee and fancy slices of cake – that I didn't really mind. He called me his mentor, and it made me feel valued. Useful.

All I was waiting for was my 'pat on the head', as Tola had called it. Proof that my work had been recognised.

So when I saw everyone gathering over one side of the office, I figured it would be good news. I couldn't see a birthday cake, and Felix hated having to make announcements. He usually got me to do it. If I was lucky, Hunter had decided he couldn't carry on without me doing most of his work and had gotten a job in Daddy's company. That would be perfect.

Tola and Eric nudged their way through to stand on either side of me, and I tilted my head.

'Bets on what this is about?'

'Someone's been nicking all the coffee pods again?' Eric shrugged.

'Maybe we're part of some big, corporate takeover!' Tola shook her shoulders, and I realised how bored she must be here if she was hoping for chaos. Change at any cost. 'What do you think?'

'Leaving or promotion, gotta be.' I shut up as Felix came out of his office, mouth in a thin line. If there were redundancies, I'd know about it, right?

'Maybe actually taking some holiday has shown Felix he needs to value you now, before you walk away to something better?' Eric offered. 'Being unavailable is the best way to make them want you!'

I shook my head and focused on Felix, desperately hoping that might be true. *Please.*

'Morning, everyone, hate to interrupt, just a quick thing, really.' Felix tugged on one side of his moustache. 'Here at Amora we like to reward hard work and dedication, and so one of your teammates will be stepping up into a new role, especially created to focus on building our clients' brands as well as their revenue. This new role will oversee the creation of brand guidelines and strategies to protect against any issues for our clients.'

Holy shit, it's finally happening. Tola grabbed my hand and squeezed.

'This is it!' Eric whispered in my ear.

'Your new head of branding is one of the hardest workers in this office and is definitely one of the friendliest amongst us!' Felix's lips twitched in a smile. 'So let's all put our hands together for Matthew. Congratulations!'

I froze. Tola muttered '*What?*' Eric moved in closer, as if trying to protect me. Or perhaps to stop me from running across the office and roundhouse kicking Felix's head off.

Matthew smiled as he walked over to Felix and shook his hand, and then gave an odd little wave to his colleagues. *Matthew.* Matthew who couldn't make a decision on anything? Matthew, who I'd had to stop using Comic Sans on professional documents . . . multiple times? Even Hunter looked perturbed.

'I . . . I just wanted to say thanks so much for the opportunity, and I won't let you down. And thank you to Aly, who's really helped me as I've been preparing for this role.' He gave me a winning smile. 'She's been here the longest, and I've really learned a lot from her.'

I nodded, puzzled. The twenty-four-year-old that I'd trained, that I'd hand-held through every decision, was going to be my *boss*?

I raised an eyebrow at Felix, who avoided my gaze, and I looked around to find all the others equally confused. But they smiled and congratulated Matthew and talked about going to the pub after work.

As people started to disperse, I fell back into my chair, staring at my screen but not really seeing it. All those years, all that extra work, those extra hours. I tried to take a step back: maybe Matthew deserved it, maybe he'd done brilliant work. He certainly loved his job and tried hard. But ... he'd been here barely a year, he didn't lead anyone, he didn't have any formal training ... if you put our CVs side by side, it would be insane to choose him over me.

And I hadn't even been told the interviews had happened ... I hadn't been given a chance.

It was like Felix was laughing at me.

'This is a fucking joke,' Eric said over my shoulder.

'Like, seriously? No shade to Matthew, he's nice and all, but the man would spend five minutes debating which end of a pencil to put in the sharpener. You've done almost all his work!' Tola hissed at me.

'I didn't *do* his work, I helped him.'

'Aly,' Eric raised an eyebrow, towering over me. 'Come *on* now. You Fixer Upper-ed him! You guided and trained and encouraged, and even though he's still pretty useless, he got the job you're meant to have!'

I closed my eyes and ran through the last year. All the questions, and support and advice. The articles I sent him, and the practice presentations I went through. I'd fixed him up and I hadn't even meant to.

I kept my eyes closed. 'Fuck.'

I felt my chair swivel, and opened my eyes in alarm, seeing Tola almost vibrating with rage. 'Aly, you go in there and talk to Felix, because this is a fucking joke. He as good as promised that job to you.'

I looked over at the throng around Matthew, then whispered, 'What am I meant to do, go in there crying "But you said!"? It'll look unprofessional. If they want to hire Matthew, then they can. That's their choice.'

'Aly, you *wrote the job spec*,' Tola said slowly, leaning down so I couldn't escape eye contact. 'If there was ever a time to lose your shit, this would be it.'

'What about fixing the Teddy Bell fiasco?' Eric supplied. 'Come on, Aly, grow a pair.'

Tola huffed, 'I agree with the sentiment but do not approve the language.'

I took a breath, adopted a calm tone of voice and smiled. 'Look, guys, it's . . .'

And then I caught Felix's eye across the room, and I couldn't tell if he was afraid of me, embarrassed or smirking, but suddenly I was the angriest I had ever been in my life.

'If you say fine . . .' Tola started.

'No, you know what? It's not fine,' I stood up, heading over to Felix's office. 'It is not fine at all.'

'Yes!' Eric punched the air. 'Aly fights for herself instead of others! Win!'

'Go and rip the shit out of him, babe,' Tola nodded,

encouraging, picking up my lipstick from my desk and throwing it over to me. Orange-red and ready for anything.

I grasped it like a talisman, pausing to reapply in the reflective window of Felix's office.

Give him hell, I told my reflection.

When I opened the door without knocking, Felix held up his hands, standing behind his desk. He already looked exhausted. 'Come on, Aly. Don't start with me here.'

I closed the door behind me, physically vibrating with rage, and simply stood, hands clasped gently in front of me.

'I just thought it would be good to have a little talk.'

'I don't have to explain my hiring practices to you, I'm your superior.'

I frowned in surprise, tilting my head. Felix had always called himself my mentor. He'd been my biggest supporter. He was always finding opportunities for me to show my worth, to prove I was . . .

'Was I even in the running for the role?' I said quietly. 'Or was it simply a way to keep me doing more work, staying motivated, cleaning up everyone else's messes?'

'Oh, OK, so I've tricked you into doing your job, is that it? Get a grip, Alyssa,' Felix huffed, leaning on his desk like he was trying to intimidate me. 'You going to get all emotional now, cry and tell me it's not fair? Because I don't want to hear it.'

'Matthew has been here barely a year,' I said calmly. 'I just want to know how he could have impressed you that much, when he is still learning about the industry. And I'd be interested to know when the interviews were, seeing as I never got the chance to put myself forward.'

'It's a promotion, not a new role.'

'It's a title and job description I wrote, based on the need for it in this office,' I countered sharply.

'See, this is what I mean.' Felix pointed at me. 'You're getting hysterical!'

I blinked, pausing for a moment. 'Hysterical? I'm asking a question.'

'You're not thinking straight. If you were, you wouldn't be in here questioning your boss.'

I took a breath and tried to lower my voice, make it softer. I wasn't shouting, or ranting, I was just pissed off. Felix once threw a paperweight at the wall when we lost a contract, but somehow that wasn't hysteria?

'Felix,' I said reasonably, smile plastered on my face. 'You've been my mentor for years, you said I was in the running. I was hoping to get some feedback, that's all. So I know what to work on for down the line.'

Felix scanned my face for a trace of anger, of loose emotion, checking my fists weren't clenched and my teeth weren't grinding. I wasn't going to let him play the *crazy female* card. Not today.

He fell into his chair like he was relieved, and his voice took on that soft, encouraging tone I knew so well from the last few months. He was trying to get me back onside. 'You need to stop taking things so personally.'

I was going to explode, but I nodded, sitting down. 'So how did Matthew edge me out? So I can know what to work on?'

'Well, he's just so *likeable*, Aly, you know how it is. We need someone in charge that the others respect and look up to. And the Big Boss knows Matthew, he sees potential in him. They've developed a rapport, so he suggested he'd be a good fit for the role.'

'Oh, wow, OK. How does he know Matthew?' I kept my face carefully neutral, my voice light and friendly, as if we were just chatting. I was mentally begging him to say *He saw him around the office, they've chatted, he was impressed.* That would be annoying, but I could live with it.

'Well, um . . .' Felix tugged at his moustache. 'Matthew is his godson, actually. He really wanted to help him in finding a career path. And Matthew only has wonderful things to say about you, Aly, so I don't think this jealousy looks good on you. Makes you look spiteful, you know?'

I felt my jaw physically drop. Was I living in some sort of alternative universe here?

'Besides, the work he did on the Digital Photography Conference was excellent, it increased brand recall by twenty-six per cent.' Felix shrugged. 'You've gotta admit, it's impressive.'

I blinked. 'Of course I agree it's impressive, it was my campaign.'

Felix looked at me, almost pityingly. 'Don't do this, kid, it's embarrassing.'

I leaned in. 'You're telling me you couldn't tell that I wrote that report? You couldn't tell that was my idea? The same framework for the campaign that I designed four years ago? Are you even paying attention here, Felix?'

'If you're accusing Matthew of plagiarism—'

'I'm not, I helped him.'

'Good—' he started.

'I'm accusing you of not seeing what's right in front of you.'

'This is beneath you, and quite frankly, I don't have time for any more of your nonsense,' Felix snapped. 'Look, if you want a better shot next time, it's not all about the paperwork. You've got to be here.'

'I'm here, I'm always here!' I yelped. 'For years, I've had no life, because my life has been this place. I'm the one working late on Friday nights, missing out on the trips to the pub, checking everyone's work!'

'Maybe before, sure,' Felix agreed. 'But these last few months? These last weeks in particular, you've been taking days off, you're always chatting with your friends, you're leaving dead on five o clock. I don't know if you're setting up your own agency—'

'—No!'

'—Or what, but your focus hasn't been here, Aly, it simply hasn't.'

He threw his hands up as if to let me argue, but there was nothing I could say. It was true. The Fixer Upper had made me take my eye off the ball. I was spending so much time worrying about Dylan's career that I'd stopped worrying about my own.

I'd thrown away everything I'd been working towards.

I didn't know if I was more angry at Dylan, my parents, Tola, or myself. Definitely myself. Well, that was it. A small voice said, *Well, at least it wasn't Hunter.*

I looked at Felix, feeling myself shut down emotionally, pulling back anything that he could cling to. No emotion, no friendliness, no excuses.

'Thank you for your feedback in this matter.'

214

I turned around without waiting for a response and walked back into the office, pulling a small smile onto my face like a shroud. I sat down at my desk and focused on my screen, when I felt Tola and Eric hovering at my side.

'I can't do this now,' I said out of the corner of my mouth, not looking up. 'Felix is watching and if I show one shred of weakness, I'm done.' *Plus I'm angry at you. None of this would have happened if you guys hadn't dragged me into this.*

'Oh Aly,' Eric started, but I stopped him.

'Please don't be kind to me right now, I can't take it.'

'OK,' Tola relented, backing away, 'but drinks after work?'

I nodded, not looking up, not breathing until they'd gone. And then my phone rang. Mama. I couldn't face it, so I sent it straight to voicemail. But she called again. When my phone rang for the third time, I answered harshly, 'Look, I'm sorry, but this really isn't a good time right now.'

'Then why did you answer the call?' a male voice asked, quizzical. I looked down at my phone in shock and saw Dylan's name.

'Hi, sorry, I thought you were my mother.'

'My watermelon margaritas are not that good, and my karaoke skills are pretty pitiful,' he said cheerfully, and I wondered if he'd realised how much he'd given away, or if he wasn't playing our game any more. 'Anyway, just checking we were still on to go through the presentation tonight?'

I closed my eyes. 'Oh shit . . .'

'You forgot? You never forget anything.'

'I am . . .' I took a shaky breath, 'I'm not having a great day.'

I don't know what I expected from our new-found peace treaty, but to my surprise he said, 'I'm sorry to hear that. Why don't we reschedule for tomorrow?'

More time away from work. More time splitting my focus. God, what an idiot I was.

'Hello, Aly?'

'Sorry.' I shook my head. 'Yeah, tomorrow sounds good. Thank you. Sorry for the confusion.'

'Are you ... are you sure you're OK?'

'Perfect, couldn't be better! Very busy, that's all!' I chirped, looking up at the ceiling to stop the tears that threatened. 'I'll text you later about a time!'

I hung up and felt like an arsehole. Now I was forgetting client meetings? And he'd actually seemed concerned. At any other time, it would have been the most natural thing in the world to let him distract me. *Tell me something true, Dyl. Tell me something I don't know. Tell me something magical.*

These days, I was starting to think the truth was more trouble than it was worth.

I didn't want to go for after-work consolation drinks. I didn't want to admit that I was annoyed about the impact the Fixer Upper was having on my life. I didn't want to blame Eric and Tola for making this happen, but a small part of me did.

'You took holiday! You're allowed to take holiday!' Tola had yelped, ordering another round. 'This is madness, Aly. You're meant to have a life as well as a job.'

That sounded so much like my mother: *When are you*

going to fall in love? When are you going to make yourself com-
pletely vulnerable and let someone destroy you? It's romantic, all
this suffering, I promise!

I really missed my grandparents, in that moment. They'd seemed to have life totally sussed. They had purpose and love and family. Work was never their main purpose. Their goal was happiness, laughter, good food and small moments. My grandmother sang songs as she rolled the vine leaves for her *koubebia*, my grandfather picked oranges from his trees and squeezed his fresh orange juice, a loud '*aaaah*' after every gulp. Maybe they lived small lives, but they were so aware of what they had, of how much joy there was in small moments.

They never seemed to have the fear of being left behind I have. I suppose some people got that chilled-out attitude, and some people got what my mama had: epic destruction.

She tried calling again while I was at the bar, and it was clear my lack of availability was annoying her. Eventually I answered while the others were getting more drinks and I felt woozy, standing in the outside smoking section, wondering how I was going to function tomorrow. And if I even cared.

'MAMA!' I answered. 'I'M AT WORK DRINKS!'

'So I need you, and you're out getting drunk?'

Panic shot through my system, and I thought I might throw up.

'What's wrong, what's happened?'

'Your father keeps asking me about the money, and I don't know what to tell him! He's taking his family on holiday next week, so he needs a timeframe ...'

I wanted to scream, *Don't you see what this is doing to me? Don't you care? This isn't love!*

'Well, I'm *very* sorry that not knowing when his firstborn is going to cough up her life savings is getting in the way of his holiday ... how awful for him!'

'Alyssa! You're meant to be helping me!'

'And who's helping *me*, Mama?' I hung up before she could reply, irritated beyond belief. I turned my phone off for the rest of the evening, unwilling to hear what she had to say. I knew I'd pay for it tomorrow; she'd be hurt by my tone, and I'd apologise, and we'd all move on. The cycle would begin again.

When it got to around nine thirty, Eric got all squirrelly and decided to slink off. Tola wiggled her eyebrows and we teased, but he just scowled at us, checked his hair in the mirror behind us, and left. *Ah, Ben.* I decided to go, too, aware that I didn't really want this day to continue for any longer than it needed to.

'Nooo, we never get time for the two of us!' Tola yelped, clinging to my arm, but I shook my head.

'Go hang out with your young friends. Tomorrow we need to have a discussion about all this stuff with Dylan. I'm ... I'm not feeling good about it.'

Tola tilted her head. 'We can always quit? If it's making you unhappy?'

'You said it would destroy our reputation!'

Tola smiled at me like I was the silliest person she'd ever met. 'What does our reputation matter if it makes you miserable? You're so odd, Aly, honestly. Go get a good night's sleep. We'll fix the world tomorrow.'

As I waited for the bus, I realised we couldn't quit – I

needed the money. And I hadn't told my friends that, which had created another problem. Everything had been so much easier when I was lonely and aloof and only had my work to focus on. When I dated men who took my energy and then left me because I wasn't fun.

No one wants to date a drill sergeant, Aly.

Why are you always lecturing me?

Stop being a nag.

I missed when my idea of a secret had been going to restaurants by myself, rather than being paid an eye-watering sum of money to turn my ex-best friend into a socialite businessman Ken doll.

I turned my phone back on and found four voicemails from my mother, which I absolutely was not going to listen to, and a few texts from Dylan:

You didn't text to reschedule. You doing OK?

I closed my eyes briefly, guilt curdling in my stomach.

Why are you being kind to me now? I'm trying to destroy you! I'm an awful manipulative bitch who doesn't even deserve the memory of our friendship. At least keep being mean to me to make it OK!

I was calling the number before I could stop myself.

'Aly?' His voice was soft, tired. 'Are you OK?'

'Sorry!' I hissed, wincing. 'Sorry, it's late!'

'Are you . . .' I could hear the curve of his smile, 'are you *drunk*-calling a client, Alyssa Aresti? For shame.'

'No, I'm drunk-calling a . . . you. It's different.'

'Is it?' he asked, suddenly playful. 'How interesting.'

219

'I just wanted to apologise for not replying. And for forgetting our meeting in the first place. And for being drunk on this call . . .' I looked at my watch, and winced again. 'At ten p.m. Damn.'

He laughed at that. 'This is very un-Aly behaviour. What's happened, is it the end of days?'

'My mentee got the job over me.'

'Not the one who shagged Bell's wife?'

I laughed, 'Hit on, and thankfully not. A different incompetent man. But he's the Big Boss's godson. Wish I'd known that before I bothered.'

'Office bullshit should come with some sort of manual.' Dylan paused. 'I'm sorry, though. It sounded like you'd been working towards that for a very long time.'

'A pathetic amount of time wasted. Anyway, I'm sorry, do you want to reschedule for tomorrow? Am I interrupting? Nicki probably doesn't get much downtime with you and work stuff—'

'I'm at mine,' he said, and the silence after that was long enough that I worried something was wrong.

'Is everything OK?' I wasn't sure if I was asking because I had a vested interest, or because it was Dylan.

'Sure . . . it's . . . sure.' I could almost *see* him shrugging.

'Oh, come on, you can spin a story better than that,' I said lightly, as if I didn't care. 'I've got a long, boring bus ride home and I need something to take my attention away from my own woes.'

There was silence for a moment, then . . .

'What do you think of Nicki?'

I wasn't expecting that. 'Me?'

'Yeah.'

I searched for the words. 'Um ... well, she's determined and hard-working, and she demands what she wants, which I always respect in a woman. She's built up her own brand from scratch, which is really impressive. I like her taste in shoes and I hate her taste in cocktails.'

'Oh, the cocktail thing drives me *nuts*,' Dylan laughed. 'Let the expert make the drink, for the love of God!'

'Why are you asking this, Dylan? Has something happened?'

'No,' he said quietly, light as a feather, 'it was just some dumb thing. She hates that I wear that St Christopher medal all the time. Says it doesn't go with my outfits. I got annoyed. It's silly.'

His mother gave that necklace to him when he was a kid, as far as I knew he'd worn it every day since she'd died. Some people had a homing beacon for their partner's most vulnerable points and it looked like Nicki was one of them. I wondered if she'd even realised what she'd done, what it meant.

Before I could say anything, he continued.

'I guess I'm assessing my life with fresh eyes. I don't know if it's what I would have imagined for myself.'

'But it's amazing!' I whispered, watching the city streets get smaller and shabbier as I got closer to home. 'You're doing this work that can help people, and it's innovative and creative and risky. You're loved by someone who is *so* hard on themselves, so open to attack in the public eye, and yet she wants you there, by her side. You, Dyl.'

'I can't help feeling someone else would do a better job,' he said.

'Of what? Turning up at events and eating free food and selling selfies to glossy mags?' I chortled.

'Of loving her.'

No, don't say that. I'm doing this to help you, to help both of you. I needed to fix this.

I needed him to see this phase as a rough spot. Growing pains as their relationship moved to the next level, and nothing more.

Worst of all, sitting having this devastating conversation was still the best thing that had happened to me in a long time. To hear him laugh, to have my friend back in some tiny, insignificant way.

'I think it would be really easy to fuck something up with a woman like Nicki. If you didn't understand why she does what she does,' I offered, hesitant.

'And what does she do?' He was annoyed, I could tell. He'd given me an in, and I hadn't taken it.

'The influencer stuff. The reality TV shows. She's a woman who's been trained to perform. It's probably harder for her to be authentic without an audience. To just be who she is.'

He sighed, 'I can see her struggling, but I don't know how to help beyond telling her to put the fucking phone down and watch the damn movie or eat the piece of pizza. Every thought she has is about harnessing an audience, what they want to see next. It's like if Jim Carrey had known he was the centre of *The Truman Show* all along. I feel like eventually she's going to have a breakdown. Which, of course, she'll leak to the press and then get a book deal for.'

I snorted, 'That sounds about right.'

'I've been trying so hard to be right for her, but ... I just can't.'

I closed my eyes, leaning my head against the window, letting it jolt me back and forth. There was no answer to any of this. *It's a rough patch, it's a phase, it'll get better. Keep trying, let me help.* He was being vulnerable, being honest, and I was using it to plan out a chess move. God, I hated myself. And yet I couldn't put the phone down. Couldn't end a conversation in which I was his confidant again.

'I'm wondering what it is that's annoying you,' I asked carefully. 'Are you jealous of her success?'

He took a moment to think about it. 'No, and it's not about having to share her, either. Sometimes it feels ... it feels like maybe everyone else is acting in a movie and I never got the script?'

'That's what growing up feels like, isn't it?' I imagined him smiling at the ceiling, lounging on a beaten-up sofa, comfortable and content.

'It's more than that, it's like everyone's pretending. Everyone's framing themselves as something else. Putting a filter on their lives. And when I hang out with them, I end up doing it too. You know what I used to say, when people asked me what I did? I said I was working on an app.'

'Which is true ...'

'Yes. But now it's *start-up, entrepreneur, tech mogul ...*'

'No one's called you a tech mogul,' I laughed, the seriousness starting to ebb away, 'calm down.'

'Nicki did! In an interview, in the hopes that it would stick!' he yelped, 'So I started dressing like one of those guys and rented fancy office space and talked as if I knew what the fuck I was doing. I went to a *polo match*, Aly. Can you imagine me with those people?'

'No, but more because you're scared of horses.'

He laughed, trailing off to silence. 'I don't feel like anyone knows me. No one knows that I'm scared of horses or allergic to mushrooms, or I still go running on Sunday mornings because my dad made me do drills. And as angry as it makes me, I can't stop pretending.'

I didn't really know what to say, so I just waited.

'God, that sounded so wanky, didn't it? Woe is me, no one knows my entire boring life story.'

'No one knows about my parents' confusing relationship, or how my grandparents used to dance in the kitchen. No one knows that when I'm sad I eat strawberry laces, or that I ask people stupid questions because I don't trust anyone to tell the truth.'

'It would be nice,' he said softly, 'to have that again.'

I thought I was going to be sick. Because I wanted that more than anything. My friend, my dear friend, back again? That person I used to be with him, the one who went off on adventures and took risks and wasn't living this grey, listless life. What did I have now, without the dream of the branding role? I had work and I had the Fixer Upper.

This would never work – I didn't get to keep him after this. I fix him for Nicki, and what, we'd never talk about it again? I'd go to their winter wonderland wedding and smile and pretend I hadn't tricked him?

Did my mother even deserve the money? Sticking plasters and concealer on Dylan and Nicki, just to pay for my mum and dad to continue their epic dance for another decade – what was this even for any more? This wasn't helping anyone.

'Aly, you there?'

I put a smile on my face and wiped away my tears, injecting that sarcastic tone: 'I'm *afraid*, Mr James, the time has come for me to get off the bus and run home so I can spend the next hour vomiting aggressively. I promise I will be incredibly professional tomorrow.'

'Now, where's the fun in that?' He laughed softly. 'Hey, Aly?'

I winced. *Please don't make this any harder.* 'Yeah?'

'You deserved that job,' he said.

'How do you know?'

'Because I know you.'

I hung up and burst into tears.

Chapter Sixteen

I groaned as the phone rang. No one tells you how awful hangovers are in your thirties. It's like you spend your teenage years and your twenties believing every movie with hungover characters is an exaggeration to put you off drinking. And suddenly you're a grown-up and throwing up into a potted plant at the office and trying to wash your mouth out with Lucozade.

If I even managed to make it to the office.

I opened one eye and looked at the name on the screen. Dylan. At seven a.m.

Oh God, what did I say last night?

'Hello?' I croaked. 'Is everything OK?'

'I'm calling about something incredibly important,' Dylan said smoothly, as if I hadn't called him half-cut the night before.

'Which is?'

He took a deep breath.

'Five things, Aly,' he said, and suddenly I was sixteen again. My heart leapt at the thought of it, even as my head pounded. And then reality set in.

'No, Dylan. No way. I have work. *You* have work!'

'Five things, or it has to be done. You know the rules.'

I scrambled on my nightstand for painkillers. 'If I don't go in today, it's going to look like I'm throwing a hissy fit over Matthew's promotion.'

'So?'

'So it's unprofessional. And you have the most important presentation of your life in two weeks. You need to be preparing.'

The phone went silent, and then I heard him hum.

'Fair point. I'm pretty good at multitasking these days. What if I promise our adventure will be educational?'

'Dylan,' I warned.

'Alyssa,' he mocked. 'It's a simple question. Can you tell me five wonderful things you're looking forward to today?'

'I couldn't give you one,' I sighed, defeated. 'I couldn't give you *half* of one.'

'That's what I thought. Make your excuses, I'll see you at St Pancras at eleven.' He went to hang up, and I stopped him, suddenly desperate.

'Dylan!'

'Yeah?'

I hesitated, unsure what I wanted to say. 'Why?'

'Because you're not happy. And it's very important that you be happy.'

He hung up, and I closed my eyes, unsure whether I should be excited or terrified.

St Pancras is my favourite London train station. There's something about the *possibility* of it all. The Eurostar, the oyster bar, the dark entrance to the Renaissance Hotel, hidden in the back corner, like there's some secret history unfolding around the commuters and day-trippers.

I sat with a coffee, pretending to read a book, but really just watching people. Greeting each other with hugs, swerving around luggage, walking at speed. Tourists getting lost, couples having arguments. You could see everything in the crowds at St Pancras.

Dylan appeared wearing sunglasses on his head and holding two coffees. He looked at my table, my cup of coffee evident, and sighed.

'Damn.'

I held out my hand. 'Gimme. There is not enough coffee in the world.'

'I *really* didn't think you'd show,' he said, handing me the cup, 'thought you'd care too much about what people thought at the office.' *I did. But I couldn't turn down this chance.*

Of course, to Tola and Eric, I made it all about the Fixer Upper. Here was my chance to get Dylan onside, to push him towards Nicki, solve all their problems. But I knew, deep down, I was lying.

Dylan looked at me, a sly smile on his face, and I panicked.

'Have you ... spoken to Eric this morning?' he asked.

I frowned at him. 'Why would I ...' He grinned at me, wiggling his eyebrows. 'Shut the front door! It *was* Ben he was meeting last night! Again!'

He held his hands up as if he had agreed he wasn't saying anything, and the two of us stood smiling at each other.

'Looks like we might be in each other's lives quite a bit,

then, if this turns into an epic romance from one of those old movies Ben loves,' Dylan said, looking up at the departures board. I was relieved he didn't see the panic that must have flitted across my face. Lies with people you were never going to see again, strangers in the street? Sure, fix them and move on with your life. But ... there was no coming back from this. I was in too deep. And now Eric was at risk, too. How long would he lie to Ben about how I really knew his friend?

'Well, let's not get ahead of ourselves, it might be nothing more than a very curable case of lust,' I said breezily, and Dylan whirled around to look at me, tilting his head like a confused canine.

'Ben took *four years* to find the perfect pair of jeans. And when he finally found the pair he liked, he bought twenty of them. Size up, size down, every colour. He waits until he finds what he wants, and he plays for keeps.'

'Bit intense?'

'I admire him, actually. It may look like he's closed off, but he just makes very ... purposeful decisions, you know? He's an analyst, he weighs up the pros and cons, waits to know what he's walking into, and then jumps in head-first.' Dylan smiled fondly. 'It's a good way to be. But if Eric's not ...'

'Not what?' I felt myself getting defensive.

'Looking for something real ...' Dylan paused, 'it's better he tells him now.'

I thought about that first night I became friends with Eric, how he'd sobbed into his pint about how much he was going to hurt everyone. I remembered the first dates and the cheeky grins and sexual jokes as he tried out different personalities and opportunities like jackets, waiting for one that fit. And I remembered the tired eyes at the end of nights at the pub as he'd hug my arm and tell me he was so very tired of looking for his perfect match.

'He wants real. But ... he hasn't had that before,' I said, and wondered if I was giving away too much, betraying my friend.

'Then it sounds like it's all good.' Dylan shrugged, sipping his coffee. 'Unless Helena doesn't like Eric. Then he's toast.'

I frowned, trying to remember whether Ben had mentioned Helena when we'd had dinner. A sister? A best friend?

'His beagle. Helena Bonham Barker. She rules that house.' Dylan grinned and tilted his head towards the trains.

'As well she should,' I laughed, jumping down from my bar stool to follow him. 'So, where we going?'

It was pointless to even try, I knew he wouldn't tell me.

'You know better than that, Aresti,' Dylan snorted.

'But you promise we'll do some work?' I heard myself and sighed. *Once a nerd, always a nerd.*

'Some things don't change.'

Get out of my brain, Dylan.

When we got to the platform, he handed me a ticket, and told me not to look. I swiped through the barrier and handed it back, as surprised as he was that I did what I was told.

We settled into the empty carriage, seated opposite each other at a table.

'While we are on this train, I promise we can work on the presentation.'

'And when we're off the train?'

230

'We have adventures. Those are the rules.'

'OK,' I said, 'work.'

We actually managed it, for two whole hours we worked together, practising the pitch, amending the presentation, researching the company. No arguing or bitching or talking in code. No mention of Nicki. I forgot about that guilty feeling in my stomach. We made progress.

And when we stepped off the train, I could smell the sea.

We walked down the hill, and it suddenly appeared, out of nowhere, full of potential and hope and the promise of summer. I smiled and felt Dylan looking at me.

'What?'

'First of five things, that's all,' he smiled, then broke into a run. 'Race ya!'

I chased him, dodging people and jumping off the kerb, exhilarated, telling myself how stupid it was even as I ran. He beat me, unsurprisingly.

'Maybe I need to start some of those Sunday-morning drills,' I wheezed, and he shook his head.

'OK, now what?'

Dylan looked up and down, as if surveying his land and looking for something in particular. Really, I was sure he was just looking for the next opportunity to present itself. Which it did when he suddenly pointed at the arcade.

It sounds ridiculous to travel for three hours only to spend twenty quid on arcade games, but being out of London was like being free of myself. I left 'workaholic fixer upper, always perfect, always striving' Aly back at St Pancras.

'What next?' I asked, wide-eyed and childlike.

'Fancy lunch!' Dylan looked so pleased with himself that I laughed.

'Oh please, not fancy. There's so much fancy in your life. Can't we just eat chips with lots of vinegar?'

'And not once take a selfie?' he replied, shrugging. 'Sounds good to me.'

Oh no, I was doing the opposite of what I was meant to be doing. I was meant to push him towards that life.

'Wait, no, we can do the fancy thing!' I held my hands up. 'It's your day too.'

'It absolutely is not,' he laughed. 'Today we do what you want.'

'When do we do what you want?'

'Probably when we're brave and drunk and ready to be honest.' He looked at me, eyebrow raised, head tilted. Daring me.

I simply shook my head, not really sure what he was asking, but certain I didn't like the sound of it.

'You never used to be this stubborn, you know?' he said conversationally, peering down side streets, hands in his pockets as if he didn't have a care in the world.

It was like going back in time. This could have been any one of the weekends we'd spent as teenagers, off on one of Dylan's adventures – music festivals, seaside towns, getting a bus to the middle of nowhere and trying to find our way home. And still him, calm, hands in pockets, strolling along like it was the easiest thing in the world to be happy.

'Well, that's not true.'

My phone buzzed.

'Hi, Nicki,' I answered the call, watching Dylan shake his head, 'how's things?'

'Well, to be honest, darling, I'm having a bit of a nightmare today. Do you know where Dylan is?'

'Dylan?' I said aloud, and watched as he shook his head more vigorously, eyes wide. 'No, haven't seen him. Why?'

I watched him scratching the back of his neck, staring at the floor as she spoke. Guilty.

'Well, we were talking about the future yesterday and I think ... I think I spooked him. I pushed too hard, and now he's disappeared and he's not answering my calls. And if he doesn't do well at this presentation, well, it's Daddy's contact, and that'll look bad ...'

'I really don't think you have to worry,' I said softly, trying to be comforting. 'He's probably taking some time to get his head in the game before the presentation.'

'We talked about marriage, and I thought he was with me on that. Why wouldn't he be with me on that?'

'I ... uh ...'

'I need this to happen, Aly.' There was a level of desperation in her voice. 'I need him. He's the only real thing in my life.'

Well, now I felt sorry for all three of us.

'Please don't worry about anything. If I speak to Dylan, I'll tell him you're trying to get in touch.'

'OK, you're right. Positive thinking. I'm going to do some meditation.' She took a breath and seemed to suddenly inflate with helium, back into her bubbly persona. 'Bye then!'

When I looked up from my phone, Dylan was smiling

like he hoped I wouldn't probe for answers. 'So, about those fish and chips, that pub on the corner looks promising!'

'Dylan.'

He ignored me, and I followed automatically.

'Dylan! Why are you hiding from your girlfriend?'

'Why is she calling you to find out where I am?' he replied, holding open the door to the pub and gesturing for me to go first. The only way we were going to have this conversation was if he was trapped in a seat, with a huge plate of food, a pint of beer, and no way out. Fine, we'd do it his way.

'Um, she paid my fee?' I retorted, picking a table and plonking myself down, waiting for him to join me.

'Right, of course, so now she owns you.'

I rolled my eyes. 'So we're back to this fun way of interacting again? Great, I'd missed the snark and all the glaring.'

'I'm gonna get some drinks and some menus.'

And then he was gone, chatting with the bartender, asking questions about ales, smiling back at me as if he knew how much he was pissing me off.

I had gotten myself stuck in the middle of this, and solving it was my responsibility. I tried to think about it as I would any other Fixer Upper situation, taking my history with Dylan out of the equation.

As much as they seemed to disconnect over particulars, Dylan and Nicki had the potential to be a power couple. They looked perfect together. He got her to chill out and eat the damn pizza, she ... got him business contacts through her dad and paid for me to improve him. OK, bad example, but ... they were two beautiful, insecure people playing out their patterns and they just needed to find a way to communicate their needs. The problem, of course, was timing.

Dylan needed to stop feeling like he was playing a part and to be able to tell when Nicki was offline. He needed to know when she was being real. And Nicki needed to remember her boyfriend was a real human, and that not every life event was a marketing opportunity.

OK, communication, empathy, smoothing ruffled feathers. I could do this.

He finally returned, placing two pints of beer on the table.

'Thanks. Menus?'

'I ordered fish and chips – that's what you wanted, right?' he shrugged, sipping at his pint, looking around the pub.

'Dylan, what's going on? Nicki said she started a conversation about your future, and you ran away?'

'Why do you even care?!' he huffed. 'You're here to fix my ailing career, right?'

'I'm here to support you before a big opportunity, when we both know you'd rather run away than take the risk of failing.'

'I can't have changed at all, in a decade?' he laughed, pulling a hand through his hair. 'I'm still the happy-go-lucky, everything's fine, hang with the cool kids guy, right? At no point in the last fifteen years could I have grown up?'

I threw my hands up. 'You're running a fucking company! I don't know what you're angry about, I thought I was helping!'

'You are! But you're helping me because it helps her,' he sighed.

That was a little too close for comfort. I took a breath, lowered my voice and leaned in.

'Dyl, she loves you. She wanted to help. That's what partners do for each other.' *She just wants a proposal in return, no big deal.*

He nodded, sipping his pint.

'Why'd you run?'

He looked at me like I was completely insane. 'Because . . . because she doesn't know me. It's like she looks at me and sees the version of me I could be in ten years.'

He gave me a pleading look like he was waiting for some big answer, but he hadn't asked a question.

'So what? That's nice, isn't it? She sees all that potential, the future Dylan. She wants to be with him.'

He shook his head, and I got the sense he was disappointed in me. The waiter came over with our plates and put them down on the table, pointing out condiments and asking if we were OK for drinks. We smiled and nodded and waited for him to leave.

I gestured for Dylan to continue.

'Right now, I'm like a puppy she bought thinking I'd grow into a Dobermann, but actually I'm part poodle and I wasn't fully toilet-trained.'

I snorted into my pint, reaching for the vinegar and pouring it liberally. I watched as Dylan sprinkled a terrifying amount of salt over his chips.

'You laugh, fine, but she's more in love with that version of me than the real me. And every time I get a little closer to whoever that guy is in her head, she rewards me. I wore the suit she picked, I went to the gala, I stopped wearing

T-shirts with eighties video game images. She's waiting for me to grow out of the things I love, and I'm not sure I'm ready to do that.'

He gave me this look, like he was trying to avoid saying something, and I massaged my temples.

'Whatever it is, say it. You're bringing back my hangover,' I sighed. 'You've got that look like you need to tell me you killed my goldfish.'

Dylan snickered, shaking his head. 'How many times do I have to say it, Mr Bubbles died of old age! It's just . . . since you turned up again, I remembered who I used to be back then. I liked that guy.'

'Eh, I thought he was kind of annoying.' I wrinkled my nose, shrugging one shoulder. 'Dylan, you wanna know what you should do here?'

He put down his knife and fork. 'Yes, actually. Oh, wise oracle Aly, fixer of such problems. What should I do?'

'Honestly?' I wiped my hands on a napkin and picked up my pint. 'I think you should stop thinking so damn much.'

He was poleaxed. His eyebrows disappeared beneath his fringe. 'What?'

I looked down at the four missed calls from my mother, the text from Tola asking if I was on track. The messages from Nicki. And then I looked at him, this beautiful man who had been my friend. He could be happy.

And then there'd be no more heartbroken calls from my mother. I could end the cycle. I could start something new – make the Fixer Upper into what it needed to be. Maybe I could teach men like Dylan, no pretence, no trickery, just a desire to grow up.

I had to help him leave me behind.

I shrugged nonchalantly, like every word wasn't killing me. 'You're in love, you're loved, you're in your thirties. Famous or not, your girlfriend is going to be thinking about marriage. Those conversations are about figuring out if you are happy plodding along, as most people are when things are good enough, or you're willing to take a step forward, to say *Yes, this is what I want long term*. That's it.'

Dylan looked so bemused I almost laughed. 'Dyl, it's really simple. Do you love her?'

'Yes, but . . .'

I shook my head. 'Nope. Sorry. The rest are doubts and insecurity and fear of change. Peter Pan is fiction, and we all have to grow up sometime.' I tilted my head at him, going in for the kill, 'Besides, you *want* to be that guy, right? The successful business type? Don't tell me you don't want to go home the day after you get that deal and tell your dad you were on the right path all along?'

He smiled that crooked smile and nodded at the table. 'I guess you're right. We are well suited, we even each other out. She's so fun. And she's shown me this whole other world I never even knew existed. I don't want to live in it all the time, but . . . growing's natural, right? Relationships develop.'

'Exactly. You two are great together. Honestly.'

Honestly?

His bright blue eyes zeroed in on me.

'So you'd be happy if I married Nicki?'

Why does this question feel like a trap?

'I'd be happy if you were happy. Isn't that the whole point

238

of our trip today? Mutual happiness?' I smiled widely, and he looked sad, shaking his head at me.

'Don't do that.'

'What?'

'That camouflage smile, it doesn't work on me. I've seen it too many times before.'

'It's not ... I'm mourning my promotion, I'm hungover and I'm dispensing the same advice I was giving when we were teenagers. Give me a break, would you?' I stuffed a chip into my mouth and chewed furiously.

He took a breath.

'Are we *ever* going to talk about it? About us?'

I winced, swallowing my food, then pressed my fingers to my lips, my voice barely audible, 'Don't do this now, Dyl.'

'We need to, because I'm going to explode. *Please*,' he reached over and held my wrist, pleading with me, 'please can we just be honest, just be *us* for five minutes?'

'You're the one who started pretending!'

'I panicked!' Dylan threw up his hands. 'Otherwise we'd have to do that whole *oh, how are you, what are you up to*, throwing around our life achievements, and I knew I would immediately disappoint you. *And* I was angry at you.'

'Well, I was angry at you, too.'

He jerked in surprise. 'Me? What do *you* have to be angry about? I'm the one who got abandoned and blocked and never heard from you again!'

I looked around at the other patrons, all eerily quiet as they listened in on our argument, avoiding looking directly at us. I held my hands up and spoke quietly.

'I think we need to stop having this conversation.'

'Please, Aly, I've been patient, but we do need to—'

'I know, but . . . not here.'

He nodded and stood up. 'OK, let's go.'

I gestured at my food. 'We need to pay.'

'Already done, let's go.'

I followed him like I was on my way to the gallows, head down and following his feet, not daring to think or talk or argue. Somehow, this was going to be all my fault. I was going to stand there, ashamed, as I told him that I'd loved him once, and I'd discovered he'd never given a shit about me. I was going to make myself weak and vulnerable and embarrassed.

He led us out to the seafront, the waves making enough noise to cover us.

'Is that to hide the sound of my yelling?' I asked, gesturing at the sea.

'Maybe I want to be able to chuck you in if you piss me off too much!'

I faced him, steadied myself and put my hands up. 'OK, fine. So let's be honest. Let's be us. What do you want from me?'

'I want you to ask me to tell you something truthful!' he yelped in frustration, and I almost laughed.

'You want me to request trivia from you? Sure, hit me with your facts about South American bird migration, I'm all ears.'

He tugged at his hair, and I thought he was going to yell at me. 'You know it's more than that! You said yourself, you asked for truths so you knew people weren't always lying to you. I need you to ask so when I say what I've gotta say, you're going to know I'm not lying, OK? *Please.*'

Well, that knocked the fight out of me.

I looked at his face, so open and familiar, so desperate to have this moment that I'd been running from.

I took a breath to steady myself.

'Fine. Tell me something true, Dylan.'

He'd clearly planned the exact thing he wanted to say, and I wondered if he'd rehearsed it, changed words until it was perfect. How many years had he been thinking about what he'd say to me if he saw me again?

'I loved you, and you ran away.'

A searing rage flowed through me, until I physically shook. I wanted to throw something at him.

'You didn't love me!' I yelled, outraged. It was like those words broke the dam. 'You had a girlfriend! You always had a girlfriend! That night you kissed me for a dare, I was drunk and I must have said something bad because you looked like I'd punched you, and then in the morning you messaged your girlfriend about what an awful burden I was and you couldn't wait to be rid of me! Don't retell this story with you as the perfect hero, Dylan.'

His jaw physically dropped. 'What the fuck are you talking about?'

I yelled, 'I remember the look of horror on your face!'

He put his head in his hands, then walked away from me and yelled at the sea, hands clenched, arms outstretched. He bellowed into the waves until it drained from him. I felt like doing the same.

When he padded back over, his face blank, he stood close to me. There was no way to avoid those eyes.

'We,' he gestured between us, 'are idiots.'

241

'None of this matters, Dyl, it was a long time ago ...'
I started.

'Are you kidding?!' he exploded. 'You told me you loved me, that you'd always loved me!'

I cringed.

'Don't try it, Aresti. All that *I was drunk* crap won't wash. You loved me.'

'Fine!' I yelled. 'I loved you, so what?'

'I loved you back, you idiot!' he shouted, and suddenly I didn't feel like yelling any more.

'No ... you messaged your girlfriend ...'

His voice was softer, his eyes mournful. 'I'd abandoned her at that party to look after you, and I didn't know if anything you'd said was real. I was waiting for you to wake up and pretend it was all a mistake. So yes, I said what she expected me to say, to keep her happy, until I could figure it out.'

'You loved me,' I said, frowning out at the sea as I dropped down to sit on the beach, grasping fistfuls of sand. 'And not in a friend way?'

'No, not in a friend way.' He collapsed down beside me, and I could feel his eyes on me. 'Is that so hard to believe?'

'Um, yeah, kind of.'

He closed his eyes and sighed, before turning back to me. 'Couldn't you tell in the way I kissed you? I thought it was a dead giveaway.'

'I was mainly focused on the sniggers of your popular friends, and your girlfriend with daggers in her eyes.'

'Right ...' he nodded, 'well ...'

'This is awkward,' I said, heart thumping, digging a hole in the sand with my thumb.

Dylan laughed, 'Yep.'

'So why did you look so horrified in my memory?'

He pressed his lips together and tilted his head, considering, playing it back.

'Well, it could have been the shock, obviously I wasn't expecting you to say anything like that. And you know what you're like when you're drunk, Aresti, so incredibly forthright and matter-of-fact ... But thirty seconds after your romantic declaration, you vomited all over my favourite jeans. And my brand-new Converse.'

I blinked, 'Ah, well, that'll do it,' before putting my head in my hands, cringing. 'I don't know if that's better or worse than I was imagining.'

'Oh, mutually in love and miserable is much better. I couldn't figure out if you cut me out of your life because you were embarrassed about what you'd said, or you'd sobered up and remembered what *I'd* said ... it was a messy time.' Dylan tapped his knees through his threadbare jeans. 'So, feel better?'

I looked at him, considering.

'I guess I feel sad for past us?' I offered, and he nodded, taking my hand and giving it a squeeze. My heart contracted a little, his thumb grazing the back of my hand.

'Me too, mainly for all the years we could have been in each other's lives if you weren't such a *drama queen*.'

I made a face at him. 'If you'd been chivalrous about my blue vomit, we could have been married by now,' I joked and stuck out my tongue.

He laughed, and it felt like I could breathe again. Like we could just be us. The boy I had loved had loved me back, and our insecurities kept us apart. And now we could move forward.

I thought about all the women who had hired me so far, how much love they had in them, how much they wanted to give, to help, that they would go through our whole charade. I thought about the wannabe rock star who was afraid to sing, the genius who couldn't speak in front of crowds, the man hesitant to demand the promotion. I had gently nudged so many of them, built them up with kind words and belief until one day they'd looked in the mirror and seen what I'd told them they were. This would be my gift to Dylan. No longer afraid of his potential, knowing he was growing in the right direction. I'd give him a life he could be proud of.

We were past this now, we were done. No more tension, no more 'what if's. He had been my best friend, he had loved me. I had loved him. And now I'd help him love her, love their life together.

It was best for everyone.

'It's been a lonely old life without you, Aly. Like I've been missing my conscience.'

'You seem to have been doing just fine without me.' I squeezed his hand and he smiled.

'You know what the best thing about all this is?' Dylan asked, pulling me across the sand towards him, arm around my waist to cuddle me close. 'No more pretending. It's been so exhausting.'

I could smell the spice of his aftershave and feel the softness of his jumper beneath my fingertips. I could see the hint of red in his stubble and count all of those beautiful eyelashes if I wanted to. I was right back where I was at eighteen, overwhelmed by the beauty of him.

No more secrets, no more pretending?

'Exhausting,' I agreed sadly, daring to rest my head on his shoulder, trying not to cry, 'it really, really has been.'

Chapter Seventeen

I imagined telling Dylan the truth a hundred different ways on that train ride home, explaining what the other part of my job included. But he'd been so happy, so eager to share everything about his life with me, like a tap had been turned on. And I couldn't resist. I wanted to collect those missing years, layer them up, and memorise them until it was almost like I had been there too.

I walked the line, telling Dylan about my dating history, my friendship with Tola. He was right, there's something about people who were there at the beginning, who can see what you overcame and where you've come from and tell you how proud they are to see how you've grown. It was freeing.

I'd texted Tola and Eric on the journey home, and they celebrated that we'd talked about marriage, that I seemed to be doing a good job. I didn't tell them we'd had it all out, I couldn't quite bear to let them think I was taking advantage of a friend. Smoothing out Dylan's love life when he was a near stranger who pissed me off was one thing; manipulating him when he was my friend again felt impossible. I visualised helping him plan a huge, fancy proposal, being there to take the photos and congratulate them at the engagement party. Standing at their wedding, one of the inner circle. How awful.

'So, five things, Aly, go,' Dylan said on the train home, drowsily tracing circles on the table between us.

'Playing in the arcades, eating fish and chips, seeing that seagull dive-bomb you.' I ticked them off on my fingers and laughed as he threw a balled-up receipt at me. 'The smell of the sea and ... getting to laugh with you again, I guess. If we're gonna be all mushy about it.' I twitched my nose in distaste. Still playing the part. *You*, I wanted to say, *You're all five today, for making this happen, for being honest, for loving me once. But you're also absolutely destroying me.*

I threw the receipt back. 'Your top five?'

He smiled at me so tenderly that I wanted to be sick. 'All of it. Every damn part. Perfect day.'

I raised an eyebrow. 'Even the seagull attack?'

'Made you laugh. Worth it.'

I rolled my eyes. 'OK, Charm Boy. You realise that shit doesn't work on me.'

He laughed, 'You keep telling yourself that ... Nerd Girl.'

'Nerds will inherit the earth one day, Dylan, we're the ones quietly doing all the research. Don't forget it.' I stuck out my tongue and he laughed again, so easy, so relaxed.

Oh God, there was no way out of this without hurting *someone*. Tricking Dylan, disappointing Nicki, potentially ruining Eric and Ben before they even got started. And Mama ... she'd be trapped in the same toxic cycle forever.

But she was the adult, right? She was the one who should have her shit together right now. What had started as sleights of hand and subtle psychology was now too big. I was messing with peoples' lives.

We settled into a quiet rhythm as the train rattled through the countryside, and I looked out into the approaching darkness.

I couldn't leave this all unfixed. I'd made this mess and couldn't just walk out halfway through clean-up. What is it they say about heart surgery looking like murder if you stopped in the middle?

I would tell my mother that I couldn't get the money.

That I'd picked Dylan over her. I'd jump straight off the train from the seaside onto the one that would take me to my mum's. I had to do it now. She wouldn't want me to hurt Dylan, she loved him too.

The train crawled along, my mind infused with memories. While there was a new wonder at this friendship, renewed and new all at once, there was also a slight fear: the idea that I'd once been loved by him, however briefly, was intoxicating. I kept imagining another life, and I knew if I allowed myself to stay in that alternate world, I might never come back.

When the train pulled into the station, I tried to back away, explaining I needed to catch another train to my mother's. I didn't escape the hug I'd been trying to avoid. He wrapped his arms around me, cocooning me on that platform, and I tried not to breathe him in. Tried to pretend that nothing had changed.

'Say hi to your mama for me,' he whispered as he let go. 'Tell her I miss those lethal margaritas.'

I nodded, lips pressed together, and then bolted across

the concourse, eager to end this torture. I was going to make it right. Even if it let my mother down.

I sat on the same train we'd always taken, and remembered Dylan's words from earlier. Wondering why we'd never bumped into each other, even though both our parents still lived in the same place. He said he never really came home. Not properly.

'What does that mean?' I'd asked, and he'd sighed.

'Once a month I drive and park outside my dad's. I save up all these things I want to tell him. How well I'm doing at work, some amazing meal I thought he'd like, beating my personal best on Sunday mornings. And I stand outside, looking at the front door for about twenty minutes. And then I drive home.'

'Why?'

'Because however I imagine it's going to be in my head, it's not,' he'd shrugged. 'He'll say something, I'll get pissed off, we'll argue, and it'll be worse than if I never went. I used to wish we had what you and your mama have. But that's not how it works for everyone.'

What did me and my mama have? I trudged along my old road, wondering. Co-dependency, resentment, love, guilt? Loving her more than anything, but fearing becoming her even more?

I paused outside the house, feeling a wave of grief. I conjured the image of my grandmother, sitting under the magnolia tree, our old cat Banana winding around her legs. I thought of the birthday parties and bouncy castles in the back garden and waiting on this front wall for Dylan hundreds of times. Riding our bikes, walking down to the cinema, sneaking out to a party.

All of those memories would be gone.

I could visualise Mama's face, trying to hide her disappointment as I apologised. The desperation as she'd start looking at one-bedroom flats to stay near her friends, or moving all the way out of town with no support system. How she'd try to pretend she was happy about it, because she didn't want me to feel bad. God, I was already exhausted.

I put my key in the lock and could smell food cooking in the kitchen, the warmth permeating down the hall. She was playing music loudly, and I could hear her singing along, laughing. Maybe I didn't have to tell her today? Maybe I could just let her be happy for a little longer? Then tomorrow I could go to the bank about a loan.

I heard Mama's laugh again as I rounded the corner. She stood sprinkling salt into a pan as my father put his arms around her waist, kissing her neck. I had seen them like this before, of course, but weirdly, never when they were married. It was only after he'd left that he started showing her affection, acting like he loved her. That had been before my grandmother lived with us. Before we promised ourselves we deserved better than men who would use us up and throw us away. And yet, here he was again.

I snapped, walking through to turn off the radio, watching as Mama jumped.

'Alyssa—' she went to make excuses, pulling her dressing gown around her. I watched the emotions chasing each other across her face. Shame, embarrassment, uncertainty, denial. Hope? She looked so happy, and I hated her for it.

'I can't tell who's more stupid, you or me,' I told her.

'Alyssa, don't talk to your mother like that,' he tried to step in, but I laughed in his face.

'You don't get to talk to me.' I turned back to Mama, meeting her eyes. 'It's definitely me, it's definitely me who's the idiot. Because I am out there compromising myself, doing everything I can to get the money to pay *this man* so you can keep your home. So that you can keep your independence and your history and your connection to your family. And you still choose him!'

'Alyssa—' Mama was horrified, her eyes wide, but I saw the anger there too.

'You know he never loved you, never loved us, right? It's a power thing. The same way it was about coming back around when he divorced you. Now he's taking your home, and you do this?'

I couldn't bear to look at her. What was I fighting for? I had been picking up the pieces he left behind for years, and she still kept going back for more. Still letting me fix everything, like I was the adult.

'Alyssa, what your mother and I have . . .' he started again, and I looked at him.

'Where does your wife think you are?' I asked, disgusted. 'Are your kids waiting for you at home, desperate for your attention, like I was when you were out fucking someone else?'

'That's not fair, Alyssa.'

I threw up my hands. 'You're an adult. Your actions have consequences, deal with it.'

On the edge of frustrated tears, angrier than I had ever been in my life, I turned to my mother.

'Do you know what I had to do to try and get that money? Money you were going to give *him?* The people I was willing to hurt, because I wanted you to be happy? No, you didn't, because you didn't ask. You just wanted me to fix it. The way I always have.'

I watched the tears roll down my mother's face as she stepped away from him, horrified at the look in my eyes. 'I'm ashamed of you, and *Yiayia* would be too. Keep your house, lose it, move back in with him. Do what the fuck you want, I don't care any more.'

I walked out of the door, slammed it behind me, and made it three streets over before I burst into tears.

The problem, of course, was that there was only one person who would understand this. Dylan.

I couldn't call him. I wanted to run to him and let him be that person for me again. I wanted to stop thinking about the fact that he'd loved me, that if I'd been a bit braver, it could be me sitting with him in a flat across town. It could be me who made dinner while he opened wine and asked for my opinion on his business. It could have been a whole life, one that didn't end in me sitting with mascara running down my face on the train back to my dingy little flat alone.

Thank you for today. So many more than 5 things. A x

I left the text sitting unsent for a few moments, wondering whether it was OK. Whether it was safe. But it was better than calling.

Oh God, there was no need for the money any more. There was no need to do any of this. I could stop all of it.

I pressed the call button, suddenly possessed.

When the call was answered, I didn't even pause to listen.

'Dyl, it's—'

'Alyssa!' Nicki yelled down the phone in extreme excitement, 'it's so good to hear from you!'

Did I call Nicki's number?

I looked down at the phone in my hand, but it said his name. 'Sorry to interrupt, Nicki, just calling about some changes to the presentation template. Is Dylan there?'

Sometimes I scared myself with how quickly and easily I could lie. My hands were starting to shake.

'Oh . . . he's taking a shower, darling, had a bit of a brutal workout, if you know what I mean?' She laughed, and I felt my stomach clench painfully. She adopted a whisper, 'I want to say thank you. Whatever you said to him, or whatever's going on. He's so much more positive about all the romance and marriage stuff. It's like it doesn't scare him any more! He's his old self again! And I'm going to get him some proper media training. Maybe Tola could recommend someone?'

I went on autopilot. 'Yep, absolutely. Happy to help.'

'OK, darling, well, I don't want him doing more work tonight, and we're about to have dinner. Dylan's trying to put in a no phones at the dinner table policy. Isn't that cute?'

'Super cute. Speak soon,' I said vaguely, and listened as she hung up.

It was then that I reached into my bag for my brush and my makeup, shook out my hair from the elastic band and put on lipstick, anticipating the juddering movement of the carriage like a Londoner with years of experience.

I stopped by my flat to change, downed a vodka with the dregs of orange juice left in the carton, and headed straight back out again.

I needed something for me. Something to remember how to feel good again. To remember what I was working towards. So I slipped into Zidario's dimly lit entrance off a side street in Tottenham Court Road, and felt myself relax at a corner table in the dark basement room.

It wasn't the most opulent of my favourite restaurants, but it was comfortable, the deep red plush carpets, and the brickwork walls, like sitting in a cave, cocooned away from the world. The waiter didn't even blink when I asked for a table for one. I ordered a huge glass of Malbec, a steak so rare it might try running off the plate, and some dauphinoise potatoes. Because today of all days, I damn well deserved potatoes cooked in cream and butter.

I got out my book, and tried to settle into that meditative space. Self-care, self-love. Treat yo'self. I knew how to do this. But after reading the same line for the fifth time, and finding most of my wine glass drained before my food had arrived, I had to admit: this wasn't working.

I didn't feel better. I kept looking around for something to distract me, to save me. I was looking for my friends. I wanted to tease Eric and joke when Tola called something old school. I wanted to make up what people were saying across the room with Dylan and I wanted Ben to take the wine I ordered from my hand and replace it with something infinitely better that he'd tell me to sip and savour. I wanted to sit in a corner with Priya and laugh about the dumb things the guys said all day when they thought she had her music playing.

My feel-good system was broken. I didn't feel anonymous and powerful and clever.

I just felt alone.

Chapter Eighteen

I had a new work rule: do your fucking job, and absolutely nothing else.

I was not there to ask about people's families or make them feel special. I wasn't there to organise birthday cakes, or soothe bruised egos or cajole or comfort. I wasn't there to cover up for my superiors' failings or try to fix the company's old boys' club culture. I was just there to do my job.

It seemed to throw everyone at first, how I could seem so friendly, I could still smile and look pleasant but I kept saying 'no'. I didn't even say sorry. It was simply: 'Oh, no, I can't.'

The first time she heard it, Tola stood up from her desk like she was a gazelle who'd got scent of a predator. Felix frowned. Hunter backed away. Matthew looked hurt.

Head down, headphones on, smile pasted on my face – I could do this. It was what I needed to stop thinking about Nicki and Dylan and their cute phone-free dinners. About the fact he'd never messaged me back. About the look on my mother's face as I told her she was pathetic.

'Aly?' I looked up and was surprised to see Becky

standing in front of me, fiddling with that engagement ring on her finger, the way she'd been doing ever since she got the damn thing. 'Do you have a minute?'

'Not really—' I started, but the tears pooled, and I sighed, gesturing for her to take a seat. 'What's up?'

She pulled her hands through her hair and took a shaky breath, leaning forward to whisper. 'I'm wondering if any of it's real, you know? Like, I tricked him into getting engaged, so does he actually want this?'

I closed my eyes, frowning at the headache approaching. 'But I did what you wanted, Becky. You wanted him to be more open to the idea.'

'I know but ... is he going to resent me? In ten years' time is he going to look back and say *I never wanted this*? He's been so worried about the money we're spending on the wedding, and ...'

I could feel myself winding up to explode. I did what they wanted. They asked me for help, for communication and support and advice and then ... it wasn't good enough? And, of course, she was echoing my doubts about Dylan. Clearly, I'd been wrong in that department anyway. Because he was happy enough to share his secrets with me and then jump straight back into Nicki's bed, getting everything he needed.

'Becky, I'm sorry you feel guilty about actually getting the things you want, but I'm afraid I've got bigger problems right now.'

'Oh.' She looked hurt, and stood up, clutching her hands like she was afraid of what I'd do next. 'Of course, I'm sorry to have wasted your time.'

I winced, but put my headphones back in and looked at my screen. When I shifted my gaze slightly, I noticed Tola stood in front of my desk, arms crossed, foot tapping. I shook my head and kept my gaze focused on the screen.

She pulled off my headphones, and tried to take my hand. 'Lunch.'

'Not hungry.'

'Don't care, you need fresh air and you need your friends.'

I laughed. 'You wouldn't even be my friend if not for the Fixer Upper.'

Tola looked me up and down, before she said slowly, 'I can see you're going through something right now, so I'm not going to hold you accountable for the bullshit you're spouting. But I've been trying to be your friend since the day I started here. It's you who holds people at a distance, not me. Now get your bag and come the fuck on.'

She tilted her head at Eric, who jumped up and met us at the lift, completely silent as we stepped in.

'Are you mute now?' I asked him.

'Nope, just trying not to antagonise the crazy lady in a confined space,' he said, blinking at me.

And then he smiled and looked so concerned for me that my stomach hurt.

'See, that's the look you get when I'm being kind, so I try not to be!' he yelped, watching my eyes fill with tears.

'Good call.' I swallowed, looking up at the ceiling until I felt confident that I wasn't going to cry.

We walked to the little park around the back of the office, down the backstreets of Oxford Circus. I loved that about London, the hidden moments of green, little pockets of joy. In summer we'd see them suddenly full, bodies lying everywhere, tanning, reading books, until you could barely see the grass beneath them. For now, the sun shone weakly and I pulled my jumper over my fingertips. Tola and I waited as Eric fetched coffees and pastries, sitting on the bench and not saying anything. It was nice to be silent together.

'I'm sorry I said that, about you not being my friend. It's just, I know you want more from me with the Fixer Upper and I don't know I can give it.'

Tola frowned in surprise, tapping her canary-yellow nails on her jeans.

'So what, you think I'll drop you if I don't get what I want? I don't do things I don't wanna do, Aly. I don't hang out with people who aren't fun. I don't date people who don't give me butterflies.' She looked almost offended that I didn't know that. 'And if I started thinking that my friends only want me around because of what I can do for them, then I'd tell them to fuck off.'

I nodded, looking at the floor.

'We love you because of who you are, not because you're a master manipulator who could make us millions.' Tola's voice softened into humour.

'I *guess*,' I said grouchily and half smiled.

She huffed, 'Millennials need to go to therapy, good God.'

I laughed, more from surprise than anything else, and nudged her, smiling as Eric approached.

'Budge up, let me join the party,' he said, sliding onto the edge of the bench and handing us our coffees. 'So ... we are gathered here today to figure out what the hell is up with Aly,' Eric said solemnly. 'Even though no one has asked me about my relationship issues in *days*, and I have things to share. But first, will this finally be the week Aly opens up to her friends and trusts them to be there? Stay tuned to find out.'

I nudged him. 'You dork. What's happening with Ben?'

'Nope!' Tola held up a hand. 'You know he's weak and wants to be the centre of attention. We are focusing on *you*. No escape. What's happening?'

I couldn't tell them about Dylan. That it terrified me to find out the truth. That I couldn't stop thinking about it.

Instead, I chose the more pressing issue.

'My mum was going to have to sell her house . . .' I said, then shook my head. I'd have to go back further than that. I'd have to explain their whole fucked-up situation, and what that house meant, and how my father manipulated her.

So I did. I told them the truth. I told them why I needed the money, and that I called Nicki to make a new deal. I told them about the hundred grand. I explained what I saw at Mama's last night, and the things I'd said and how ashamed I felt.

And then I sat there before them, completely vulnerable, waiting to be judged.

'That's so shit.'

'I'm sorry, Aly, that must be so hard to deal with on your own.'

It was the kindness that got me, once again. I closed my eyes and tried to stop the tears leaking out.

'I said some awful things.'

'Were they untrue?' Tola asked, rubbing my back like I was a child talking about a nightmare.

I shook my head. 'But they were designed to hurt her.

I wanted to wake her up. I've been trying to wake her up for years.'

They curled themselves around me, protecting me, knowing me. Accepting all without question. Well, there was one question.

'A hundred grand, though,' Tola whistled. 'That's some top-level bullshit. I love it.'

I shrugged. 'I don't. I just wanted to do something good and hang out with you guys in the process. I didn't want all of this . . . mess.'

'Are we *sure* we don't want to carry on fixing Dylan and then we can all go on a really nice holiday? Like whatever's fancier than first-class kind of holiday. I'm only half joking.' Eric grinned at me and squeezed my shoulders. I tried to smile.

'What can we do, my lovely?' he asked, so intensely earnest that I felt a bit odd.

I wiped my eyes. 'You can forgive me.'

'For what?!'

I met his eyes. 'I introduced you to Ben. What's going to happen when this is all over, Eric? What if you've met *your person* and I've turned you into a liar before you've even gotten started?'

Eric tilted his head and smiled at me. 'All the best romances start with a few well-placed lies. And I wouldn't worry too much about me and Ben being the love story of the century anyway. He's putting a few roadblocks in without any help from you.'

Apparently there were wobbles on the road to true love and co-ownership of a sassy beagle.

261

'What does that mean?'

'He won't date me because I'm a baby gay,' Eric huffed, 'but he wants us to be friends. Just my luck for this to happen when I finally find someone who's hot and smart and kind and funny and has good dress sense and is a dog person . . .'

'What's a baby gay?' I asked.

'Ben's been out forever, right?' Tola asked, and Eric pointed at her.

'Exactly.'

'Whereas you . . .'

'I was engaged to a woman for three years, have only been in a relationship with a woman and only my immediate family members know I'm gay.' Eric splayed his hands. 'Baby gay.'

'That's not your fault!' I yelped. 'He's being unfair!'

'He thinks I need time to figure myself out before jumping into something.'

'You've been figuring yourself – and other people – out for a year and a half! What more does he want?' I asked, completely affronted.

Eric glanced at Tola. 'Uh-oh, we woke the beast.'

'No, I'm being serious,' I replied, taking his hand. 'You are wonderful. You're funny and smart and handsome and loyal, and you've been wanting a real connection with someone, and you find it and he feels the same way but you don't have enough experience for him? What the hell is that?!'

Eric looked concerned. 'Aly, breathe. You've got problems enough right now, I was just having a moan. We're going to hang out as friends, and my animal magnetism will win him over. There's only so long you can pretend to be friends with someone when you really want to jump them.'

Tola looked at him and burst out laughing, then tilted her head towards me.

'Unless you're Aly, then you can survive that way for at least ten years.'

I really didn't want to laugh, but I couldn't help it.

'You guys are the worst.'

'Lies, terrible, terrible lies,' Eric said, giving me a brown paper bag. 'Now stick this doughnut in your mouth and cheer the hell up. We've got our first Matthew-run meeting this afternoon, and without you to run to, Hunter has been coaching him. It's marionette theatre in there, and we're going to need a robust sense of humour.'

Thank goodness for my friends. I had no idea what I'd do without them.

The key to happiness was avoidance and a smile.

Avoiding my mother's phone calls. And texts and emails and voice messages. Hanging up on my father and blocking his number. Letting Tola take the lead on the remaining Fixer Upper sessions and ignoring her when she asked about booking more in. When she asked what I wanted to do about Dylan.

Dylan, who kept appearing in his girlfriend's photos and videos online, peering over her shoulder, kissing her cheek, making her giggle. Doing exactly what I'd wanted him to. Dylan, who messaged me every single night with his list of five things for the day, and number five was always *That we're friends again*. He was killing me. I was right back where I'd been all those years ago, watching him be the perfect boyfriend to another girl, helping him do it, and pretending I didn't care.

I needed to put this energy into myself.

I didn't want anything else to do with the Fixer Upper. I couldn't keep wearing some parts of myself like a suit of armour.

I had to call this off. I had to tell Nicki we were done with all of this. I would help Dylan with his business stuff, Nicki would take what she'd learnt from us and keep beavering away at making him what she wanted (maybe she'd succeed), and I'd get to keep my friend. And maybe lose this sick feeling in my stomach where that betrayal sat.

It was time to face the KLP and be prepared for her claws.

I was writing a plan of attack, a carefully curated bullet-point list (*How To Get Out Of This Bloody Mess*) when Eric called. I answered with suspicion.

'You don't call me at the weekends. Are you OK?'

'Please, please don't say no,' he begged, and I was immediately on edge. I put down my pen.

'What?'

'Nicki has invited us all glamping.'

'Glamping. Right.' I blinked. 'Why?'

'She thinks it would be – and I quote – a *super-fun bonding experience.*'

'And why do you know about this but I don't?' I snorted, tapping my notepad with my pen.

'Because she wanted to invite you, but I asked if I could do it,' he sighed, 'because I knew you'd say no.'

I closed my eyes briefly, looking around the coffee shop

and wondering if any other clientele were currently battling intrusive influencers who wanted to take you on fancy holidays. Probably not.

'And why would I say no?' *Of course I'm saying no.*

'Ugh, I don't know, morals or some other ridiculousness? Aly, come on. I need this.'

'You need this?' I laughed, taking a sip of my coffee. 'You need to go glamping with a reality TV star slash heiress. Because ...'

'Because Ben's going. And my current plan relies on proximity.'

'And this plan is ...'

'To hang out with him until he caves and sleeps with me again. And then keep sleeping with him until he falls in love with me.'

I exhaled. 'Oh good, completely nuts, excellent. Why do I need to go? Go without me. Godspeed.'

'Because I need you, OK? I need the support. I am doing what you said: fighting for my man. And if you don't come, I'm going to cave. I need you to help me be brave, OK?'

I smiled, feeling a little teary. 'You need me?'

He laughed.

'How is that surprising? I am throwing myself at your mercy. Please help me trick this man into loving me.'

'No trickery, no fixing—' I started.

'I know, I'm joking,' he said warmly. 'I need moral support, that's all. I love Tola, but she's young and people fall all over themselves to date her; she doesn't get what it means, how rare this stuff is when you find it. Us oldies have got to stick together.'

I exhaled slowly, rubbing my forehead. 'Eric . . . the stuff with Dylan and Nicki—'

'I know, it's awkward, and you feel weird about it, and you want to call the whole thing off. But they are super loved up right now. Like she could not stop going on about him on the phone. She's really happy. He's really happy. They've got their big presentation, it's all happening the way you planned.'

I'm not sure it is.

But it was true, social media told the story of the UK's most beautiful, enamoured couple. There he was in her bed, naked from the waist up, breakfast tray settled next to him, hair looking perfectly mussed. He'd clearly stopped overthinking, stopped worrying they weren't right for each other. The perfect boyfriend was back again, and I knew I should have been happy, but it killed me a little.

'You really need me to do this?' I asked, dreading his answer.

'Please, this is *it*. Love, white fences, marriage, beagles. Morning coffee and matching pyjamas and getting old and wrinkly together. He's my someone, Aly.'

It was the first time I'd heard Eric that sincere. And that vulnerable.

'Well . . . fuck. Like I can say no after that, you utter bastard.'

I heard him sigh in relief, and then laugh.

'Good, we go on Thursday.'

'If I take more time off, Felix will kill me.'

'You know why he won't?' Eric replied. 'Because it's your entitled holiday, you're not a senior staff member and, oh yeah, *you're allowed to have a life*. If he wanted you to be chained to your desk, he should have incentivised you when he had the chance.'

I sat up, as if he'd just shaken some sense into me. 'You're right. Thank you. Yeah! OK, this could be fun. Glamping with an heiress. At least it's a story, right?'

And a chance for me to have a one-to-one chat with Nicki and put this whole thing to bed once and for all. Operation Unfix It.

'One we'll be telling our kids!' Eric laughed, suddenly energised. 'OK, I've gotta go shopping! I need something that says *I'm crazy about you and I'm out and proud, and also I'm good at being in nature.*'

I laughed, 'Erm . . . your birthday suit?'

'World enough and time, sweetheart. See you tomorrow!'

Chapter Nineteen

Two days later, I sat on my front step waiting for them to pick me up, scrolling through social media. I had six missed calls from my mother already that morning, and a bunch of messages I hadn't opened. It was too raw and, quite frankly, I wanted to stay angry. I wanted to punish her a little longer.

I kept returning to that photo of Nicki and Dylan in bed, their perfect breakfast tray, the adoring smiles on their faces. I couldn't figure out what about it was disturbing me. Was it a weird filter, had they photoshopped it?

It took me a minute to realise – there was no St Christopher around his neck. Since his mum died, I'd never seen him without it. And she'd told him she didn't like it, that it didn't fit her brand. Maybe this was real for him then, he'd completely thrown himself in head-first, no doubts. No excuses. Just like I'd told him to. It should have been a win.

He wanted us to be like we were when we were kids, but I couldn't do that. I needed distance, space. Some time to figure out how to be this version of myself with him. Not to give everything away and let him … be Dylan. He couldn't be the most important person in my life this time round.

Best to take a step back, be professional, not let him get too close.

Which wasn't likely to be easy in a tent …

I heard a car honking loudly and looked up in shock. It was a goddamn limousine. I had severely underestimated this lifestyle, clearly. But hey, I'd wanted a good story to tell. I painted on a smile and hiked my bag over my shoulder as I stood.

'Hi, guys!'

They waved, all of them inside, already drinking bubbly and playing music entirely too loudly.

The driver took my backpack and put it in the boot, and I immediately regretted my practical clothes, as I'd known I would.

I slid into the car, the disco lights blinding me slightly, and laughed at them, dazed.

'Are we going glamping or are we American teenagers going to the prom?' I said, and Ben winked as he handed me a glass of Prosecco.

'This is just for effect,' Nicki said, smiling too widely at me, that mermaid-to-piranha vibe emanating from her. She draped herself around Dylan. 'I want you guys to feel special. To know how much I truly appreciate you, and everything you've done for Dylan and Ben.'

I looked around. 'No Priya?'

Nicki pouted, but covered it with a smile. 'Childcare issues.'

'And she'd rather eat glass than go camping,' Ben supplied.

'I told you, it's *glamping*,' Nicki started, and Dylan put an arm around her.

'And she's going to be very jealous when we're all having a lovely time and she's missing out,' he placated her, and she looked at him with such gratitude and relief that I was a little stunned. Who was the real Fixer Upper here?

'Besides, I thought it would be so nice for us all to hang out together, before the big presentation and it all coming to an end!' Nicki said innocently, and I looked at her, trying to figure out what was happening.

'Before the most stressful meeting of our life is over?' Dylan laughed, pulling Nicki in for a hug. 'I don't think we're going to be upset at that being done, babe. In fact, if I never have to wear a suit and do a presentation again, it'll be too soon.'

Nicki frowned, quizzical. 'But you look great in a suit.'

'He also looks great in jeans, it's really unfair,' Ben said, and everyone laughed. 'But at least that way I don't feel like I'm about to be told off by the big boss.'

'But ... he *is* the big boss,' Nicki frowned again, before smoothing out her forehead.

'I think what Ben means is, once we've got this funding, we won't have to worry too much about the look of things any more. Hopefully, we'll have the backing to do what we want, to build stuff that matters. And we can do that looking mighty fine in jeans and a T-shirt.'

'And in a less expensive office.' Ben smiled pointedly, and I wondered why he thought now was the right time to push this issue. Nicki looked aghast.

'Well,' I smiled, 'definitely something to chat about when

270

the time comes, but you never know how life can change when these deals come in! So here's to success!' I held up my glass, and everyone joined in.

Dylan sent me a grateful look, and Nicki looked between us, suddenly suspicious.

'It's such a shame we won't all be hanging out like this after the presentation,' she said again, and I realised immediately what she meant. She wanted me out of the picture. She didn't want the proof of her subterfuge sitting around with a loaded gun after she got what she wanted. At any time, I could turn on her, tell Dylan the truth, destroy her relationship. Of course she wanted me far, far away.

I clearly wasn't the only person scheming on this trip.

Nicki was looking at Dylan like he was everything she wanted, and when she looked at me, it was like I wasn't the person onside any more ... I was the one standing in the way of it all. She *knew*. She knew I wanted to call the whole thing off.

There wasn't enough air in the limousine, and I could feel every bump in the road as we sped along. Surely we couldn't get on the motorway in this thing? I needed fresh air and a place to hide.

I felt Tola's eyes on me, and I smiled, trying to let her know everything was fine, even as the nausea made me shake.

'Here,' Dylan passed back a bottle of lemonade, trying to catch my eye. 'Should help with the carsickness.'

I nodded, sipping gratefully.

'You get carsick, Aly?' Eric frowned, and suddenly I felt their eyes on me. 'You've never been ill in my car.'

'Only on the motorway,' Dylan said, and the car was silent for a moment.

I rallied and looked over at Eric. 'Besides, I puke in the glovebox of your car when you're not looking. You know, just to be polite.'

That smoothed it over, but still, Nicki was watching me as though she didn't like what she saw.

I looked at Dylan, and I knew he was thinking the same thing – he hadn't told Nicki about our friendship when we first met, how could he tell her now? What a mess. I glared at Eric, because obviously this was all his fault.

'What?' he hissed at me, and I pointed at my phone as I texted him.

If I'm not maid of honour at your wedding after this, I'm never speaking to you again.

Of course, the glamping site was unlike anything I'd ever seen. It was Instagrammable, an influencer's dream, and obviously they were prepared for Nicki's arrival. It was all porters and luxury cabins, little pastel bicycles parked at different stops. We were driven in golf carts around the grounds, shown the different events available, and the woodland spa, until we were finally deposited outside our yurts.

I'd been camping before, on school trips, and with my family abroad. At festivals with Dylan. This was a world away from all that.

Our names were on the tents, and I noted with interest that Ben and Eric were sharing. Tola and I shared a look with Nicki, who wiggled her eyebrows and smiled, and for a moment, it felt like everything would be all right.

And then Dylan looked at their names on the plank of wood outside the biggest bell tent. 'Wow, the honeymoon suite!'

'Maybe it's good inspiration!' Nicki said coyly, fluttering her lashes at him. I held my breath, wondering how he'd react. That pressure, so casually mentioned. He'd been a world away from that when we talked. And yet, something must have changed, because Dylan laughed, threw her over his shoulder, slapped her on the behind, and disappeared into the tent.

I wanted to throw up, not from motion sickness this time.

'You did it! Somehow you did it!' Tola grabbed my hand and pulled me inside the yurt. 'What did you do, what changed?'

I shrugged. 'They needed a little room to understand each other, I think.'

'The Fixer Upper strikes again!' Tola tipped an imaginary hat, but I shook my head sadly.

'I don't think it was me.'

'I bet it was.'

I didn't want to take credit. Dylan was happy, Nicki was happy, the presentation would go well, and then I would fade out to stage left. I couldn't stay his friend, Nicki wouldn't allow it. It compromised her. And Dylan would make the choice that made her happy. He'd survived all this time without me, he didn't need me. We'd be those people who occasionally liked each other's social posts. That would be fine.

Tola and I looked around the room for a moment, taking it all in. Two beautiful four-poster beds dominated the room, covered in knitted throws, each with a treat basket ready with our names and a card welcoming us. There were hammocks and chairs and a little changing area behind a painted room divider. In the centre of the yurt hung a huge chandelier. It was beautiful.

And then I heard Nicki giggle.

'Let's jump in the hot tub and order fancy cocktails from cute barmen?' Tola offered, patting my hand in sympathy.

'I think I'm gonna go for a run first,' I said. While I was changing, my phone rang.

'It's your mum,' Tola yelled, 'shall I answer it?'

'No.'

'Come on, eventually you're gonna . . .'

'Eventually, T. On my terms, OK? I'm not ready yet.'

She held her hands up as I emerged in my running gear. 'Fair enough. So you're just going to leave me here like the limp lettuce, sandwiched between two shagging couples?'

I laughed. 'You're very good at making your own fun. By the time I've come back, you'll have charmed all the staff and made a group of lifelong friends at the bar.'

'True,' she nodded, surveying her fingernails. 'Fine, go if you must, but no calling work.'

I held up my hands. 'That's the old me. New me is not that person.'

'Good to hear it, babe. Though, for the record, I liked old you too.'

'You're the only one.' I shook my head, disappearing from the tent.

I'd never really liked running. It was something I did because it was good for me, because it felt like being a grown-up. Because it was important to do things you didn't like and just get the hell on with it. But being away from Nicki and Dylan, unhooking that clasped feeling in my chest, that guilt in my stomach ... running was the best thing I could have done. The grounds were beautiful and with each inhale I felt a little more in control, a little more like myself. I nodded and smiled as I passed a few others running together in the other direction.

Maybe I should join a running club? Maybe that's where I'd been going wrong, with the solo dining and the insistence I could do everything on my own? Maybe actually what I needed was other people. Friendly faces and mindless conversation as we all moved in the same direction. Separate but united. Feeling like a part of something, but still feeling like myself.

When I arrived back and had my shower, I felt calmer, like I wasn't about to shake apart at the seams. But Tola wasn't in the tent, and when I ventured outside and round the back, I found her setting up the hot tub.

There was champagne chilling in a bucket on the side, an array of snacks on a side table, and two fluffy robes. I looked at her. 'You got a hot date I don't know about?'

She pointed at me. 'I told you one day I was gonna crack that head open and see what was inside.' She gestured to the hot tub. 'That time is now.'

I considered fighting, but at this point, I was too tired. I changed into my bikini and came back out, slipping into the warm water with a sigh. She topped up my glass and got in too, clinking our glasses.

'It's not too shabby, this rich-girl lifestyle,' she said. 'I think I could manage it.'

'I think you'd do fabulously.' I smiled at her, but caught that glint in her eye. 'Uh-oh.'

'Yup,' she agreed, 'enough avoidance. What the hell is going on with you?'

'I told you the stuff with my mum ...'

Tola nodded. 'And I'm super-honoured that you trusted us with that. But that's not what I'm talking about. And it's not work or the promotion. I don't even think it's the Fixer Upper.'

Quite the number of messes to choose from. I sunk down until the water was up to my chin. 'OK then, smarty pants, what's it all about?'

'Dylan James.'

I looked around in panic, as if she'd conjured him, but she waved her hand. 'They're all in the forest bar getting cocktails. That's why I wanted us to have a chance to talk *alone*. Because you aren't great at ... feelings.'

I frowned. 'That's not true.'

'Oh, don't get me wrong, you're excellent at other people's, knowing what makes them tick, how they think, why they're hurting. But I think you're not being honest with yourself or with us. Why's it different with this project, Aly? Why is *this* the one that's breaking you?'

I pressed my lips together, sighed deeply.

'Because it's him.'

Tola nodded.

'He loved me, back then. I'd loved him, and he loved me, and I fucked it up because I was afraid ...' I rubbed my forehead. 'And I can't stop thinking about it. I can't stop thinking about what would have happened, and if we'd still be together now, and if . . . if we would have been happy.'

'Happier than he is with her?'

I winced, thrashing in the water. 'I *made* this happen. I told him what he needed to hear, what he needed to do, and now look at them, they're perfect! I did exactly what I was meant to do, and it *kills me*.' Once I'd started, I couldn't stop. 'Because I don't get to keep him. You know what this trip is to Nicki? A last hurrah, so she can get rid of the evidence. You don't keep around the person who cleans up the dead body.'

Tola quirked a smile. 'Melodramatic. So you're gonna tell Nicki it's all off?'

I nodded, gulping down my champagne and waiting as Tola refilled it. 'Yes, I'm gonna call it off. I'll help Dylan with his presentation because he's my friend, and then I will fade into the background. Maybe I can prove to her I'm not a threat, in time. She can't out me without outing herself, after all.'

'And we're back into the plotting and scheming and controlling!' Tola yelped, frustrated. 'Aly, you're honestly telling me you're not going to fight for your man?'

'He's not mine. And he's happy!'

'Because you made him that way!' Tola said. 'He knew you got carsick on the motorway. He knows when you need to be taken away for the day, he knows what to ask you to make you feel better. When have you *ever* had that from one of those projects you dated? When have you ever let one of them know you enough to look after you?'

I looked at her, frozen in horror. How didn't I see it all along? I took a deep breath and laughed.

'Damn, Tola. Two shots straight to the chest. Savage.'

She snorted at that, holding up her glass in recognition of her triumph.

'Tough love is a good kinda love, and I don't think you have anyone else in your life to offer it. Because they're all too scared of you.' She grinned. 'But I see you. Also, you are very pretty and nice and deserve good things. So there. It's a love sandwich.'

'But do you think I'm doing the right thing, with Dylan?'

'Oh, absolutely not. I've never gone in for self-sacrifice-for-the-greater-good thing. Being miserable for the sake of it isn't really my brand, you know? And it's arrogant to think you know how he feels about you.'

'I know how he feels about Nicki.'

Tola rolled her eyes. 'Well, I wouldn't have approved anyway. Loving someone you kissed *once* when you were eighteen. You don't even know if the sex would be good. What a waste.'

I splashed her, laughing as I closed my eyes. If nothing else, I had good friends. Excellent, ridiculous, real friends.

'So can I bring up something while you're in this super-chilled state of being, with me as your spiritual guide?' Tola assumed a saintly expression.

'I'm not gonna like this, am I?'

'Well, that positive attitude lasted about thirty seconds!' she huffed. 'We've gotta talk about what we're doing with the FU, babe. I don't think we should be fixing men for women.'

'You think we should be teaching them how to do it directly, efficiently? Like a "teach a man to fish" approach?' I asked.

'No, I think we should be teaching women that they deserve better.'

Like Amy and her writer boy. Of course.

Tola was so striking most of the time, but I'd never seen her like this: almost bare-faced, glowing with booze and the light of the water, smiling at me with determination. None of her style to distract from the glorious substance. It might have been my stupid skill that launched the idea, but it was Tola, her vision, her drive that had brought us here. And it could be her who took us in a new direction.

'You know I've got four sisters, right?' Tola said, and I nodded.

'One of them married a nice guy, just *one* of them. And even he's pretty useless,' she laughed, shaking her head. 'But it's like they put up with it, for love. For someone to look at them and own them and demand things from them, for the rest of their lives. They all wanted so badly to be chosen . . . and now it's like it's normal. It's normal to belittle the person you marry, and expect them to be a crap dad and a lazy partner and not expect more of them or more for you? I don't wanna be like that, babe. And I don't want any other women to be like that either.'

I nodded.

'Well . . . I *did* like telling that girl her stupid boyfriend wanted her to be eaten by sharks . . .' I said, 'but I don't wanna be a PI, dealing with cheating and stuff. What are you suggesting? We become relationship counsellors?'

'I'm suggesting we do something that writes women as the main characters in their own stories,' she nodded at me, wiggling her eyebrows, like she was trying to sell me something. 'Sounds good, right?'

I took a moment to think about it, considering all those projects I'd dated, and what I would have done differently. What life would look like if I wasn't pretending to be a different main character, that New York woman eating alone. What would it look like if I was just me, if they were just them?

'Saying no,' I said suddenly, thinking of Mama. 'Building self-esteem, rebuilding after damaging relationships. Equipping them with the language to ask for pay rises and promotions.'

Tola bit her lip and nodded. '*Now* we're talking.'

'But that's so many things! There's so many things we could do . . . what is it actually going to look like, this vision of yours?'

She grinned and shrugged. 'I don't know yet – stay tuned for more news as it arrives. But when it does, I want you with me.'

When it got too hot, we pulled ourselves out and sat on the edge, looking at the darkening sky.

'Can I ask you something?'

'You can try,' she smiled.

'The way you are . . . how *good* you are with yourself. The confidence, the drinks from strangers, the people fawning all over you – has it always been this easy for you?'

She thought about it. 'I have my moments, my wobbles. But I feel best when I'm being true to myself. Doesn't mean

I don't feel vulnerable sometimes, doesn't mean I don't worry that my friends will get tired of me. I know I'm a lot for some people. I can be painfully honest at the wrong time, I can hurt people. I don't always get it right. But, no, I don't have shame or regret in my choices.'

She flickered, and I had to know what that exception was. 'What?'

'I mean ... there are a few regrets, I guess. I have this mate, and we like each other. We've liked each other for a long time, messed each other about a bit in the process. But the idea of fucking it up, of losing her in my life, it doesn't seem worth the risk. So we mess around, and then I go off and screw some guy because it's easier, and she pretends she's not hurt and I pretend I'm not annoyed, and we start it all again.'

'Whoa,' I said. 'That sounds ... complicated.'

'Yeah, I'm not a fan of complicated. Not for me, anyway. For rampant over-thinkers and over-feelers, like you and Eric, sure. But I prefer things simple. Primary colours, you know?'

'So what are you going to do?'

'I'm going to avoid it until it's unavoidable. And, I'm going to go dancing. You wanna come?'

I looked up at the stars as she swung her legs out of the hot tub and slipped her feet into her flip flops. 'There'll be dancing and drinks and probably semi-famous people. You in?'

I shook my head. 'You go and have fun. I'm enjoying this quiet time.'

I resisted dunking myself back under the water until

after Tola had left, waving goodbye as she ambled up the path. And then I fully submerged my shoulders, revelling in the warmth after the crispness of the evening air against my skin. I wondered if Tola would come back to the yurt that night or if she'd be swept up in some love affair. An emotional palate-cleanser.

I reached across the tub to top up my glass and sighed in satisfaction, eyes closed. Perfect silence, the dark sky and no worries. No need to pretend to be someone else, no hiding, no secrets.

'Hey, there you are!' I heard a voice, and when I blinked my eyes open, Dylan was pulling his T-shirt over his head. 'The others are dancing at the forest bar, but I wondered where you were. Pour me one of those, would ya?'

I busied myself reaching for a new glass, and filling it, so I didn't have to look at him as he pulled his jeans off. I waited until I heard the splashes before I turned back, smile on my face.

'Why thank you.' He clinked his glass against mine, and sipped, looking around us. 'Well, this is the life.'

'It's certainly very fancy,' I admitted, resting my head on the edge and looking up at the sky again. 'I like feeling small and insignificant. A whole world starting anew every minute. Inconsequential problems.'

'Aly, come on. You could never be insignificant.' Dylan frowned at me like I'd said something wrong.

'I didn't mean it negatively,' I shrugged, my eyes drawn to the lines of his arms as he stretched out.

And then I saw that silver St Christopher around his neck and smiled, relieved.

'What's the smile for?'

I shook my head. 'The fact that some things stay the same. It's comforting.'

He gave me a searching look, bright blue eyes on mine. 'Some things do stay the same, you have no idea.'

I felt my breathing speed up and struggled to look away.

'Five things,' I blurted, like a safe word. Anything to stop him looking at me like that.

Dylan nodded, thinking about it, tapping his fingers on one edge of the hot tub. I put my drink down and pulled my legs up under me, cuddling my knees.

'The view from the skywalk,' he said slowly, like he was carefully curating his list. 'The little caramel wafers in the gift basket. Seeing Ben finally falling for someone ...' He raised an eyebrow at me, a look of mischief crossing his features before bringing his finger to his lips. 'Shh, it's a secret.'

My grin was impossible to stop. I nodded.

'That's three,' I prompted, waiting for him to mention Nicki, throwing her over his shoulder, spending the day with her. The person who made this all possible. Falling more in love with her by the day.

'The bartender who made me an incredibly strong cocktail with a twenty-year-old rum,' Dylan whispered loudly, and laughed at himself. 'Shh, it's another secret.'

I giggled, shaking my head and watching as he shifted closer, until his arm reached along behind me, until I almost slotted into his side and he was near enough that I was breathing his air. Those eyes still killed me.

'And number one, with a bullet,' he said softly, raising

a hand to trace a piece of hair near my temple, 'is how this one piece of your hair still manages to curl like that, a corkscrew that can't be controlled, even after fifteen years.' His lips quirked, eyes focused on that strand of hair, 'it's a tiny, beautiful miracle.'

My breathing became shallow again, my heart raced, and I closed my eyes. *What the hell are you doing?*

'You're drunk?' I shouldn't have made it a question.

Dylan smiled at me, shrugging one shoulder. 'Doesn't matter, we don't lie about five things,' he said, and then slid back away, reaching for his glass. 'We lie about everything else, but not that.'

'And that's *my* fault?' I asked, clasping my hands into fists under the water to stop them from shaking. '*You're* the one who pretended you didn't know me. *You* started all this.'

'Oh, I know,' he laughed, shaking his head at himself. 'I didn't want to give you the satisfaction, and now I can't say to my girlfriend, *Oh, by the way, darling, this person you introduced me to is actually my best friend.*'

'And she's not intending for us to stay friends when this is all over,' I said thoughtlessly.

'What does that mean?'

I gestured between us, 'She doesn't like this thing. And I don't blame her, because how would you explain two people who hated each other suddenly knowing intimate details about each other's lives?'

'She thinks we slept together?' Dylan blinked, like the idea had never even occurred to him.

'Or that we want to, which is potentially worse.'

He did a double take and frowned at me. 'How is that

worse, Aly? Thinking about something is worse than doing something?'

I breathed slowly. 'Potential is always worse.'

He shook his head again, as if it was the maddest thing he could imagine.

'That's nuts. Besides, you may as well tell me to stop breathing,' he laughed, tipping the last of his champagne down his throat.

'What?'

'Wanting to be with you, it's always there. Like tinnitus or the way my wrists click when I stretch. It's part of me. Some days it's louder and some days it's a whisper, but it's always there. That's what happens when you love someone for fifteen years: it lives in your bones, like an echo.'

I closed my eyes, and my chest contracted.

'I should have asked you exactly *how* drunk you were, shouldn't I?' I stood up to get out, reaching for the robe on the side, while he stared at me.

'What? What did I do?'

'You're being inappropriate,' I whispered, unsure whether I was making a scene.

'Because I fancy you?' he laughed. 'Newsflash, Aly: fancied you for most of our friendship. Didn't stop us being friends. Didn't stop us dating other people.'

'*You*,' I said, '*you* dated other people. And now you're swanning around flirting with me and saying things when you're clearly on your way to making a real commitment to Nicki. That's not good-guy behaviour.'

I saw him take a breath, nod as if getting himself back into character. 'You're right. You're absolutely right. I thought we could get to that flirty friendship straight away, and I was wrong. Sit down. I promise to sober up.'

I lowered myself down carefully, eyeing him.

'So is there someone special in your life? We haven't discussed your love life at all, and you know all about mine,' he said pointedly.

'Dylan.'

'What? I'm being friendly. I'm asking about your relationship, that's what friends do.' He held his hands up.

'I'm not seeing anyone, no.'

Dylan tilted his head. 'Why not?'

'Because it feels like a waste of time right now. Every man I've dated has benefited from being with me, has grown and changed. And I haven't changed at all.'

I'm still here, fifteen years later, looking at you like you're the answer to my problems, too scared to tell you the truth. Because I'm in love with you, still, and it's fucking killing me, you arsehole.

'You've changed,' he said, considering his words carefully. 'You're someone who never found what they were looking for and is patchworking it together instead.'

I didn't want to ask what that meant, whether it was a compliment, why it made me feel as if I wanted to cry. I could only shake my head, and we sat in silence for a moment. Sometimes it was easier to go backwards than to go forwards. That was safest for us, living in nostalgia and not thinking about our future. We didn't have a future.

'Tell me something true, Dyl.'

He made a face, pointing to his pile of clothes. 'Damn. I had a really good one about flamingos, but it's in my jeans back pocket.'

286

He's got another Aly list? My stomach clenched.

'OK, then tell me what's going on with you.'

'I'm—' he went to deny, and I held a finger up.

'Something true.'

'I lied to Nicki about my dad. She wanted to meet him and was so excited about it. I couldn't tell her we don't talk any more.'

'Why?'

'I didn't want to disappoint her. Things have been so good these last couple of weeks. I've been following my Aly advice, just like I always did.' He threw me a grateful smile. 'I'll arrange something and have him mysteriously call to cancel at the last minute.'

'I'm sorry,' I said, and felt his hand reach for mine, squeezing my fingers under the water.

'My fault. Been playing the happy-go-lucky fella for so long, can't expect people to take me seriously straight away.'

He smiled softly, shaking his head at me, and I laughed, letting go of his hand, but he reached for mine again.

I let him, but watched, desperately alert.

'You know I had a really clear plan for what I wanted with my life,' Dylan said suddenly, and I looked at him in surprise. He laughed. 'I know, right? Not like me at all. But these last few years, I had this vision of what my perfect life would look like. Of me running my team and making things that mattered, stuff that made people's lives better. And I'd have like a basic office, nothing fancy but near a good coffee place, and every day I'd have a nice chat with the barista and tip really well and find out what was happening in the area, be part of the community, you know?'

I nodded, closing my eyes as I listened, still holding his hand.

'And I'd have this little house near a park and go running on Sunday mornings. Maybe my dad would come and meet me, and we'd run together like when I was younger, but we wouldn't fight after. And I'd make a huge Sunday roast, have all these friends around me. I'd get a dog, I'd drink sangria in the garden. Paint my living room walls bright orange. List more than five things every day.'

I was getting dizzy.

'Sounds perfect,' I said faintly, feeling his thumb trace my palm, my breathing becoming more shallow. I opened my eyes. 'You're right on track.'

He looked at me. 'Am I?'

'What are you doing here, Dyl?'

His thumb stroked my knuckle, and I looked at him, pleading. But I didn't let go, and I didn't move away.

'I feel like every decision I'm making right now is taking me further away from that life. Sponsored posts and photoshoots and fancy office buildings. Credit cards for holidays and huge bunches of flowers and always, *always* apologising. I'm exhausted, Aly. I'm so tired of pretending.'

The slow strokes up my wrist were killing me. It was too warm, and I was too drunk.

'You said you were happy,' I breathed, and he tilted his head at me.

'I'd forgotten what it was like, how addictive it is,' he said quietly, eyes averted.

'What is?'

'You and me. Having history. Having everything make sense.'

I shook my head, pulled my hand away, and stepped out of the hot tub, wrapping the robe around me.

'Fair enough,' Dylan said, holding his hands up again. 'I broke the rules.'

I crossed my arms, shaking my head at him.

'I know you're just doing the same dance you always did, so I can't really blame you for that, but you can't curl up around her, and make her feel special and make love to her, and then come to me for advice. You can't give her the public boyfriend part of yourself and then save the broken bits for me. I know that was how we always worked, I know. And I'm sorry. But it killed me then, and I won't let it happen again.'

He stood up. 'Aly, I—'

'Don't worry about it. I'm glad we're friends again. Let's keep it that way, OK?'

At that moment, the others stumbled back, giggling together. They stopped when they saw us.

'Ah, Aly and Dylan arguing again. Good, the world has turned back to making sense!' Ben laughed. 'Are we getting in?'

I smiled at him. 'You guys go for it, I'm a shrivelled prune!'

Dylan wore a matching smile, nodding as Nicki asked him if he was OK.

I walked away and didn't look back. The way I should have done right from the beginning.

Chapter Twenty

I woke up with Tola next to me, clutching my arm like a determined koala. I wondered why she hadn't slept in her own king-sized bed, but when I peered over, I saw it was piled high with clothes.

She looked so sweet, gold shimmer eyeshadow smudged across her face, wearing an oversized Guns N'Roses T-shirt. Like an angelic child who'd crawled into her big sister's makeup case. I extracted myself and changed into my running gear, unzipping the tent carefully and finding Nicki already up in full makeup, taking selfies outside the tent.

'Good morning!' she stage-whispered, 'Just getting some shots.'

I took a breath. She looked so normal, suddenly. Like any other woman who'd come to me because her boyfriend didn't see her, or make an effort for her, or want to grow up. But she had someone who did all those things, who tried harder than anyone, and it still wasn't enough.

'Nicki, actually, I was hoping to catch you—'

'Of course, darling, it would be so lovely to have some

one-on-one time, but I've got to get this done, OK?' She knew what I wanted to say, and she was going to put me off for as long as she could.

'It really won't take long,' I said, smiling my shark smile. 'Why don't we go and get some breakfast, just the two of us? Catch up on where we are with our projects?'

That caught her interest. She smiled, a little confused, and nodded.

'Very well, twist my arm. I've given the chef my nutritionist's recipe for buckwheat waffles, so let's hope he knows what he's doing!'

We settled in the garden at a table, Nicki smiling and waving at everyone like she was the bloody queen.

'Sorry, it's so embarrassing but it comes with the territory,' she smiled, eyes back to her phone. I put my hand over the screen, and she looked at me in shock.

'I was hoping we could have a little chat.'

'About Dylan?' she asked, placing the phone on the table, but continuing to look at it like it might hold the answers to the universe.

'About Dylan.'

Nicki finally nodded and gave me her full attention.

'You've made good progress, I'll give you that.' She sipped her green smoothie thoughtfully. 'When I saw how much he *hated* you at the beginning, I had my doubts, but it seems as if the two of you found some common ground?'

'I don't ...'

'I mean, he's been so loving and attentive recently, so I have to credit that to you.' She smirked at me. 'All those long sessions working on the presentation, and I thought he'd

291

be exhausted, but he'd run over to my place, so suddenly *enthusiastic*, so ... passionate.'

She knew what she was doing to me. How obvious must I be to her, the woman who fell for her mark?

'Well, anyway, darling, I'm not really sure we need to continue with our arrangement any more. I think I can take it from here.' Her face was a mask. 'You can keep the money, of course, I understand that you really did help with the business side of things. Clearly that's where your skills really sit.'

'I don't understand. *You* want to call this off?' She adjusted herself, flicking her tresses over her shoulder. I wondered how early she had to get up to straighten her hair, if she ever resented it. She picked up her phone again, flicked through absentmindedly, smiling at the number of 'likes' she got. I'd never realised how much of a junkie she was, how you never got her full attention. That must be why it was usually so alluring when she offered it, like a gift. Like you were special. I wondered if that was how Dylan felt.

'It seems in working together, Dylan has developed ... an attachment to you.'

She threw up her hands like it was ridiculous. 'I'd mentioned setting you up with a friend of mine, kind of like as a thank you for all your help, and he got all annoyed. *You can't organise people's lives like that, Nicki,*' she mimicked, then rolled her eyes. 'Ironic, right? And *then* there's all the in-jokes.'

'In-jokes?' I wracked my brain. Nicki looked at me like I was a moron.

'In the car? He knew you were carsick!'

'That wasn't a joke,' I said, trying to laugh it off, 'and I looked pretty green. I must have mentioned it at some point.'

Nicki looked at me, really staring, as if she was trying to siphon the truth out of me by sheer force of will. I'd seen her do this on reality TV, staring for an uncomfortably long amount of time. I'd always assumed it was an editing trick to try and eke out the drama, but now I figured some producer had told her it was powerful.

'Look, I agree. I think we should call it quits,' I said. 'You can take the money back, the whole hundred grand – I won't charge for my time spent. I don't . . . I don't feel right about it.'

Nicki nodded like it was what she'd expected: weakness.

'It's a shame. If you could have delivered what you were promising, you'd be a millionaire. An icon,' she laughed. I wanted to scream. 'I thought we were on the same page here. Men need to be sculpted, encouraged. Reinforce good behaviour. We all do it, try to train them. But it's so time-consuming, so exhausting.'

The server stepped in to clear our plates, carefully averting her eyes as she leaned past. Her body was rigid, her eyes wide as she recognised Nicki. I thought her hands trembled a little. I smiled and mouthed a 'thank you' as she left.

I turned back to Nicki, shaking my head.

'I just . . . I don't understand why he's not enough for you the way he is,' I argued. 'He's attentive, he's sweet. He cares about you, he respects your career, he pays attention to what you need. He's tried really hard, going to the events, being that person you need him to be. Why isn't it enough?'

Nicki looked at me again. 'Because it would be enough for you?'

I tried not to wince. 'We're not talking about me.'

'I think we are.'

She let the silence sit again, and this time I refused to be bullied. I sipped my coffee daintily, taking my time, and then I put the cup back on the saucer and smiled. 'I'm going to go. We don't have to talk about this ever again.'

She gave me a look like she knew she didn't have much time left. One well-aimed shot was all it would take.

'Darling, I say this because I don't want you to get hurt. But you realise you don't have a chance with him, right? I mean, you're lovely, don't get me wrong, but you have a certain . . . unpolished quality. He might feel protective towards you, like a sibling, he might even like you as a person, but Dylan is, through and through, just another guy. He likes his women toned, tanned, waxed and wearing lingerie. He can pretend he's not into all the effort I put in, but believe me, when we're alone he makes his preferences clear.'

I took a sharp breath, and smiled, leaning in to whisper to her.

'And I'm saying this because I don't want *you* to get hurt, Nicki – if you have to manipulate him into proposing, you're going to need to manipulate him into every decision for the rest of your lives, and he's going to resent you.'

'As long as he can hold out until after my TV deal, that's fine with me,' she bit back, and I looked at her in shock. 'When we get home, the flat will be set up with a hugely romantic backdrop, with all of his favourite foods, good champagne, and a photo montage. All the fantastic holidays, all the wonderful times we've had. And when he turns around, he'll find me holding a pendant on a chain, a replica of the one his mother gave him, but in 24-carat gold. A proposal gift.'

I closed my eyes, it was so painful. 'Nicki, come on. Did you get him a puppy too?'

'I *know him*,' she argued. 'I know what he likes. What he cares about. He wants the beautiful apartment and the sharp suits and the big office and the perfect wife.'

'So that's why we came on this trip? So your assistants could set up the proposal?' I laughed, not even surprised any more as I scraped back my chair to leave.

'Alyssa...' she widened her eyes, sweet as pie, 'if you tell him about any of this, you'll look just as bad as me. Stick to the script or get off the stage. I don't want to see you again after this.'

She assumed a sweet smile. 'OK, darling?'

Don't give her the satisfaction, Aly. You know how to play the game, so play it.

I smiled as if we'd had a perfectly lovely conversation. 'Thank you for such a *memorable* experience, Nicki. It's been mind-blowing. I'll see you at the car for our journey home.'

'I've booked you all a separate car,' she said cloyingly, thrilled to get that final win. 'After all, Dylan and I have somewhere important to be.'

As I walked away, I comforted myself that I'd done what I set out to do. It was over. No more fixing, no more lying or trickery. And no more Dylan. I had to trust that there was still enough of him in there to make the right decision. The Dylan who would look at a more expensive, fancier version of a gift from his mother, and wince.

But either way, it was done now. It wasn't my problem to fix any more.

I had more than enough problems of my own.

The drive home was muted: Tola quietly dozing, Ben and Eric wrapped around each other, and me clutching a bottle of water and trying not to imagine what would be happening a couple of hours from now. I'd watched as Dylan waved at me as we left, one arm around Nicki, not a care in the world.

I looked down at my phone to find a text from Priya:

How was the nightmare group trip? Did you all have group massages and bond? Is everyone Team Nicki now? P x

I wanted to laugh at the timing of it. I wanted to think that Priya's feelings and Ben's tense looks and that nagging bit of doubt was enough for Dylan, but it wouldn't be.

There was no doubt about what he'd do. I knew exactly how this was going to play out.

I was going to watch as they announced their engagement online, and I was going to trawl through the pictures and the articles and let myself have one night crying and drinking. Just one night to say goodbye. Enough now.

And then I was going to find another job and stop fixing things and people.

I had a plan. I kept repeating it in my head. *I have a plan, I have a plan.* It's going to be OK because I've got a plan.

When I got in to the flat, nearly running in without a backwards glance, calling my thanks over my shoulder, I

296

shut the door and gave a sigh of relief. No lies, no pretence, no feelings. Just quiet. I fell into bed and slept for the rest of the afternoon.

A few hours later my phone rang, and I searched for it under the duvet, discovering I had eighteen missed calls. Tola, Eric and Mama. Tola was calling.

'What's happening, is everyone OK?' I asked, panicked.

Tola sighed, 'Thank fuck you're answering, where have you been?'

'I was asleep! What's the emergency?'

'Go to Twitter and look at what's trending,' she said.

'Social media? So I can assume no one's dead or maimed?' I put her on speakerphone and opened the app.

'Not yet,' Tola said darkly.

There were two things that concerned me:

#theKLP

#fixerupper

'What the fuck am I looking at, Tola?'

She sighed, 'Read the articles and call me back. We need to do damage control.'

Fix up or Stitch up?

Kitty litter heiress pays one hundred grand to get 'fixer-upper' tech boyfriend to propose.

The old saying goes that money can't buy you love, but Heiress to the Happy Kitty fortune and reality TV show royalty Nicolette Wetherington Smythe is not going to let that stop her. Nicolette has been in the public eye consistently since the fifth season of Posh London aired, but it's only more recently her tech entrepreneur boyfriend Dylan James has been seen in the limelight.

A source has informed us that was all part of an elaborate plan to make Mr James a more worthy partner for the influencer, increasing his audience in preparation for a big tech deal and a proposal.

But unlike most women, the KLP isn't a fan of waiting, so she hired self-confessed boyfriend fixers, Alyssa Aresti and Tola Ajayi, AKA the Fixer Upper, to speed up the process. Under the guise of business support, Aresti and Ajayi have been prying into Mr James' personal life and attempting to fix him up to Wetherington Smythe's high standards. As you'll remember in season four of Posh London, the KLP dropped biscuit billionaire and heartthrob Landon Hawthorne for failing to see her 'entrepreneurial vision'. Well, no one's missing it now.

I scanned a few other sites, looking to see how much people knew:

Aresti and Ajayi have been running the Fixer Upper for almost a year, and their website promises a range of packages, from career support and general hand-holding, to commitment and communication. Hidden on a website accessible only with a password, there are real secret society vibes here. Plus, we love their kickass tote bags and sassy badges. Ladies, we salute you!

So what do we think, girls? Would we pay someone to fix up our man, and is it worth a hundred grand to get them to use a washing machine correctly?

I threw my phone on the bed and put my head in my hands. *Shit.*

I immediately called Dylan, but it rang once and then went to voicemail. I had to find him, I had to explain. But what could I say, except *It's true, I'm sorry?*

Tola rang back, but I didn't answer. She kept texting about making a plan, preparing a statement, trying to talk to Nicki. But I couldn't face it. I couldn't face any of them.

The server, the one at the restaurant that morning at the glamping site. She hadn't been rigid and nervous because Nicki was famous. It was because she got hold of some gossip that she knew would be worth something.

I pulled the covers over my head. Oh God, the office would see. All the people who had used the Fixer Upper would see. Nicki had a whole PR team to spin this, but we were toast. We were done.

Dylan would be so hurt.

I tried one more time to call Dylan, still no idea what I'd say, and this time it didn't go to voicemail, it simply said: '*The number you dialled has not been recognised.*'

Chapter Twenty-One

I couldn't stop watching the drama unfold, even as I refused to do anything. Tola was at her best, ready to push, promote, respond, but I couldn't. I couldn't do anything but sit there and scroll:

Who the fuck do these bitches think they are? From the look of them, they could use fixing up!

More bra-burning feminists trying to destroy men. Someone needs to teach these bitches a lesson.

This isn't ethical! I don't like what this says about men, they're not dogs to be trained! Lots of them have their lives together! #notallmen

How about accepting people as they are, with all their faults? Isn't that what love's really about?

The ones that had a point were the worst. There were more hopeful pieces, though, women who got what we were doing, understood what it meant. But they were few and far between, and didn't make up for the vitriol.

On Saturday night came the big bang – an interview with Nicki herself. I'd been following her approach through all of this with an eagle eye, surviving on chocolate and coffee as I refreshed, refreshed, refreshed. Scanned hashtags, looked through photos, poisoned myself with other people's opinions.

She'd posted an image of a broken heart and asked for time to mourn her relationship. A couple of hours later, she'd posted about the terrible exhaustion of being an ambitious female and dragging your partner along with you. Then there was a crying selfie, perfectly wet eyes dripping mascara, but her face not at all puffy, her lips plumped and slicked with gloss. I wondered how many shots she'd taken to get that one, and how she'd decided it was more authentic than the others.

And now here it was, a real-life interview, recorded on social media but likely to be used in clips across the news as more and more people picked up the story. Ex-customers had come out of the woodwork, explaining why they'd used us and what had happened. Some had been found out when the story broke with our photos and were out for their five minutes of fame.

Nicki's agent had got this so perfectly right. Even as I hated it, I noticed the details, the oversized knitted jumper (even though it was warm for spring) and leggings, showing how vulnerable and normal she was. The light makeup, the tears ready to spill. The camera loved her, and the interviewer had clearly been pushed to make her seem sympathetic. That's what she paid the big bucks for.

'So, Nicki, why'd you do it? You and Dylan seemed so in love, why bring in a professional?' The interviewer leaned in, chin resting on her hand, like she couldn't wait to get the details.

'Well, I think as a modern, ambitious woman there is an exhaustion at trying to carry your partner. At trying to make them reach their full potential. I'm sure women all across the country understand that. We're the care givers, the emotional support, the career advisers and everything else. And so when I found the Fixer Upper, I felt they really understood that. They were there to help.'

OK, maybe she won't screw us. Though she's definitely hanging Dylan out to dry . . .

'So, what went wrong?'

Nicki assumed a wounded look. 'I believe that the woman I hired to do the majority of the work, Alyssa Aresti, developed feelings for my boyfriend.'

'Wow! Not very professional!' the interviewer prompted. 'Do you think she's done that with other clients?'

Nicki looked as if she was considering it, while I clenched my fists. She shook her head, and I breathed out, relieved.

'I knew Alyssa had history with Dylan when I hired her,' Nicki said simply, 'but I'd assumed they were just friends. In the end, attempting to help my boyfriend with his career and his future meant I put him back in the path of someone he'd once loved.'

She knew? She knew the whole time? How? Why?

'That must hurt . . .'

Nicki adopted a brave smile, tilted her chin, and let a single perfect tear roll down her contoured cheekbone.

'It's a great step for their love story, but an unfortunate one for mine. But that just shows you, if you need to fix someone, maybe they're not the person you should be with.'

The interviewer nodded sombrely and then assumed a sly smile, 'And what about the rumours that your ex, Landon Hawthorne, has been a great part of your support system since you and Dylan split? Photos were shared online of you two hugging this morning.'

Oh yeah, absolutely heartbroken. Already looking for the next angle, nice one, Nicki.

She smiled coyly. 'Landon's always been a great friend, and we're very close. He's been my rock through all of this.'

'Well, there you have it, folks: secret deals, clandestine affairs, and potentially a new love sprouting from a failed relationship. Just another day in the life of the KLP. Don't forget to vote in the poll: Would you use a Fixer Upper on your boyfriend?'

I wanted to throw the laptop across the room, but I restrained myself. How did she know we had some sort of history? Had she'd hired me as an experiment? A good scandal? Perhaps this had all been a trick, to make Dylan suffer. But I couldn't see the point.

The doorbell rang, followed by impatient knocking, and I trundled over to look through the peephole, suddenly fearful that the journalists calling my mobile had found my home address. But it was only Tola and Eric, waiting until I'd opened the door and then leaning on it so I couldn't shut it again.

'Let us in. We have pizza, and you look terrible,' Tola said, gesturing for me to lead the way. Eric nodded seriously, and I did what I was told.

'Jesus, Aly, it's only been a day and a half!' Eric surveyed my flat, things strewn all over the place, open wine bottles and food left out on the side, blankets piled up on the bed. 'Or do you always live like you're having a breakdown?'

I glared at him, and he crossed his arms and glared back.

'No, we needed you to do damage control, and you let us down. So you don't get to be mad. Now, go and jump in the shower and when you get out, we're going to eat dinner and talk about this mess.'

I rolled my eyes like a teenager and stomped off to the bathroom.

'Huh, you're kind of hot when you're being all in charge,' Tola laughed at Eric's tone.

'You with an authority kink, does not surprise me at all,' he responded, and started clearing the breakfast bar. I watched them for a moment, my two friends, tidying my home, coming to rescue me. This was the first time they'd been to my flat. We were real friends now, and that much I could rely on.

I emerged from the shower refreshed, put on clean clothes, plaited my wet hair, and went back into the room to find the place transformed. They'd set out plates, poured wine, lit candles, and both turned to smile as they saw me.

'There she is,' Eric said, patting the stool, 'Come sit down and eat something.'

'You don't have to parent me, you know,' I said, doing as I was told and reaching for a slice of pizza.

'No, but it's nice to be the one who's looked after sometimes, isn't it?'

I chewed slowly, and then sighed. 'OK, tell me, what happened?'

'The story broke when we were still in the car after dropping you off!' Tola winced. 'Ben saw it on his phone.'

'How's this affecting you?' I asked Eric, and he shrugged.

'Ben is as protective of his friend as I am of mine. He hasn't completely cut me out, but we've agreed to talk when things have calmed down a bit.'

Poor, kind Ben who had grasped my hand and said *Don't let him refuse your help.* More people I'd hurt. Oh God, what about the business deal?

'Have they still got the chance to pitch, or has that all gone?' I asked, suddenly desperate.

'That's what you're worried about?' Tola raised an eyebrow.

'They've been working on this for years, if they don't get what they need now, they're all going under. Priya and Ben and Dylan have worked so hard to rebuild. I don't want this to ruin things for them.'

'As far as I know, it's still going ahead,' Eric said, and I nodded, relieved.

'Did you see Nicki's interview?' I asked, and they nodded. 'What do you think she meant about knowing mine and Dylan's history? She knew we knew each other.'

'*Apparently*, it was a good angle. When her and Dylan had their inevitable shouting match, he told her you wouldn't do something like that, that you were old friends,' Eric said. 'Ben was willing to give me that much information.'

I winced.

'Could all be bullshit, though?' said Tola, sipping her wine. 'I know from my contact at her agency, she's been offered a book deal for the whole thing. Six figures.'

'Of course,' I laughed. 'I thought I was a master manipulator, but Nicki really is exceptional.'

'Have you tried talking to Dylan?' Eric asked, and I shook my head.

'I think he's blocked my number, and it's no more than I deserve.'

'So I'm guessing you told him how you felt? And this is Nicki retaliating?' Tola asked. 'Did I give bad advice? I didn't think you'd take it!'

'I didn't tell him anything. This was just Nicki protecting herself.'

Eric widened his eyes. 'Hello, excuse me, I think I've missed some key information here.'

Tola gestured for me to get on with it, reveal the whole mess.

'I'm in love with him.' I closed my eyes and took a breath. 'I have always been in love with him.'

'Of course,' Eric laughed, 'because you'd pick the most complicated, unavailable person possible. I told you to stop picking projects, I didn't mean start choosing car crashes!'

I actually laughed, wiping my eyes with a paper napkin. 'Can't you see how this kills me? I control everything! And I couldn't control this.'

Eric nodded, and paused, as if he wasn't sure whether to say anything. He leaned in, 'So I'm assuming you acted in a completely Aly-like fashion here and bottled up your feelings as if they didn't matter?'

'I don't steal people's boyfriends!' I yelled. 'He was happy with Nicki!'

'He was trying to make *you* happy, idiot! You're trying to fix everything, and he's trying to keep a smile on his face for everyone, and neither of you talk and *my God* I do not want to date ever again.' Eric sighed. 'I hope Ben forgives me. It's horrible out there.'

'This is what he wanted, Eric.'

'Someone who lied to him and paid someone a hundred grand because he wasn't good enough as he was?'

'How is that different to what we were doing all along?' I yelped, 'I don't understand! Before it was OK, it was helping, it made sense! And then this ... this was all wrong, and I don't get why?'

'Because, sweetheart,' Eric said patiently, 'Dylan is the sort who didn't need to be tricked. He just needed to be asked. To be trusted. So, does he love you?'

'He did, back in the day,' Tola filled him in, taking a delicate bite of pizza, 'before this one thought the worst of him and ran away like a little scaredy cat.'

'Well, isn't that a mood?' Eric looked at me, then turned to Tola. 'That's right, right? A mood?'

She nodded. 'Well done, babe.'

'He was happy with Nicki, he was! She was building a future for both of them ...' I trailed off.

But that wasn't true, was it? Because he'd told me what he wanted. He wanted Sunday-morning runs and a little house and a dog, and a place to drink sangria in the garden ... the kind of life that Nicki wouldn't stand for at all. Quiet and beautiful, no script to follow.

'I almost wish you were the boyfriend-stealing trollop she's painting you out to be,' Eric huffed. 'At least I'd know you'd put your happiness above a job well done!'

'Do you think ... do you think he'd forgive me? I mean,

could I . . . could this be for me? The whole . . . love thing.'
I watched Tola's head tilt to the side in confusion, and Eric
blinked. They didn't get that I'd only seen two types of love,
complete devotion and complete devastation. That loving
someone made you weak, made you risk yourself.

'Aly, honey, have you never been in love before?' Eric
asked gently, trying to keep the awe out of his voice.

'Sure,' I started to laugh. 'Once. Fifteen years ago.'

The laughter collapsed into hysterical giggles, and suddenly I was crying, tears streaming and finding it difficult
to breathe.

'He's never going to forgive me for this. I took all the
things he's most insecure about and used them. I picked
money over him.' *But surely he'd understand? If I told him
about Mama's house, he'd know what that meant? He was the
only one who'd really know what that meant.*

But he'd ask me why I hadn't trusted him with the truth.
And I didn't have an answer for that.

Tola closed her eyes briefly, and the look of sorrow and
sympathy on her face got me again. I hid my face with my
hands as I cried, and they shushed and cuddled me, stroked
my hair, held me close.

After a few moments, I got my breathing under control
and reached out a hand, eyes still closed.

'What on earth are you doing?' Eric asked.

'That just happened, and no one's even going to hand me
a goddamn glass of wine?' I snorted, wiping my eyes, 'and
you call yourselves my friends.'

Tola smiled and went to grab my glass, topping it up.

I reached for it, but she held it out of reach.

308

'You can have it when you come up with a plan. Aly is the lady with a plan.'

'Fine, I'm thinking.' I wiggled my fingers. 'Wine, please.'

I gulped half of it down.

'OK, so the million-pound question: What are you going to do about Dylan?'

I made a face. 'Wait for this to all blow over and go on with my grey, sad life?'

Eric made a buzzer noise, 'Uh uh. Wrong answer. Try again.'

'Apologise?'

'Sure ...'

'Try to explain why I needed the money, make him understand?'

'Warmer ...'

'Tell him he's perfect the way he is, even with his fears and *always all right* attitude and terrible taste in music and terrible taste in girlfriends, and he doesn't need fixing because I love him?'

Eric tapped his nose. 'Got there eventually.'

'And when he tells me I betrayed him and our friendship and he never wants to see me again ... ?'

'You'll know you have been honest and that you have friends who will take you out to get really, really drunk until you forget all about it.'

'Lucky me,' I smiled at them, and though they took it as sarcasm, I was more grateful than they would ever know.

Chapter Twenty-Two

I couldn't quite face going into the office, not yet. I knew I needed to be honest. I needed to speak to Dylan. I needed to grovel like I'd never grovelled before.

I spent the day tidying my little hovel, taking pride in my space again. Trying to figure out a plan. I logged off social media, and I didn't look at any of the glossy magazines in the corner shop. I kept checking the time, counting down to when I knew his meeting was.

I called Tola on her lunch break, unable to deal with the nerves. 'How's the office?'

'The usual stagnant hellhole.' I could almost hear her shrugging. 'Hunter asked me to fix him up with someone. He thought it was a dating site. The man can't even read an article, no wonder his reports are trash. Why do you sound like you've had eight coffees?'

'Because I have,' I replied, 'the presentation is today. I was wondering if he was preparing, if he felt confident, nervous.'

I just ... I wished I could tell him that it was a good idea, really. That I believed in what he did, in how he protected his colleagues, in how he'd worked so hard for so long to get them here. That he deserved this opportunity. That I'd always believed in him, for him, not because I was being paid. Just because he was Dylan James, and he could do anything.

'Text him.'

'He's blocked my number.'

'You don't know that,' Tola huffed. 'That's the point. Anyway, he might unblock it and see it. Or maybe you can just send all that good energy out into the atmosphere so you can move the hell on.'

'I don't want to move on. I want him.' *God, that sounded weird to say out loud. As if the universe would hear and snatch away any opportunity.*

'You know, life was a lot easier when you dated losers with a clear expiration date.'

'Well, it would have been if I'd known they had an expiration date at the time,' I said. 'What a waste. But at least it was easy. No messy feelings. I feel like my stomach's in my throat and my head's up my arse.'

'Such a poet,' Tola said. 'Text the boy. Something simple. Nothing mushy. Nothing longer than a sentence. Then get your head back in the game, Aresti.'

In the end, I settled for a simple:

I hope the presentation goes well. I know you'll be wonderful. A x

Of course there was no reply, and of course I counted down the hours and then stalked everyone's social media looking for some nugget of information. I even called Eric in the hope that Ben would tell him something. But it was radio silence. I'd betrayed the team, I didn't get to hear the final score.

I really needed my mother. I took a breath and made the call. The first of all the hard apologies I'd have to make.

'Hello?' She sounded wary, like she was waiting for me to launch into another screaming list of all her faults. It made me ashamed.

'Hi Mama,' I said and waited for her to scold me for ignoring her. To start defending herself.

Instead I heard her exhale in relief, and then burst into tears.

There is something about being the reason your mother is crying, especially when you've always been the one to comfort her, that is particularly brutal. Being on the other end of the phone was not enough.

'You called, you finally called!' she yelped, sounding suddenly so young, and then sobbed again.

'Mama, it's OK.'

'It's not OK,' she said fiercely. 'It's not OK at all. You were right, about all of it. Who he is, what he's made me. How—' she swallowed another sob, 'how disappointed my mother would have been.'

'I didn't want to be right,' I said, 'and I didn't want to be mean.'

'I keep thinking about when you came home from university and you weren't happy. You hadn't dated, you hadn't made friends. You didn't talk to Dylan any more ...' I stared up at the ceiling, trying to hold it together. 'And I

312

was talking to your *yiayia* about what we could do, how we could help you.

'I remember it so clearly: we sat at the kitchen table, and you hadn't come downstairs in five days. We sat with two glasses of red wine, and I said, "Why doesn't she want to fall in love, to meet somebody? She's always being strong, always on her own! I just want her to fall in love!" And my mama looked at me, so sad . . .' She trailed off.

'What did she say?'

'She said, "She sees what it's done to you".' Mama's voice broke.

The breath I took then felt like my first real one in a long time.

'I thought I could fix everything. If I could be a better mother and a better wife. More fun, more loving, more independent. I'd fix him, fix you, fix us. But it doesn't work that way.'

'So I'm learning,' I half laughed.

'This was not your fight, my baby, this was mine. And I'm going to win it. If he wants this house, he can fight me for it.'

I'd been let down before by Mama's big moments of confidence, her assurances that *this time*, it would be better. But she sounded certain of herself, strong, and that was impressive enough.

'OK, Mama.'

'You don't believe me,' she said softly. 'That's OK. You'll see.'

'I hope so,' I said, my throat sore. 'I've made a few mistakes of my own.'

'Yes,' she said, reproachful, 'it was very annoying to be

in the doghouse so I couldn't tell you off!' But she laughed, and I laughed along with her. 'Oh my darling, what are you doing? Tricking Dylan? Working for kitten princesses?'

'Kitty litter, Mama.' I waved it away. 'It doesn't matter. It was a mistake.'

'Dylan always tried the hardest to be whoever you wanted him to be. You could see it with his father. He'd be strong, he'd be invisible, he'd be sensitive. Play the joker, the fool. That boy tried on every personality to find the one that would make people love him.'

I winced. 'Don't, I feel awful enough as it is.'

'What was there to fix?'

'Nothing.' I shook my head. 'I just wanted to be with him again. I just wanted an excuse.'

I imagined my mother nodding sagely. 'I know there were times when . . . I let myself fall apart and I let you hold everything together. You cooked dinner and tidied and got your clothes ready for school. You asked me how I was and did everything you could to fix my heart. That wasn't fair of me.'

I said nothing.

'But Dylan was there with you, too, wasn't he?' she said softly. 'Making you laugh, holding your hand, burning all my good frying pans. He was there, by your side, making sure you were OK. That's love, darling, that has always been what love is. What I've wanted for you. What your grandparents had. Caring and being cared for. Equals.'

I pressed my lips together. 'He won't forgive me for this.'

'That's fear and shame talking, Alyssa. Never be too proud to apologise. To make things right.'

'To fix it?' I hiccupped wildly, the words bubbling up.

'Just one more thing for you to fix, sweetheart,' she said. 'But only because it was your mess in the first place.'

I exhaled, feeling the tears well up again. 'Yes, Mama.'

'Come to dinner tonight, I miss you. And we'll make a plan together. What to do about the house, what to do about Dylan, all of it. You and me, we'll make it right.' I didn't realise how long I'd been waiting to hear those words until she said them. The tears tracked down my face as if they'd been hoping for permission to fall.

And so I got on the train back home, that journey tied up in nostalgia, like everything about my life lately.

I was ashamed of how I'd treated Dylan, ashamed of how I'd let myself fall again. More than anything, I was ashamed that I kept asking him for truths when I kept feeding him lies. If I'd been the friend I was fifteen years ago, I would have told him the moment I saw him: *This woman doesn't get you, doesn't know the truth of you. You deserve someone who loves all of you.*

My mother greeted me with a huge hug, wrapping her arms around me and swaying me side to side. She breathed relief, and I clung to her for a long time.

She ordered pizza, and we sat at the table with a good bottle of wine while I told her the whole tale. All of it, no hiding how lonely I'd been, how worried I was that I'd given everything I had to these men who moved on to better lives without a second glance. How powerful I'd felt, ever so briefly, when I started the Fixer Upper.

'You helped people, Alyssa. Now you need to find the right way to do it. Not all this tricking and scheming and controlling people. You can't help people who don't want to be helped,' she gestured at herself with her wine glass, 'look at me.'

I went to argue, but she smiled, tears in her eyes as she looked up at the photo of her parents on the mantelpiece.

'Love is only meant to be terrifying right at the beginning, right before you fall,' she said softly. 'Then it's meant to feel like home.' I reached across and squeezed her hand.

At that moment, the doorbell rang, and we looked at each other in surprise.

Mama laughed, wiping her eyes as she went to open the door. 'Maybe the pizza is here early? Rom coms on the sofa, I'm thinking *Dirty Dancing*, yes?'

But when she opened the door, I heard her voice harden. 'Yiannis.'

Dad.

I stood up, gearing for a fight, terrified she was going to fall back into the pattern.

But then Mama peered round the doorframe and said, 'Your father and I are going to talk.'

She walked across the room and kissed my forehead. 'Go for a walk, yes? Half an hour. You can go out the back if you'd rather?'

I blinked at her, the first sign of this new person she promised she was becoming. Then I picked up an old hoodie from the chair, pausing to grab her wrist. 'That's not what love looks like, right?'

Mama nodded, repeated our saying back to me.

I kissed her cheek and escaped into the back garden, not even bothering to open the garden gate, instead swinging my legs over the low part in the wall and jumping off into the alleyway. I'd smoked my first cigarette here, with Dylan, of course.

I knew before I even stepped onto the street that my wandering half an hour was going to be a walking tour of our history. How could it be anything but, when he was the only thing on my mind?

You didn't give me the chance when you disappeared, Aly, I could hear him in my head. *Fair's fair.*

I walked past our old school, impossibly small now. I could still see where I'd hid from the other kids at lunch, reading my book, afraid to make friends. This lanky boy had rolled in front of me and put his finger to his lips, shaking his head. I heard the other boys coming looking for him and then wandering off. He'd managed to piss off a group of kids in the first two days of school.

'Can I stay here? Just until they're gone?' he'd asked, pushing back the dark fringe that kept flopping over his eyes.

I'd closed my book, narrowed my eyes in consideration and said, 'Sure, but you've got to tell me something interesting. And it has to be real!'

He'd thought about it for a good thirty seconds and then said, 'I'm deathly afraid of watermelons.'

It was the first time I'd laughed in a long time. He'd spent the rest of lunch telling me about growing a watermelon tree inside your belly, and I didn't pick my book up again. We were eleven.

My chest hurt thinking about it, so I ambled down the next street, looking at how the houses had changed, passing the bakery that made my favourite little lemon pastries, covered in powdered sugar. I passed the coffee shop where all the teenagers got iced coffee in the summers, holding up the street with the queue. The pharmacy where I'd had my ears pierced, and the corner shop where we'd paid some twenty-year-olds to buy us beer and they'd returned to give us a pack of Haribo and our full change, saying we should enjoy being kids.

I let my feet decide the route, but I knew where I was coming up to – Dylan's street. I couldn't stop myself. I wanted to stare at that house, the one I hadn't seen since I snuck out in the morning full of self-loathing and shame and loss. I would just peek at it. Wonder what might have been. Stare from across the street for an outline of Mr James in the living room, the flick of the tail from the ancient cat next door. One moment, that was all I needed. To say goodbye to our past.

And there he was.

Leaning against a beat-up blue car, staring at his house. He was wearing his blue suit, the crisp white shirt, top buttons undone. He looked every inch the businessman. But he didn't walk up to the front door.

He never did, did he? He turned up, stared at it for half an hour and left, never getting what he came for. Whatever that was.

I sidled up, unsure of whether I was ready for the onslaught, for what I deserved. Something real.

'You going in this time?' I asked, staying a safe distance away, and he didn't even look round, just shook his head and exhaled, like he was saying *Of course. Of course it's you*.

'I never do,' he said, eyes still zeroed in on the front door. 'Did you come looking for me?'

'It's the last place I would have looked,' I replied. 'How did the interview go?'

Endless questions, batting back and forth. We could manage this, as long as he didn't look at me.

'Well,' he nodded, 'they're going to take EasterEgg into the fold, put their funding and backing behind the projects ...'

'That's amazing!' I yelped, a little too enthused for the situation.

'And ... they've offered me a job.'

'I thought the meeting was the job. They're investors.'

Dylan swallowed, clenched his jaw. 'They will invest in EasterEgg. Priya and Ben will stay here and take on new staff. And I'll be working on the promotion side. They thought ... they thought I was suited to it, with my recent "exploits". I'm famous now, after all.'

I winced. 'Is that what you want?'

'I figure it's time for a new start. Where I'm not the guy who ... well, the guy who needed fixing. The guy whose girlfriend would go to extraordinary lengths to make him good enough.'

'Dyl ...'

'The job's in California. Silicon Valley. I leave in a couple of weeks.'

I inhaled sharply, then tried to cover it.

'That's soon.'

Dylan shrugged and said nothing.

'I need to explain everything, and apologise. It was complicated—'

'A hundred grand's a lot of money, I'm sure you had your

reasons.' I hated that dull, dry voice. The way he pretended it didn't matter.

'Mama was going to lose her house, and I, well, I . . . tried to undo it. I called it off, gave the money back at the end.'

He looked at me then, seriously. 'Is she still going to lose it?'

I shook my head, and he nodded, speaking quietly, 'Good. That's good.'

I tried to figure out where to start, how to explain it all. I didn't have my flash cards or a playbook. I didn't have a plan. All I had was the same words going around in my head like a mantra: *I love you, I love you, I love you.*

'I need to apologise, Dylan, and I'm not really sure where to start . . .'

He shrugged, looking across at his old front door, back to that guy I met again last month. Guard up, unimpressed, aloof. Saving his smiles for everyone but me.

'I can't really blame you, Aly. I was always a fixer upper, right? We knew that from the beginning . . .' He paused, trying to decide if he was going to say any more. 'It's just hard when it's the one person who always made you feel like you were enough.'

I made a noise, but Dylan didn't let me interrupt. 'It's fine. The guys will stay here and live their lives, and I'll start over in the States. No more running a team, worrying about letting people down or trusting the wrong people. I can try something new. Paint a different picture.'

'You were a good leader,' I said softly. 'It suited you.'

He shook his head. 'No, it suited her.'

I was suddenly desperate for him to look at me, to stop

resolutely pretending that I wasn't there, that he was just quietly talking to the air.

'What about the little house by the park? Your dog, and your orange walls, and Sunday roast dinners?' I said. 'Don't think they do a decent Yorkshire pudding in California.'

He shrugged again. 'Dreams change.'

'I ... is this really what you want?' I asked.

He exhaled a laugh. 'Oh, it matters what I want, now? Here's the real question: what do *you* want?'

The minute he turned, I took back my wish. He was looking at me with such disappointment. It wasn't that mocking dislike from when we'd first seen each other again – this time he might actually hate me.

'This isn't about me.'

'Well, no, that's not really true, is it? Because it's *always* been about you. It's about you fixing people and making them better. Fixing your parents, fixing me. Drunkenly making declarations fifteen years ago and then running off and leaving everyone else to pick up the pieces! What part of this hasn't been about you, Aly? And you *still* don't know what you want?'

His voice was rough and his eyes demanded an answer. We faced each other, and I found myself unable to move.

I wanted to say it: *I want you, I want us.* But I'd already ruined his chances here. He had the opportunity to start over in the US, be someone new. Be free. I'd already taken enough away from him, I couldn't take his fresh start, too. Love was letting people go if it was best for them.

So I stayed silent.

When I shook my head, Dylan half laughed again.

'You know what the hilarious thing about all this is?' he

said, shaking his head. 'If you'd told me, I would have gone along with it. I would have done as I was told, tried to be Mr Perfect, because I figured that was the only way anyone gave a damn about me. And it *still* wasn't enough.'

'That's not—' I moved closer, but he cut me off.

'If you'd trusted me with the truth about your mum's house, I would have helped. You know that.' He met my eyes, and I couldn't argue. My beautiful friend.

'I know it's not enough, but I'm sorry. At first you hated me, and I hated you, and then ... it was a chance to be a part of your life again.'

He shook his head.

'You didn't do this for me! You did this for her!'

'I thought you were happy!'

'And I thought seeming that way was the only way to keep you,' he sighed. 'Seems I'm still a mug, all these years later. And now I get to start all over again, new life, new friends, new job. A whole bunch of new people to pretend in front of, to make them think I've got the script, that I know what I'm doing.'

I couldn't help myself.

'You don't have to go.'

He met my eyes, holding my gaze and I fought the need to look away.

'Be brave, Aly, you gonna give me a reason to stay?' He tilted his head. 'How many months of training would I need for that?'

'No, it's not ...' I put my hand to my mouth. This was my fault. There was no fixing this. Not this time. I didn't deserve his forgiveness.

Dylan looked at me with disappointment, his voice hoarse, 'You realise you're the one with this sad, small life, so desperate to control everything and keep yourself safe that you're not actually living. More concerned with how it looks than how it feels. You're still pretending.'

I pressed my lips together and nodded. I couldn't argue.

He stepped away from the car and opened the door, painting a completely blank look on his face. 'Well, I'm giving you a gift, Aresti, more than you gave me. You actually get a goodbye. A proper ending.'

He got into the car and I watched, wordless, from the pavement as he drove away.

When I got back home, my father was gone, and my mother was upbeat. Not jittery, faux-positivity. Actually upbeat. We ate pizza up on the sofa as promised, her arm around my shoulder, and we curled up under a blanket as we watched a movie. When I trudged up to my childhood bed, unbelievably exhausted, she tucked me in and swiped my hair away from my face like I was a child.

'I am going to sell this home,' she whispered like she was telling me a fairy story. 'And I'm going to buy something that I can make beautiful, something that will have *my* memories. Someplace you'll come and visit, and we'll drink wine on the patio. Somewhere that isn't tied up with you and me and your father.'

'Even though it means letting go of *Yiayia*?' I asked.

Mama smiled and nodded. 'I have thousands of memories of my parents, littered across the world! It's time for me to do something for me. Just like it's time for you to do things for you. Good things are coming for both of us. It's time to be bold, yes?'

I nodded.

'It'll be a little scary, but I'm ready,' she said to herself, and I was suddenly overcome by how proud I was of my mother. Finally, here she was, ready to shine.

I thought of Dylan, his beautiful, angry face under the street light as he waited for me to give him a reason to stay. How I thought letting go was a gift. But I still hadn't been honest. I still hadn't jumped.

'Yes,' I said, 'you are.'

And so am I.

Chapter Twenty-Three

'Aresti! Get in here!' Felix yelled when I arrived the next morning, which didn't help with the stares I was getting around the office. It was mainly the men, lips curled and eyebrows raised.

The women had known and had been on my side when it was their sisters and cousins and hairdressers I was helping. But now the men knew, it was like they wanted nothing to do with me. They couldn't afford for their secrets to get out, that they weren't happy with their lot, that they were exhausted and disappointed and unfulfilled. I was proof that we were all pretending, and it was easier to turn away. To show off engagement rings and holiday photos and tiny pastel onesies. The accessories to a life that didn't tell the full story.

I slipped into his office and into the chair opposite Felix.

'Morning,' I smiled stiffly. 'What's up?'

'I saw about your little side hustle in the news yesterday. The top dogs aren't exactly *thrilled* by the association.'

I pressed my lips together and nodded, 'I understand.'

Felix tugged at his moustache, and I wondered whether he was allowed to fire me for this. Like, legally, could he get rid of me for a bit of bad press?

'Surely we could spin this for the PR?' I said lightly. 'Make it look like a campaign for one of our female-first brands?'

'The crazy woman who thinks men are beneath her?' he snorted. 'You think there's an angle for that?'

I smiled tightly. 'If you're good at your job, there's always an angle.'

Felix sighed, shaking his head. 'I vouched for you, I said you were brilliant. I said you were a hard worker who was dedicated to this place, you'd be here forever, making it tick over, doing whatever it takes.'

I blinked, wondering if that was meant to be a compliment.

'But now ...' Felix trailed off, and I frowned at him. All his actions seemed so caricatured somehow, as if tugging at his moustache, putting his head in his hands, sighing deeply, would convey this deep level of disappointment that I'd never recover from.

But I suddenly found that I didn't really care what he thought any more. How odd.

'So ... what do I need to do?' I asked, and apparently it was the right question, because he beamed at me.

'Good girl,' he said, pointing a finger. 'That's the right attitude. I need the Aly from a month ago. The girl who got it done, who didn't complain, who gave two hundred per cent. I need my Girl Friday back, kid, you know? It's like you suddenly started to think you were too good for this place after Matthew got that promotion.'

I blinked at him. 'Oh, is that so?'

Felix rolled his eyes at me. 'Come on, Aly. Be real for a second, would you? You ... you're a packhorse. A hard worker, solid, dependable. But you're never going to be a leader. You haven't got the balls for it.'

I burst out laughing, shaking my head.

Felix frowned. 'Be serious for a moment. You're in the shit here and I need you to—'

'To go back to being the perfectly helpful, amenable, selfless person I was before? The person with no life outside this office. The person who lived to prove herself?' I asked, expecting him to get the sarcasm.

But Felix missed it completely. 'Yes, exactly.'

I threw my head back, and pressed my lips together, trying to contain my laughter. Eventually it escaped.

'My God,' I said. 'I've wasted my life.'

'What?'

'I quit, Felix.'

I felt calm and refreshed as soon as I said it, as if a cool breeze had descended upon me.

'Don't be stupid, where are you going to go? You just made a PR mess of yourself and your reputation, sweetheart, don't be an idiot.'

'I told you, when you're good at your job, any mess can be an opportunity.'

'So you're serious?'

'As a heart attack,' I said, standing. 'Expect my letter of resignation in a few minutes.'

'And what about your notice period? Aly, you're not thinking straight!' Felix laughed.

His face gleamed, like he was being so accommodating, talking to me as if I were a child.

'I have more than enough holiday to cover my notice period, thanks, Felix.' I smiled widely at him. 'This has really been a learning experience for me. Until now, I didn't realise how many shitheads were at the top. Like you said, I never would have made it.'

I opened the door and walked out, just as he started yelling.

'You get back here, young lady! I'm not done with you! I won't give you a reference!'

I got halfway across the office before I paused and turned back, watching his little red face scowling at me. I adopted an apologetic expression.

'Felix, don't be so hysterical, you're making a fool of yourself.' I wiggled my eyebrows. 'See ya!'

I walked across the room to grab my bag, left everything else at my desk, and as I walked to the lift, I caught Eric's eye and winked. He nodded.

When I got to the hallway, I was surprised to see Tola next to me, holding a box.

'Is that my stuff?'

She shook her head. 'It's mine. I handed in my notice two weeks ago. I was kind of hoping you were going to be brave enough to follow my lead. Turns out you followed your own.'

The lift opened, and we got in, and I nudged her with my elbow.

'You were brave,' Tola said suddenly. 'I'm really proud of you.'

I shook my head. 'Getting mad at my boss and walking

out after a PR nightmare, with no job to go to, no references, and no idea of what I'm doing next? I'm not brave, I'm an idiot.'

'Pssh, you are not. Besides, you and me are going to start a business.'

'Oh right, and do we know what type of business that is yet?' I asked, amused.

'Absolutely no idea,' she replied.

'Oh good. Excellent.'

I couldn't help grinning. I felt like I could run a marathon or scale a building.

'We're mad, you know?' I said in awe. 'We're stark raving mad.'

Tola smiled at me, shaking her head. 'We're not mad. We're *brilliant.*'

I spent the rest of the day with Tola, in a coffee shop around the corner, with two brand-new notebooks, making plans. We talked about the kind of business we wanted to run, what we'd learnt from the Fixer Upper, how we could move forward.

We wanted, quite plainly, to create our own agency. We knew we wanted to run a business that supported female companies. No fixing up, only building up. Glowing up. Growing up.

At one point we just sat without speaking, listening to the women in the coffee shop talking to each other. It was like when we first started the Fixer Upper. But where before we'd heard only about the pandered-to boyfriends and babysitting dads, we realised it was bigger than that. It was not being taken seriously at work, it was lacklustre maternity pay, and no one talking about miscarriages, and never quite getting over that feeling when you saw a cover model and pinched your thighs. It was every ridiculous thing you'd ever believed about yourself and about being too damned exhausted to fix it.

'What problem do we need to fix?' Tola asked me, and I shook my head.

'For now, we just need to listen.'

'*You're* OK with not being in control of everything all the time?'

'It's meant to feel scary when you're falling,' I repeated my mother's words. 'And then it feels like home. We'll get there. We've just gotta do the scary bit first.'

Tola shook her head at me in utter surprise. 'I love you. I absolutely love you right now.'

It was hours of double-shot lattes and ridiculous slogans, words written in capital letters, Tola getting louder as she said, *Yes, yes, that's it, that's the one!*

It was the most excited I'd been for a long time, possibility stretching out like a new, unseen road that had suddenly appeared from between the trees.

And I didn't know how to fix it all. But I knew where to start, with the two guiding principles that I'd forgotten until someone had brought them back to me: Tell the truth and find wonderful things.

Chapter Twenty-Four

'Thank you for agreeing to see me,' I said, sliding into the chair in the EasterEgg office the next day. Ben sat across from me, stern and unyielding. 'I have a lot of explaining and apologising to do.'

He nodded. 'Well, yeah. I'm mad at you.'

'And you're right to be. But please don't take it out on Eric. He's so crazy about you and this whole mess was not his fault.'

Ben's facade cracked a little. 'Oh, I know – the man is a terrible liar. Which is odd, considering he's such a good actor.'

I looked at him, suddenly hopeful.

'OK, so ... you guys are good?'

Ben narrowed his eyes at me. 'I'm not sure if we're there yet, Aly.'

My heart sank a little. 'Right, of course. Of course.' I looked at the table, trying to figure out my next move.

'We'll get there, though,' he said gently, and when I looked up, he gave me a little smile. 'Eric told me what you said, about my rules. About how unfair I was being on him.

331

You were right. I was scared to take a chance on someone who might hurt me. Who might not be ready for me. I was scared to give up good enough for something better.'

I nodded, not wanting to jinx this.

'You're actually pretty astute when you're not scheming and manipulating,' he snorted, and I smiled, relief flooding my chest. 'When you're honest with people, you talk sense.'

'Well, that's what I'm doing here, as well as apologising. I really am sorry,' I said, looking at the office, half packed up.

'I know.'

I nodded, taking a deep breath.

'When are you moving out?'

'Tomorrow, to something a little more low key. Now we don't have to impress anyone any more, we can be ourselves.'

I looked out of the window at the perfect skyline. 'But without Dylan.'

Ben considered me, a slow smile building across his face. 'Alyssa, are you scheming again?'

'If he really wants to go, if he's excited to start over in a new place, a new life, I will leave right now, and we never had this conversation . . .' I watched him carefully as he took his glasses off and wiped them on the corner of his shirt.

'And if he's miserable and heartbroken, and running away to save face?'

'Then I've got one *tiny* little scheme left.' I shrugged mischievously, holding up a thumb and forefinger. 'Barely a scheme, a . . . *petit subterfuge* followed *immediately* by honesty and absolute embarrassment on my part.'

Ben nodded for a moment, thinking it through.

'You love him, as he is?'

332

'I love him, as he is.'

He exhaled, relieved. 'Thankfully that's been the only fucking obvious thing since this entire charade started. I'm glad you're finally brave enough to admit it to yourself.'

'To you, to him, to anyone who will listen. He asked me to give him a reason to stay,' I put my palms together and smiled angelically, 'and I'm hoping you can help me with that.'

'Planning big romantic gestures and potential public humiliation? My absolute favourite way to spend a Friday,' Ben said.

It wasn't just about showing Dylan that he was perfect as he was. It was about showing him that I would fight for him. That I trusted him. That I wouldn't run again. So it was kind of poetic that we were staking out his running route.

We were in the park where Dylan ran on Sunday mornings, near his flat. Ben had arranged to run with him, he knew the route, and had agreed to be a diversion. Along the path, there would be five boards, painted with my words. My five things for Dylan. Five chances to get him to stay. I just had to hope five would be enough.

I looked over to Eric, who was standing at the edge of the park with Helena the beagle. Ben stood next to me, smiling at them both.

'You ready for this?' he asked, and I felt my stomach clench in anticipation. I was about to make a fool of myself for this man. And he might turn away, tell me it was too late. But I had to take a chance. It's only scary while you're falling.

Tola jogged back over to me, saluting. 'OK, all the boards are in place. We're good to go.'

I was going to be sick.

'Right, I better go meet him at the other entrance,' Ben said, watching me get more and more nervous. I twisted my fingers. What if he walked straight past me? What if he saw me, pounding heart open, and ignored it all? What if I never recovered?

'Your face, oh darling!' Ben gave me a hug and a kiss on the cheek. 'I don't want to give you too much confidence in your schemes any more, but you're being vulnerable and I'm really proud of you.'

'Thanks,' I said in a small voice, suddenly terrified. 'Put in a good word for me, please?'

'You got it.'

He jogged over to collect Helena Bonham Barker from Eric, and I saw him head across to the entrance.

'Hey, he's here!' Tola whooped, pointing.

'Shh!' I pushed her gently, trying to stop her from snagging his attention. Which was pretty difficult considering her vibrant gold T-shirt and bright green three-quarter-length trousers. Tola clutched my hand, and I felt Eric arrive and take my other one.

I watched as Ben and Dylan started to jog, and as he approached the first wooden sign, the words painted in orange:

1. You've always been my best friend.

He was too far away for me to see his expression, though I saw him look around, confused.

He slowed down, his whole body tensing when he saw the second one:

2. The way you still listen to the stupid music we loved when we were teenagers.

By the third, I saw him speed up, eager to find it, and the look on his face, the laughter that exploded when he read it. The way he lit up.

3. You make me want to run toward things instead of away from them.

At the fourth sign I had a clear sight of him, running towards me, looking for those words, my truths, my five things.

4. You still have the best laugh I've ever heard.

And there he was, standing straight in front of me, face flushed, those impossibly blue eyes daring me to be brave, just as they always had.

I let go of Tola and Eric's hands and walked over to the last sign, the tin of paint and the paintbrush at my feet.

5. I want to paint that orange room with you.

He walked over and I held my breath, waiting for him to say something.

He paused in front of the sign, hands in pockets, head tilted to the side like he was assessing an art project.

'Kind of a cryptic one to end on, Aresti.'

'Five wasn't enough,' I said, trying to hold back tears, taking a breath. 'I can give you ten. I can give you a hundred. But I want that life with you. I want your house by the park and your Sunday runs. I want a dog with a name to rival Helena's and I want to make an absolute mess painting our walls orange. I want to invite your dad for a Sunday roast even if it's quiet and awkward and you don't know what to say, and I want to make my mum's watermelon margaritas and sit in the garden with you reminiscing about all the stupid stuff we did when we were kids.'

'Aly—'

'And I want you to run this business that you've worked so hard for, and I want to be the person you talk to about it, not to fix anything, but just to remind you that you're good enough.'

I took a shaky breath, meeting his eyes, so desperate for him to know I was being honest.

'You're it for me. No matter what happens, no matter how much I mess up and try to fix it or however you try to be perfect. I see and love all of you. That's my true thing, my something real. Always has been.'

He blinked, then stood there and stared at me, this half smile on his face like he wasn't sure what was happening.

'Say something, Dylan,' I begged. 'Words, please.'

'Don't think I've ever had a big romantic gesture before.' He smiled at me, rubbing his hand across his eyes. But when he looked up his eyes were shining. 'A guy could get used to this treatment.'

I took a hopeful step forward. 'He could?'

He shook his head and raised his eyes to the sky, as if he still couldn't believe me sometimes, before putting an arm around my waist and pulling me in close.

'Ask me,' Dylan said, those blue eyes bright, our noses almost touching.

I smiled and took a breath, whispering the words, 'Tell me something real, Dylan.'

He closed his eyes briefly. 'I really wish I had something more clever to say. All I've got is I love you. I've loved you forever.'

I laughed. 'Clever enough for me. Would you kiss me already, please?'

The first time Dylan kissed me, I was eighteen. It had been chaste and sweet and friendly. He had stroked his thumb across my cheek, and all around us his friends jeered and whispered.

The second time I kissed Dylan, I was thirty-three. Our friends whooped, strangers clapped, and it was not friendly at all. I ran my fingers through his hair, tasted his smile and sighed against his lips. He held me close and kissed me like he was making a promise.

There would be problems, of course. Arguments about whose turn it was to deal with the puppy's vomit or who forgot to book the fancy restaurant of the month, and maybe even one day who had to get up at six a.m. on a Saturday to take the kids to whatever awful sport they ended up enjoying. There'd be missed flights to decidedly budget destinations, and start-up struggles and stupidity from both of us as we learned how to live. But it wouldn't need fixing. Because we'd have each other. And we'd have our friends there to celebrate and commiserate and laugh with us through it all. Seeing the reality, no filter. It was allowed to be hard sometimes. There's beauty in that too.

Because it's only scary when you're falling.

And then it feels like home.

Acknowledgements

This book was something new for me, so huge thanks to my magnificent agent Hayley Steed, who jumped on my pitch email with an immediate response in full capitals with lots of exclamation marks – your skill as an editor, negotiator and hand-holder blows my mind every time. I'm so grateful to be on Team Hayley.

To the wonderful team at Piatkus, and my editor Sarah Murphy – I'm just overwhelmed by the enthusiasm and love you have for the book. It's been so delightful feeling that someone 'gets' your characters and loves them as much as you do.

To my writer buddies in the Savvy Authors group and the TSAG who are always there to offer advice and hand-holding – I couldn't do this without our wonderful community. A special shout out as always to Lynsey James, the other half of Team Cheerleader who, true to the name, always waves a pom-pom, whether it's during editing hell or publication week.

To the friends and conversations who sparked this book,

who happily shared their stories of emotional hand-holding and boyfriend babysitting, and have worked through their own shit over the years to become even more amazing people – thanks for sharing, and I love you big time.

To my family, who don't always get the writing and publishing world, but are always standing by to be as proud of me as possible. This book exists through the support of my family, in particular my mum (who thankfully is nothing like Aly's mum!) and my husband, who will gladly admit that he was a bit of a fixer upper when I met him, but has grown on his own, and dragged me along for the ride too.

And finally, to you, dear reader! Thank you for reading this book, I hope it resonated and made you laugh and think and start conversations. If you found you enjoyed this particular style of sassy feminist rom com, I hope you'll stay in touch!